BODACIOUS

by Sharon Ervin

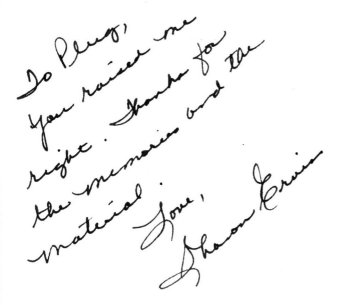

AmErica House
Baltimore

First printing

ISBN: 1-58851-494-3
PUBLISHED BY AMERICA HOUSE BOOK PUBLISHERS
www.publishamerica.com
Baltimore

Printed in the United States of America

To my husband, Bill,

Ever prodding me to reach beyond my grasp,

and

To Brandi, Joe, Cassie, and Jim,

our finest achievements

Acknowledgments

The Lesser North Texas Writers, Plano, Texas, all of whom contributed, but specifically:
Randy Thompson, devil's advocate and loyal detractor;
Steve Copling, for defining the Stockholm Syndrome;
Mark Benedict, my champion even when I am wrong;
Carol Woods, the voice of reason;
Pam Askew, for challenging every assumption;
Cathy Spaulding, for remarkable insights;
Doug Stevens, for vigilance;
Ed Davis, for causing, then breaking the tension;
Everett Isaacson, mitigator/referee;
Sami Mikhail, for the occasional hug, and
Florine Hager, for getting me there.

Francis Thetford, my dad, posthumously, for the genetic gift

Lolly Thetford, for enthusiasm beyond the call of duty

Jacques Chatenay, the quintessential computer guru

Jane Bryant, Glenna Herzer, Connie Gordon, Marilyn Pappano, and McAlester's McSherry Writers, for unwavering friendship

Chapter One

A shotgun blast jarred the isolated convenience store, shattering plate glass windows. Women screamed. Men yelled. Sara Loomis crouched, curled over her knees, and covered her ears.

Some of the half dozen customers remained upright, paralyzed. Others, like Sara, dropped to the floor. Muffled voices shouted commands, but Sara couldn't understand a word they said.

Suddenly, fingers bit into her upper arm and yanked her to her feet. She tried to jerk her arm out of his grasp and yelled, "No."

Her ears rang at a second gun blast. The fingers pinching her flesh lifted and shoved. She lurched forward, her feet doing a quick stutter step to keep up. Her purse strap dropped off her free arm. Before she could catch it, the satchel plummeted, scattering contents that clattered and spun, skittering over the floor behind her.

"No!" she shouted again, tugging, trying to tear her arm free of the pinching fingers. "No, no!"

The masked man with the biting fingers bumped and bulldozed her out into the brisk October afternoon, past the first set of gasoline pumps to the far driveway.

She flailed with her free hand to keep her dress from billowing over her head as the wind swirling through the Ozark mountains licked at her clothing.

Shoved into the cab of a cannibalized pickup truck, she struggled to get out of their way as a gang of shouting, shooting, smelly men piled in, around, and on top of her. The driver gunned the engine and peeled out, toppling the occupants who tumbled against each other shouting obscenities.

"Wah Hoo!" the man with the pinching fingers yelled, yanking off his ski mask, and righting himself. "Did you see that porch monkey hit his knees when I pointed my gun at him? 'Bet he peed his pants." His laugh sounded phony.

"Hey, fool," the driver shouted, pulling pantyhose from his head. Sara shivered. "Queenie said no shootin'."

"Cappy done it, Holthus," a muffled voice volunteered.

7

Free of his pantyhose hood, the driver had heavy jowls, bright red hair, and a beard. "Joe Lee, was there any bills in that ATM?"

One of the skinny guys on Sara's lap answered, removing a ski cap. "Hell, I thought we was drawing cop fire, Holthus." She couldn't see his face, only the acne-riddled back of his neck. "I didn't get to the damn machine. Shit, I thought I was fixin' to be dead."

Smashed into the seat with two sweaty men on top of her and others crammed on either side, Sara blinked hard. The air was putrid with the stench of booze, tobacco, and unbathed bodies. She swallowed, trying not to retch.

Pulling off caps, stockings, and ski masks, the other occupants all talked at once. She didn't move, hoping to remain invisible.

"If the cops *had* showed up, someone'd be shovelin' their guts up off that pavement 'bout now," one bragged.

"Holthus, how much'd we get?" said another.

The driver swung a hard left to avoid a chunk out of the roadbed. His passengers resettled before he said, "How the hell do I know? Gilbert, did you get the cash drawer?"

The man in the passenger seat stiffened. "Yeah. Got the whole wad right here in my pocket." Patting his jeans pocket, he caught his elbow in Sara's rib. She flinched, but bit her lips to keep from making a sound. His eyes widened and he stared at her. "What's *she* doin' here?"

Necks craned and eyes glowered. Sara cringed. The driver leaned around to peer at her and scowled. "Cappy?"

"B-B-Beer's all I g-g-got. Franklin got the g-g-girl, Holthus. You know it weren't me. Weren't me doing no sh-shootin' neither. I ain't c-c-carryin' no gun."

Holthus shouted louder. "Franklin!"

Smushed next to Sara, pinchy fingers puffed up. "Holthus, I had that there clerk lickin' floor the whole damned time. Don't be hollerin' at me. I done my part exactly like Queenie told us. Didn't see him settin' off no alarms, did ya?"

"The girl, Franklin. What a dumb ass thing to do. We come away with a couple of six packs, a pocket full of change, and the feds looking at us 'cause of her. You damn fool. You're all the time screwing us up."

Franklin sneered. "We got away, didn't we? Free as birds, ain't we? And we can do the same damn thing tomorrow or next week or any damn time we take a mind to."

The driver slowed the truck. "I'm gonna let 'er out."

"No, Holthus. She done seen us. She can point to us in court. No. We gotta keep 'er."

Sara trembled. She wasn't supposed to be here. Pinchy was right. She'd seen their faces. She could identify them. Her heart sank to the pit of her stomach and a tremor ran through her body. She knew one way they could guarantee her silence.

But they wouldn't kill her. Murder her over pocket change. No. Surely not. Not in this day and time.

She cleared her throat. The putrid smells sickened her. Her mind darted irrationally. She should have flattened herself against the floor in the convenience store when the commotion started. She shouldn't have let that stupid Franklin bully her. If he'd shot her there, she'd have been better off than letting herself be hauled out here with the five of them.

How could she defend herself? Against all of them? Alone?

Her mind swirled. *Get a grip. Don't panic. Think!*

When the truck's other occupants turned their attention from Sara, Franklin's small fingers wriggled onto her leg. She slapped his hand and squirmed as far away from him as she could. He grinned.

She reconsidered. Maybe she wasn't going to die. Maybe she was just going to wish she had.

Think of something else. Their names. If she got away, someone would want to know their names. What did they call each other?

Holthus, the big red-headed one behind the wheel, seemed to be the leader. She prodded herself to the mental exercise. Peculiar name, Holthus. First or last? She didn't know.

Gilbert, the skinny one in the passenger seat, sounded the most intelligent but didn't seem to have much influence.

Joe Lee was on top of her. She'd seen only the back of his head. Stealing another look, she saw white particles moving in his dark, unkempt hair. She shrank as far from him as she could. In her lap, he was inescapable.

Cappy, the young one who stuttered, was also partially in her lap,

9

squeezed between Joe Lee and the steering wheel. She wondered why they'd brought him.

And Franklin, the leering groper with the twitching, pinching little fingers, kept touching her and grinning his toothless little grin. Ugh! It was obvious what was on his mind. Reflux rose in Sara's throat. She swallowed hard and coughed.

Her ears popped. They were gaining altitude. The truck sputtered, the engine missed, but kept going. The tires squalled around curves that wound up and up. She peered out the side window. They turned onto a dirt road. The stench inside the truck seemed to be getting worse.

Sara peered between Cappy and Joe Lee to see ahead. The pitted roadway had dissolved to little more than a cattle trail.

Franklin grinned at her. He didn't appear to be over twenty years old, but he had no teeth in the front of his mouth. Strands of hair dangled from his upper lip. Chills pebbled Sara's arms and she trembled involuntarily. His leer made the muscles around her mouth quiver.

Eventually when the vehicle slowed and pitched to a lurching stop, bony fingers again clamped onto her arm. Franklin yanked Cappy and Joe Lee off her lap with his other hand before he jerked her out of the truck.

Her feet on the ground, Sara found herself looking squarely into the toothless grin of Franklin's flushed, misshapen countenance. Only a little taller than Sara, the man was spindly. His head and face festooned with scraggly patches of matted hair, he seemed to be the source of much of the stench inside the truck's cab. She looked around. They were in a mountain clearing surrounded by trees.

"I get her first." Franklin eyed Sara hungrily. She felt an energizing boost of adrenaline shoot to her arms and legs.

She was a college-educated woman with a future. She'd been with two men in her life—with Jimmy Singer the whole, long, miserable summer. If she cooperated, if she didn't fight them, would they let her live? Five of them? She didn't think she could endure it.

Jerking her arm out of Franklin's grasp, she spun and darted for the woods.

"Let 'er go!" Holthus shouted, but Franklin caught her in a dozen steps, threw her on the ground, climbed on top, and straddled her. She kicked and flailed and screamed with all her strength.

Franklin shrieked, trying to protect himself from her flying fists and unbuckle his belt at the same time. "Come on, some of you hold 'er for me." No one moved. "She's done seen us. You know what that means. You know what we gotta do."

Sara squeezed her eyes shut, bucking and twisting and pummeling him.

Suddenly, soft hands grabbed Sara's arm, yanked her out from under Franklin, and straight up onto her feet. Whoever had helped loomed behind her as Sara stood facing Franklin, again eye to eye.

He leered at her a moment before his gaze shifted to the person behind her. He narrowed his eyes and set his jaw stubbornly as the person spoke. "'Thought I'd find you up here." The husky voice sounded female. "How much'd you get?"

All eyes turned on Holthus. "Don't know yet, Queenie. Gilbert, count what's in your pocket."

Out of the spotlight, Franklin pulled a piece of hemp from his pocket and wrapped it slowly round and round his hand, never taking his eyes from Queenie who remained behind Sara.

"I'll do the killin'." Franklin's voice was quiet.

"Nooo." Queenie's objection sounded more like a belch. Sara was afraid to look at her. Before she realized what he was doing, Franklin dropped the rough rope around Sara's wrist and yanked. Recoiling, she took a swing at him. He dodged. She kicked a knee at his groin. He side-stepped nimbly. With no objection from Queenie, Franklin snagged Sara's free arm. She slapped and kicked at him as he danced around knotting the cord and yanking it tight.

"She's gotta be kilt, Queenie, you and all of us here knows that."

The belcher hesitated before she spoke again. "Cappy'll do it."

"It's not his turn." Franklin's voice became a whine. "I got 'er. She's mine. Anyway, it's my turn."

"Franklin, Cappy's gonna do it, d'you hear me?" It was a rhetorical question; not a question at all, but a thinly veiled threat. "It'll make up to him some for that buck."

Franklin clenched his jaws, glowered at Sara, and gave the rope a yank. It tore her flesh. She gritted her teeth and trembled with the effort not to scream. She wouldn't give him that satisfaction—or any other—if she could help it.

"She's a handsome woman." Franklin arched his thin little eyebrows. "Nice all over. *Real* nice tits. They're her owns. I already felt of 'em. I like pink cheeks and black hair, too. I always did like black hair on womens. Queenie, her and me, we'll have us some fun. I'll get her wore out proper before I..."

His words dwindled as he looked at the imposing form behind Sara. "Come on," he wheedled, "Cappy's too stupid. He'll forgit somethin'. He'll be too embarrassed to strip her bare. He'll leave something on her they can trace if they find her. Me, I'll see she's stripped proper. Do it right. Enjoy the doing of it." He continued leering. "Maybe together her and me'll have a lotta' fun. Might let her live a couple of days, if we're havin' a real good time."

The woman's voice was a snort. "I said it's Cappy's turn. He'll peel 'er right. He just got rattled and forgot before."

"Hell, Queenie, Cappy's too stupid to hardly find his way home after he gets her kilt."

Queenie hollered, "Cappy, come on over here."

The wiry stutterer who had been partly on Sara's lap in the truck and appeared to be maybe fourteen years old, shuffled closer. When he reached for the rope binding Sara's wrists, his hands were so badly stained that the filth looked permanent.

Franklin refused to give up the lead at first, staring at Sara and giving the rope another savage yank. The hemp burned, and again Sara bit her lips to keep from crying out. She stiffened as a gun cocked beside her ear. Franklin's eyes bulged and he shoved the tether into the younger man's hand.

"Queenie, you wouldn't..." Franklin gazed at the gun barrel suddenly propped on Sara's shoulder. His expression turned docile, pleading.

Sara looked at Cappy's triumphant, snaggle-toothed grin, and exhaled a sigh of relief. His pale eyes were blank, his face full of giddy appreciation as he stared past her. Grinning, he turned his dull orbs to Sara's face.

The boy's straw-colored thatch of hair was cut in short bangs at the top of his forehead as if the job had been self-inflicted by a four-year-old. Like Franklin, Cappy was only slightly taller than Sara and spindly. He began to jitter on his toes, dancing and touching the front of his filthy trousers with his free hand, as if he needed to pee, soon.

Sara hurried to obey Cappy's wordless bidding as he pulled on the rope. She would do anything to get away from the vicious, leering Franklin.

Leash in hand, the youngster, without uttering a word, turned, brushed by Sara, and plodded toward a path which appeared to go directly into the woods. He tugged her along behind him like a toddler with a pull toy. She stepped briskly to keep up.

Franklin took one stride as if he planned to follow, but Queenie's deep voice resonated again. "Franklin, I brung you into this world. It's only right I be the one to see you out. I expect I'll be the one to do it, when the time comes."

"Ah, Ma..."

* * * *

Maybe a quarter of a mile into the woods, Cappy squared himself with a blackjack tree and undid his pants. Sara turned her head rather than witness the event.

They had walked probably a mile, the tether slack between them, before Sara spoke. "Cappy, I can cook."

"You c-c-can?" He stopped in the middle of the narrow path and turned all the way around to study her. His clouded eyes were rimmed with red. She nodded, looking directly at him with her most respectful expression, a look usually reserved for dignitaries and annoyed bosses.

"And I can clean. I'm a real hard worker. I could do your chores for you."

He looked puzzled. "You c-c-could? What ch-ch-chores?"

"Whatever chores they make you do."

"Oh." He nodded but obviously didn't know what she was talking about.

"I work on newspapers, Cappy. I write stories about interesting people. I'm on my way to a new job, on the *Gazette*, down at Overt. When I get there, Cappy, I'll write a wonderful story all about you."

"Yeah? C-c-can you type-a-write on one of them elec-tronic ma-ch-ch-chines?"

"Yes I can."

He swallowed hard. Sara supposed he was trying to slow his words to avoid the stutter. "I bet y-y-you even learnt to run one of them com-com-puter outfits. Am I r-r-right?"

"You're right, Cappy. Absolutely right." She wanted to keep him talking. If he liked her, maybe she could find a way out of this. It was a chance.

He stared at the ground. "It's a sh-sh-shame to kill someone with so much l-l-learning." He gazed woefully at an anthill, staring, standing absolutely still in the dappled sunlight filtering through the trees.

Watching his movements, his expressions, Sara saw his indecision. "Yes, you're right again, Cappy. I'd say it's a terrible waste. You're pretty smart, for a kid."

He bit his lower lip and squinted at her face. "I ain't smart and I'm nineteen, if I'm a day. I ain't l-l-lying neither." He thought another long moment. "Yes, ma'am, seems like it s-s-sure would be...wasteful, I mean."

A glimmer of something sparked his eyes and they darted to Sara's face. "You're not th-th-thinking I'm so s-s-stupid as to turn you l-l-loose, are you?"

She shook her head studying him with feigned concentration. "No." She hesitated. "But maybe you could think of something else, some way we could get me out of this, something besides killing me, I mean. I'm depending on you, Cappy." That's right, she told herself, let him be your hero. "Can you figure out any way you could save me?"

He studied the path and shook his head periodically, as if considering and rejecting ideas. With each shake of his head, his narrow shoulders curled forward and down a little more. Then, suddenly, he straightened.

"I know." He grinned at her a moment before his expression wilted and he slouched again. "No. Wouldn't be r-r-right. Be b-b-better if I kilt you myself."

"We could talk about your idea." She bobbed her head affirmatively to encourage him.

He sighed. "Th-Th-This one's n-n-not hardly worth the t-t-talk."

"Come on, let me hear it. What are you thinking?"

"I c-c-can't do it. You'd be better off with Fr-Fr-Franklin."

14

"That big mouth guy back at the clearing?"

"Yeah, the one who w-w-wanted to do you hisself."

"Cappy, no matter what you're thinking, it *couldn't* be worse than him?"

Cappy rolled his eyes and spread his mouth in a broad grimace. He lowered his voice to a whisper. "I was th-th-thinking I might could j-j-just carry you to Bo. He's cr-cr-crazy. Bo'll kill ya q-q-quick, th-th-that's for sure."

Mountain terminology, *carry*, meaning take, Sara mused. "Is Bo a friend of yours?" Cappy shook his head. "You are talking about a human being, aren't you?"

Again Cappy looked dubious. Sara waited. "N-N-Not for certain. The p-p-pumas and the b-b-bears is scared sh-sh-shitless of Bo. S-S-Snakes don't even go 'crost his path."

The boy obviously was delusional.

"Cappy, maybe you could just leave me here in the woods. I've got no sense of direction. I'll probably die in a day or two, without even a sweater. How cold does it get nights in the mountains this time of year? Down in the twenties, I'll bet."

He shrugged, obviously intent on capturing another thought. Finally, he looked up as if the idea eluding him had been snared and startled him. "But, m-m-ma'am, I'm supposed to take my pl-pl-pleasure with you first."

She was getting impatient with this rube, but she needed to keep her cool.

"I imagine you get to take your pleasure with women a lot, don't you, Cappy, a strapping young guy like yourself?"

She tried not to wince as he slurped up a thread of spittle dripping from his mouth and swung his head woefully from side to side. His scowl turned into an intense, puzzled look.

"None of 'em'd even sh-sh-show me how. I got me a town gal last spring and carried her up here proper, but she wouldn't show me. Bitch. I ast her just to please take off her shoes. She wouldn't. I just wanted the p-p-pleasure of looking at them long, skinny, pink little feet—naked."

Sara stared at Cappy's face. Surely he was kidding? She didn't think so. Stammering, he rushed to continue.

"I pr-promised her I wouldn't touch 'em or nothin' but she wouldn't. Franklin said it's 'cause she's frigid. Franklin says 'most all women is—frigid."

Sara nodded. It was easy to understand that these guys might meet a lot of frigid women.

"Well, Cappy, the truth is, I don't get or give much pleasure with men myself. I'm afraid I'm one of those frigid women Franklin told you about."

Sara looked at the ground, sobered by what was probably the truth. Twenty-six years old, she didn't have a very good track record at sex. Each occurrence had been an ordeal.

The men in her experience were hurried. They took off their pants, grudgingly put on condoms—angry that she insisted—rammed themselves inside her, said it was great, and apologized for having to rush.

In the aftermath, Sara felt dirty, humiliated and alone. She bathed repeatedly to get rid of the peculiar odors that lingered afterward.

Cappy interrupted her reverie. "You mean you d-d-do know how to do it?"

"I guess I don't know how to do it *right*, Cappy. It's probably better not to learn a thing from someone who can't do it right." She watched his puzzled look deepen. "How would it be if you learned to shoot a gun from someone who hated guns and who didn't know how to shoot one? What would be the use in that?"

He brightened. "I'm the champeen squirrel shooter and skinner anywhere around here. If you want me to learn you to shoot and skin squirrel, you can just up and ask me."

The stutter was gone, at least temporarily. "I will, Cappy." She wondered if he realized he'd implied she'd be alive long enough to learn to shoot. "I sure will. Now, what about this Bo?"

Cappy's expression darkened. "I'm not for sure whether Bo's any good at squirrel shootin' or not."

Sara suppressed a groan. "I mean what kind of man is he?"

"Well," Cappy's mouth twitched, "I'm not for sure 'bout that neither." She was getting confused. He brightened with a new thought. "All I know for sure is, he's old. He's awful old, 'pears to me."

16

She wanted to pursue the other. "What else could he be, Cappy, if he's not a man?"

"They say he might be part man and part somethin' else."

Her smile of disbelief nearly escaped. He had to be kidding. But his face remained serious as he shook his head and rolled his shoulders pitifully. "A mix 'tween a man and a bear or a razorback hog or somethin'. He don't talk words, just barks or h-h-howls at a person. When he catches somethin', he roars 'fore he t-t-tears its head off. I hear'd him do it two, three times, then hear'd the shrieking of the thing he 'as killing."

Cappy shook his head as if trying to shake something off the top of it. "T-T-That sound give me chills running p-p-plum up my back. That shriekin'll give a man nightmares." He hesitated, staring at her as if he had made a decision. "It'd be better for me to go on and kill ya my own self."

Sara felt a vibration in the ground. It rumbled like a truck gearing down to negotiate a curve on a road somewhere nearby. She needed this hillbilly to let her go. She must stay calm, keep her head. She could find her way to a road, if she could just talk him into releasing her. She got an idea.

"You don't have a gun, Cappy. How're you going to kill me?"

He pulled a knife from a sheath at his side. She waited for his eyes to meet hers. His began to tear, and he drooled badly.

Sara drew a deep breath and sighed. "Sticking me will be gruesome. I guess it'd probably be quicker, easier for you if you cut my head off. Is that what you're thinking?"

He shuddered and turned his back.

"Of course, cutting my head off is going to make an awful mess." Sympathy tinged her words as she pressed her argument. "Good thing we're way out here." When he looked back at her, she cast him a pitiful glance.

"I'll try not to scream, Cappy. I'm afraid the sound of my bodiless head screaming and all that blood will haunt you every time you try to sleep for probably the whole rest of your life. It might even be worse than the nightmares you get from hearing Bo's victims because these screams will be coming from your own victim instead of his."

Cappy blinked back tears and sniffed.

"You're a tender-hearted person, Cappy. I can tell. Murdering me by hand'll be awfully hard on you."

He shivered and his expression twisted with misery. "Th-Th-Then what am I s'pose to do with you?"

"Leave me here in the woods, Cap. Let me die of my own stupidity. Put your guilt and the blame for my passing where it belongs, right here on my shoulders."

He shook his head and wiped his nose with the back of his hand. "I ain't leaving you here alone for the varmints to eat you. No, ma'am, I ain't the kind to do something cruel as that. There's snakes and ticks and chiggers."

"The crawling things probably aren't so bad, now that the weather's turned." Was she reassuring him or herself?

He pondered a long moment, sniffing and snorting, mopping drool with the back of his hand. Finally, he set his mouth in a grim line, rolled the slack in the tether around his hand, and began walking, his carriage decisive, again tugging her along behind.

"Where are we going?" He looked back and pursed his mouth. "Come on, Cappy, how much farther? I'm tired. And thirsty, too. Please, could I have a drink of water?"

She kept talking, knowing he could hear her, but he refused to answer. It was obvious by the set of his jaw and the sorrow on his face that her fate was sealed, in his mind anyway.

Sara lost all track of time and distance and direction as they trudged through brush and a forest of blackjack, cedar, and pine trees. Night was coming. The north wind, lazy before dusk, suddenly had a pitiless bite to it.

Just before sundown, they came upon a crude shed. Beyond the shed and an outhouse stood a primitive cabin which looked to be deserted. The buildings were made of logs and topped with corrugated metal roofs.

Obviously nervous, watching all directions, Cappy hurried to the side of the cabin and yanked the rope down. Sara dropped to her knees exhausted. She scarcely noticed as Cappy ran the length of rope from her wrists between two rough-hewn logs of the cabin's outside wall. She was glad to be off her feet, even briefly.

Before she realized what he was doing, Cappy was inside the cabin.

From the other side of the wall, he jerked the rope and pulled her wrists tightly against the structure. He secured the rope to something inside.

She watched him closely as he emerged, a shadow in the creeping darkness. He didn't raise his eyes, but paused a moment in front of her, then plunged into the underbrush, going back the way they had come. She guessed the hesitation was his way of saying good-bye.

Struggling, she got to her feet, a difficult proposition without the use of her hands.

With her wrists bound tightly against the wall only about two feet above the ground, she was not able to rise to her full height. She dropped back to her knees, staring at the rope.

The hemp ripped against the already chaffed and broken skin of her wrists. She bit at the merciless restraint, snagging it with her teeth, snarling at the pain, spitting the bristling strands, determined to free herself.

The last vestiges of sunlight disappeared and with it, her anger cooled. She could taste blood trickling from her rope-ravaged lips. A relentless wind and unforgiving cold arrived with the darkness. She braced herself, but there was no escape from the icy-fingered gusts that rendered her short-sleeved denim dress all but useless.

As if to compensate for the cold, the moon rose; a bright, illuminating harvest moon.

In her distress, Sara continued gnawing at the hemp halfheartedly, occasionally taking a break to rake the rope back and forth against the logs.

Something rustled leaves at the edge of the clearing and she froze, paralyzed with a mix of hope and fear.

The wind sent leaves scurrying. Sara thought she heard twigs and leaves crunching beneath footsteps. She couldn't tell how far away the sound was but it seemed to be moving closer.

Straining eyes and ears, she stared into the night but couldn't see anything.

The rustling grew louder.

Suddenly a hulking shadow emerged from the trees and assumed the form of a man or a large, two-legged animal. She heard its breathing as it lumbered closer and closer.

Chapter Two

Sara shrank into the cabin's shadow, ducked her head, hid her eyes, and tried to be absolutely still.

The shuffling feet hesitated in front, just around the cabin corner from her. She heard him snuffling at the air. Could he smell her? She held her breath.

He slammed the cabin door wide. It sounded as if he paused again, listening. Finally she heard him go inside.

Panic swelled. Cold, tired, frightened, Sara pressed herself against the cabin wall. Moments passed. She heard no sound, no movement inside. She twisted her wrists, squeezed her hands to make them as narrow as possible, and pulled. The rope bit deeper into her seared flesh. Then the restraint moved ever so slightly and she heard the snuffling again, directly on the other side of the cabin wall. There was a muffled growl and an intake of breath. The rope slid back and forth between the logs, raking her wrists along the unfinished bark. She shuddered, biting her lips, trying not to cry out.

Then the binding was still.

The creature shuffled toward the door. He was coming.

Desperately Sara clamored to her feet, bent, yanking, twisting, and turning, trying to pull the rope through the slit. It held fast. Giving up, she dropped to the ground, curled over her knees, ducked her head, and waited.

She whispered, "Oh, God, don't let this be happening."

The door slammed. She heard him approaching, shuffling around the corner. He stopped immediately in front of her, the toes of his boots inches from her face.

Boots?

Her mind reeled, chasing an elusive thought. She felt him peering down at her. She squeezed her eyes shut, expecting any moment to be mauled, shredded.

Terrified by a low growl, she pressed her forehead into the dirt, cowering as close to the earth as possible.

A series of guttural noises echoed back from the woods, startling her. Her eyes popped open. She turned her head sideways trying to get a glimpse of the form looming over her.

Standing on two legs, its glistening eyes leered down at her.

Sara did not faint easily. It was an attribute for which she was usually grateful. Facing the brute in front of her, however, she wished for the sweet solace of a swoon.

Think, damn it, think. Cringing, she peered out and something she saw calmed her. Leather trousers rose from the worn boots on his feet.

Boots and trousers?

Reason took hold. No wild creature wore boots and trousers. This being was not an animal, at least he was not the mad mutant Cappy had suggested.

Sara looked higher, over a burly fur coat to a face. The upper face was camouflaged by the mass of hair which spilled over his forehead, framed his eyes, and cascaded to his shoulders. The lower part of his face was effectively concealed by a bushy, unkempt mustache and beard.

Neither Sara nor the other moved as they regarded each other in heavy silence.

She heard movement and strained, lifting her head a little to see, then shuddered as he drew a knife, and ducked again.

One step put him almost on top of her.

The scream she had suppressed earlier emerged as a croaking sob.

He raised the knife. She planted her forehead in the moist dirt. She heard a swish and a loud THWACK!

Still bound together, her wrists were suddenly free of the tether attached to the cabin.

Astonished, Sara attempted to leap to her feet, thinking to run, escape into the darkness. Instead, she wobbled. Her legs were asleep from being folded so long beneath her on the cold ground. She staggered. Before she could either steady herself or fall, the creature looped one massive arm around her middle and lifted.

Her long-muted screams erupted, rending the stillness of the night. She shrieked herself breathless again and again, but the noise had no effect.

Her nearly one hundred-thirty pounds seemed of no consequence to the brute as he shifted her from one side to the other, grabbing things

22

with whichever of his hands was free as he plodded toward the shed.

He gathered tools, a length of rusted chain and, finally, what looked like a cow's nose ring from a workbench beside the shed. He carried the collection and Sara to an anvil beneath a tree beyond the shed. He and his collection were clearly illuminated in the moonlight. Spellbound, she calmed as he stood her on her feet. His movements were decisive; he, coordinated.

He dropped the chain and shackle, which clattered to the ground beside the anvil. She was standing, but her knees quivered as the knife suddenly reappeared, glinting. She was aware of the man's huge hands, which emerged from the long sleeves of his animal-skin coat. The hands were thick with big, square fingers.

She kept reminding herself to think. Cappy was wrong. This guy was not part bear or razorback. He was a man, perhaps one of the mountain men remembered in Ozark ballads or myths. Sorting through her memory, she tried to recall Paul Bunyan fables that might serve her now.

Her thoughts darted frantically, but slowed as she became curious. She stared at the hair-enshrouded face. She could make out a hawkish nose and a broad thin line of lips, barely discernible beneath the bearded growth. Her survey stopped at his dark, angry eyes glowering into her face.

Black, they were clear, attentive eyes, not Cappy's dull ogle or even the shining leer of a madman. The eyes were alert, but so dark they seemed like two chunks of coal sunken into sockets bordered by the mass of hair.

No, Cappy didn't know what he was talking about.

Still, he had told her this guy was large. That part was true enough. And old. Cappy obviously was right about that, too. Stooped, the man walked slowly, as if deferring to the stiffness of age. Still, he was several inches taller than Sara, who was five-foot-eight.

Avoiding his glare, Sara continued to study her captor.

His knee-length coat looked like some kind of animal pelt; effective, she supposed, against the Halloween chill. His leather trousers were like leggings and the size of his calves indicated he probably did a lot of walking. Worn, low heeled army boots encased large feet.

He might be ancient and uncivilized, but he *was* a man. That realization soothed her and she drew a deep, ragged breath. She could deal with a human, one-on-one. She could cultivate him, influence him, eventually perhaps manipulate him.

A good news reporter grooms her sources and she was a damned good reporter. A dud at sex, Sara otherwise had excellent people skills. She would lull him, woo him, win him.

She risked another peek at his face, which provided no clue as to how to get through to him...yet.

Strategy. Sara drew another breath. She needed to use her head. Think. Caught up in her observations, she'd lost track of his movements.

What was he doing, still looming over her, looking every bit a predator?

First requirement: she must remain calm.

He grabbed the back of her neck and shoved her to her knees. He was terribly strong. His heavy hand kept pushing her down, forcing her to grovel on the bare ground beside the anvil. She wasn't struggling—she bit her lips, swallowing her objections—why was he being so rough?

She yielded, gulping to keep herself from crying out, staying where he positioned her. He grabbed the rope still binding her ravaged wrists, lifted, and stretched her hands over the anvil. Terror consumed her when she saw the hand axe he wielded as easily as most wield an eating utensil over a plate of food. She watched in horror and disbelief as he raised the instrument. She screamed as it began its descent.

"No!"

He brought the axe down with a resounding clang and Sara whimpered, expecting excruciating pain to follow the amputation. There was no pain. No amputation.

She raised her eyes slowly to look as she wriggled her fingers, intact. Nothing had been removed, rather the nose ring had become a metal shackle around one of her bleeding wrists. He'd used the flat side of the axe as a hammer.

She felt light-headed but didn't flinch when he ran the rusted chain through the ring at her wrist. She needed to focus on something, to keep her mind clear. Later she could react. Now she must concentrate.

All that rust must have weakened at least one link.

The man gave the arrangement a yank to inspect its integrity, rapped twice more with the blunt side of the axe, and tested again before he was satisfied. He tossed the axe on the ground.

Without allowing her to gain her feet, he grasped Sara's upper arm in one huge hand and pulled her to a nearby tree. A heel broke off one of her shoes as she shambled along on the sides of her feet trying to keep up.

From a pocket, he produced a screwdriver and pried open the link at the far end of the chain. He looped the link through a rung in the tree, apparently one where animals were sometimes tethered. His massive hand strained only slightly as he used pliers to pinch the link closed.

Turning, the man again wielded the knife. Sara shrank from him as far as the rusted chain allowed.

Grabbing her free wrist, he positioned the knife and sliced the hemp that had torn her scalded flesh. The torturous rope fell away.

She quickly presented the manacled wrist, indicating he should remove the hemp from that one too. He turned the hard, dark eyes on her for a moment, then relented, and cut away the second piece of rope as well.

He glowered at her a moment in the darkness before he turned and lumbered back to the cabin, probably a hundred yards away.

Then she was there in the dark, alone.

"Be thankful for the little things," Sara whispered to the night. "You're alive, appendages intact. It's better than you thought." She again inhaled deeply. The delayed fatigue rendered her suddenly very, very tired. And cold. This was no time for self-pity. She had to get out of here.

Sorting through twigs and sticks on the ground around her, she found a stout one, squatted, leaned against the tree and, trembling, laced the stick through the rusted links of the chain one at a time, twisting, using leverage to test them, looking for one which might yield.

The boy, Cappy, spoke of this man almost reverently. Sara hammered suspect links with rocks, trying to bend or break them. In Cappy's mind, this guy was the lone acceptable alternative to murdering her himself. He would take her to...to... What was the name?

25

What did Cap call him?

"Bo," she whispered to the pervading silence. "This neanderthal's name is Bo."

The links toward the middle of the chain were the most corroded. She found the weakest. Link thirty-four was rusted thin on one side. She placed that link on a slab of rock, located a heavy, jagged stone and hit it sharply. The sound reverberated, a muted clang. She looked toward the cabin. Light filtered through seams between logs. There was no sound nor any sign of movement.

She hit the link again, then again, and over and over until she became annoyed by the stubbornness of this new, inert enemy. She pounded harder and harder, venting her frustration and anger.

Take a breather. Rest a minute. Think. You can do this. You can get out of here. You just have to keep your head.

No wonder she was tired. Hysteria was fatiguing. It had taken all of her energy to cope with the shocking events of this day. She slumped against the dependable girth of the tree trunk and shivered, again aware of the chill air whipping around her.

This whole situation was ridiculous, like a time warp nightmare. Here she was, city born and bred, well educated, launched in her career and, here in the Twenty-First Century, waylaid by a pack of ignorant hillbillies, thrust into the hands of a mute madman, and chained to a tree in a land left a hundred years behind.

"But it's temporary," she said out loud.

The air was growing colder by the minute.

Laying the chain aside, Sara wrapped her arms tightly around herself. The north wind seemed determined to cool her fury and defeat her spirit as it penetrated the denim dress and her skin, wending its way straight through to her bones.

Struggling to her knees and stretching the chain to its fullest, Sara moved to the leeward side of the tree. Using her hands, she raked leaves, dried grass and weeds into a meager pile amid the gnarled tree roots that coiled on top of the ground.

Covering herself as much as possible with the folds of her skirt and folding her arms and legs beneath her torso, she nestled into the tree's unyielding underpinnings.

Despite her fatigue, the long walk through the woods and, finally, relief after the fear that had devoured all that remained of her strength, Sara was not able to rest or even to relax. Muscles all over her body throbbed and cramped their objections to the day's treatment.

The cold and dark were menacing, the night alive with strange noises. She heard hoots, animals skittering among dry leaves, wind whispering through the pine branches high overhead.

Would rescuers come? Could they find her?

No, they wouldn't be coming to this remote outpost, she supposed, not unless one of the hillbillies told them where to look; not unless her hypothetical rescuers could make Cappy show them where she was. And they would have to find Cappy first.

From what Sara had seen, the little backwoods village where the thieves lived seemed overpopulated with mentally deficient folks, probably the result of unchecked inbreeding.

Was Bo one of them?

She didn't think so. His eyes were more alert than the others.

As to her prospects for rescue, who might come? The police? Eyewitnesses would tell them the robbers had taken a hostage. That's what she was, actually, a hostage. But would they know *who* she was?

Of course. She'd left the contents of her purse strewn all over the convenience store. With her driver's license and credit cards, even a backwoods policeman probably could determine her identity.

Also, her car was parked at a gas pump there. It wouldn't take much of a cop to figure out it belonged to her or, more accurately, to her and the bank.

Why hadn't she suspected something when she emerged from the restroom into silence? Usually she was more observant, more aware of her surroundings than to blunder into the middle of an armed robbery.

If only she hadn't been in such a hurry to get to Overt.

Funny, she thought, that stop was the last time she had used the bathroom and she felt no need to go now. Of course, she'd had nothing to eat or drink since...

Since when?

What time had she stopped? Probably two-thirty. What time did that make it now?

Dark came at seven-thirty-five last week at home. They'd gone off daylight savings over the weekend. It had gotten full dark as she huddled beside the cabin. How long had it been since then?

She was too confused to try to determine what time it might be.

She wouldn't be signing in at the *Gazette* business office tomorrow after all. Would they get word? They'd probably hear about the kidnapping. Would they realize the victim was their incoming woman reporter or would they simply assume Sara Loomis had gotten a better deal and stood them up? They might not even bother to inquire as to her whereabouts

Would anyone come looking for her?

Maybe Jimmy?

No. She'd been brutal. She doubted Jimmy Singer would care what happened to her.

But her parents would. Despite the fact they had finally gotten the point, yielded to Sara's demand for a little space, they probably would try to find her. But with winter coming, if this Bo person kept her staked outside, she might not last until they found her.

How could anyone find her among the mountains and ravines of the Ozarks; track her over rain-cut back roads to that little mountain clearing where she had been forced to follow Cappy into the deep woods.

The prospects for rescue didn't look good. Her escape was probably entirely up to her. She groaned.

The excited optimism of a new job in a new place was gone. Fatigue and gloom settled over her. She was too tired to cope. She'd wait, think in the daylight, when her mind was fresh. She felt the sharp edge of an oncoming headache and buried her face in her hands. Salty tears slipped between her fingers, trickled down her arms, burning the scrapes and abrasions. She twisted her head, peered at her poor wrists and began to weep in earnest, making no effort to muffle the sound as her anguish escalated to low, forlorn wails.

Her bawling stopped as quickly as it began when she heard what sounded like an answering cry. Frozen in place, she listened to hear first one yelp, then another.

Voices began yipping off in the distance then, gradually, closer, coming from every direction, their plaintive yowls echoing up and down the valleys.

She needed to blow her nose and picked up a dried sycamore leaf to use as a tissue. It didn't work. She caught up the hem of her skirt to mop her eyes and nose, wiping away the worst, listening to the voices coming closer.

When she heard distinct rustlings in the leaves from the darkened woods, she got to her knees, watching, waiting – adrenaline pumping hope into her limbs.

Suddenly she was peering into a pair of bright eyes. Someone was there, watching her. Someone had come.

"Help." She tried to keep her voice low, not wanting it to carry to the cabin. She needed to coax the watcher closer, to prevail upon him to rescue her. But the fellow was timid. He blinked but he didn't move. Others joined him, their bright eyes also staring at her.

"Help me!" She opened her arms to welcome them, shaking the restraining chain to show them her plight. "Please help me."

They seemed frightened of the chain. Maybe they were afraid of the man, Bo. The wind blew Sara's voice away from the cabin. What would it matter if he heard anyway? This was a large group. There were enough of them to clobber him.

But the onlookers stayed back, milling, keeping themselves hidden, peeking out from behind the trees.

"Don't be afraid." She tried to keep the excitement out of her voice. "You can get me loose before he knows you've done it. If he comes, we can jump him, catch him by surprise."

She shifted position but continued kneeling. They seemed diminutive, perhaps they were the Ozark version of pygmies. She leaned forward coaxing, encouraging them.

Suddenly one of the rescuers let out a high, peculiar yip. Maybe they were a tribe of Indians and those sounds were their signal. She leaped to her feet.

"Come on. But be quiet. If you yell, he'll hear you. Bring a knife. Pry this link open. I can go with you. Come on. Hurry up, before he hears. Don't be timid. I'll help you. He can't fight all of us."

The leader crept forward a few steps and crouched, staying in the deepest shadows. Suddenly he leaped into the open and Sara was able to see his form in the dappled moonlight dancing through the tree limbs.

She gasped. Hairs prickled warnings along the back of her neck as she staggered back a stumbling step.

He was neither a pygmy, nor an Indian. Shaped like a large, gangly dog, her hoped-for deliverer appeared to be a coyote, salivating, his bright golden eyes ravenous.

Sara stumbled again as she scrambled to the back side of the tree, putting the trunk between her and the animal. Terrorized, she screamed into the night. "Help. Someone. Help me."

The coyote crept forward, sniffing the air with his long nose, sidling, sizing her up.

She yanked at the chain, struggling to keep the tree trunk between herself and the pack, which was advancing behind their leader, emboldened.

She could hear herself shrieking. Her screams sounded hysterical, shattering the silent night. She picked up handfuls of sticks, dirt and rocks and flung them at the approaching band. Some hesitated at her pitiful bombardment, then lifted their noses and resumed their approach.

Inhaling, her breath burned her throat. She knew the animals could smell her fear. It probably impelled them, but she didn't know how to extinguish it.

They split up but kept coming, one by one sporadically darting forward, retreating, advancing, circling.

She let out another ear-splitting shriek as a hand touched her shoulder. She spun. The hulking old man crouched behind her. He leaned his gun against the tree and hunkered in the shadows, waiting. She tried to move, to get behind him but he caught her arms and held her in place, shielding himself from their sight. Her heart knocked against her rib cage and pounded in both temples.

The lead coyote snarled as he darted forward several paces, baring his teeth. He stopped and crouched and appeared to be grinning as he minced his way toward her. She shrank back, reaching for the man, but her groping hand fanned the air. He was gone.

Too afraid to watch the approaching coyote, she squeezed her eyes shut. Would she suffer long as the animals tore her to pieces? Her hope at that moment was to die quickly.

The coyote snapped and snarled, apparently working up his courage. She felt the warmth of his body as he came, leering into her face, close enough for her to smell his breath and see the saliva stringing from his exposed fangs.

Mesmerized, she watched in horror as the animal crouched, then leaped. A man's huge hand flashed in front of her face. His fingers grabbed a handful of fur at the coyote's throat. As he lifted it, the animal's growl of triumph became a squeal.

The man caught its tail with his free hand, released its throat and, grasping the tail with both hands, swung the animal, lurching away from the tree to give himself space to heave the creature in a full arc.

Bo hurled the coyote round and round, gathering momentum as he moved toward the pack, laughing maniacally. Eying him uncertainly, the coyotes danced a wary retreat. One yowled, then the others joined the cry and they scattered, running every direction, their tails between their legs, in a frenzy, an all-out rout.

Still spinning the leader over his head, Bo suddenly released its tail. The coyote flew a dozen feet before it hit the ground with a thud. Stunned, the animal wobbled, righted itself, took several drunken steps, and dropped onto its side, pawing the ground. Finally it gained its feet and ran, lurching sideways in its flight.

The baying faded, swallowed by the earth and the trees.

In the ensuing silence, Sara remained hunkered down, struggling to quell urges that ranged from uncontrollable sobs to hysterical giggling. The whole scene had been outrageous. One unarmed man sending a half dozen coyotes squealing into the night.

Using the tree for support, she staggered as she wobbled to her feet. The man's behavior must have appeared as irrational to the coyotes as it had to her. She found that thought sobering.

He had a definite swagger as he walked toward her. She half expected him to beat his chest and bray his victory to the wind. Instead he shot her a look of smug triumph, but when his eyes read her expression, his joy vanished. A squint and he looked away from her.

She cringed as he drew his knife. He dug the blade into the chain's link looped into the rung in the tree and twisted. The chain dropped to the ground. He picked up the loose end, wound it around his hand and tugged. She followed as he led her to the shed. He lifted the brace, threw the door wide, and pulled her inside. It was dark, but welcoming with the innocuous smells of leather and newly cut grass.

Bo dropped the end of the chain and picked up what appeared to be large pliers. The open door beckoned and Sara took a step toward freedom. The man growled a warning and she froze. He put the pliers against the metal nose ring at her wrist and cut. She was free.

She could bolt, run into the dark—follow the coyotes—but she hesitated. Instead she looked at these new surroundings, straining to see in the darkness. Lord, she was tired.

Without looking at the man, she whispered, "Thank you," and wondered if she were thanking the man or God.

From the corner of her eye, she saw him nod once, acknowledging the words. He strode into one of the two stalls in the shed and rolled a large black motorcycle out, then pitched forkfuls of clean hay into the floor of the newly vacated stall. When the hay was mounded to three feet or so, he caught Sara's upper arm and shoved. Stumbling, she fell forward to find herself swimming in the fresh hay.

She turned to regard her captor in disbelief.

He ignored her, pushed the motorcycle outside, returned for an implement leaning against the wall, then left again, slamming the doors. She heard the wooden brace fall into its brackets, securing the doors from the outside and shutting off all of nature's night lights.

No longer exposed to the wind or the elements or the attacks of vicious predators lurking in the woods, Sara sat stunned, reconnoitering. The hay was clean and sweet. The silent man had not murdered her, had not even injured her, really. In truth, he had protected her, provided a warm, safe place for her. She felt thankful to be breathing and relatively uninjured.

Sitting on her legs, she touched her wrists and stretched her arms up and to the sides. She seemed to be all right. She stood. Her legs felt okay. She twisted from her waist, was sore but generally sound.

Moving slowly, she felt her way to the double doors, pressed her ear to one and listened.

All she heard were nighttime rustlings of creatures and wind. She pushed on both doors. They didn't give. She didn't plan to leave until dawn, but she needed to find a way out and be ready to go at first light.

She bumped one door with her hip. Nothing. She kicked it, then butted it with a shoulder. Still nothing. She retreated a step and banged the door harder, then again, battering each door with one shoulder after the other, again and again, until her eyes teared with pain and frustration.

Breathing hard, Sara glared at the unforgiving doors, turned her back, walked a wide circle then hurled her body forward, ramming them with all her strength.

The rebound knocked her off her feet and sent her sprawling, face down on the hard-packed dirt floor. She lay there, gasping as she doubled her fists, knuckles together, to pillow her forehead. Too tired to cry, she lifted her head and banged it against her fists.

Finally, brutalized, exhausted, she made her way back to the hay mounded in the second stall and collapsed. She pulled her knees up and curled around them into a fetal position.

She thought idly of Bo laughing out loud. The sound resonated from vocal chords that obviously worked. Her eyes popped wide in the darkness. Bo didn't speak. Why not?

Tomorrow she would make him take her back to civilization. She didn't want to risk it alone at night against the coyotes and other wildlife prowling the forest, looking for an easy meal. Nor did she want to run into that hideous Franklin, eager to rape and murder her.

"Tomorrow I am out of here," she promised herself, "one way or another." She might need a weapon to force the brute to do what she wanted. She thought of the gun the man had carelessly leaned against the tree beside her when the coyotes were circling. She could have grabbed it. That was a stupid thing for him to do, if he considered her his enemy. And he must. Chaining her to a tree was no way to treat a friend.

Was the gun a stupid oversight or was he testing her?

No, it was no test. It was stupidity. Rank stupidity.

Okay, he was stupid. What was her excuse? Why hadn't she taken advantage of the opportunity?

If he put the gun there as a test, it probably wasn't even loaded.

Or maybe he thought if he should be overcome by the coyotes, she would use it to rescue him. Mountain women probably knew how to shoot guns. She, on the other hand, knew nothing about weapons, couldn't have shot it if she'd wanted to. But if he thought she could save him...

The pitchfork! He had tossed the hay into this stall with a pitchfork.

She scrambled to her feet and groped around the stall, then out into the main part of the shed. She stumbled, caught herself and continued feeling her way along the wall to the doors. Nothing.

He had come back after he removed the motorcycle. Had he taken the pitchfork out with him? She hadn't paid attention. Maybe he was smarter than he looked. She smiled to herself. What was the old gag? He could be a whole lot smarter than he looked and still not be very smart.

Okay, the chance at the gun and the pitchfork were gone, but there would be other opportunities. She needed to be alert for the next one. Just because he didn't speak, she must not assume Bo was more or less intelligent than Cappy. Maybe he could be manipulated more easily than the little half-wit.

Or maybe not.

This was all just so much mental chewing gum.

"Lie down." She spoke the words out loud into the darkness. "Rest. You've got a long walk back tomorrow."

She wrapped the full skirt of her dress around the lower part of her body, mounded hay over her and burrowed into her nest.

Chapter Three

Friday, Day 1: Sara opened her eyes in the windowless shed. Thin shafts of light filtered between seams of vertical logs. She thought timbers were supposed to be laid horizontally in log buildings. Sitting, aware of the pleasant smells of hay and animals and leather, she sneezed.

Stiff and sore from yesterday's adventure, she moved gingerly, testing soft, pampered muscles. She examined both wrists, scalded raw from the rope—the right worse than the left. They both stung.

She needed to use the facilities but there were no facilities, except for the outhouse. How strange to be here in this place left a century behind the rest of the country.

She struggled to her feet, stretching to get the kinks out, peering around, able to see outlines of things in the filtering streams of sunlight. Her bladder prodding her, Sara stepped out of the stall, moved across the shed, backed up against a wall and hesitated, listening.

Hearing only the sounds of nature, Sara flipped up her dress, dropped her panties and squatted. She relieved herself, consoled by the thought that farm animals probably had done the same thing in the same place many times.

Her most urgent problem solved, Sara straightened her clothing as she paced the shed's perimeters. There had to be a way out. If there were, she would find it.

She found a pole among scraps of wood in a corner. She used it to dig at the base of each upright, except those barricaded by a stack of crates and pasteboard boxes and the ones inside what appeared to be a tack room. She'd have to investigate those walls later, if it came to that.

She broke her pole off twice trying to pry it between logs. She dug and kicked and pushed against every accessible log before she plopped back down in the hay, winded.

Someone rapped twice, hesitated, then lifted the brace outside from its hasps and opened the doors.

Sara jumped to her feet as sunlight flooded the dreary interior of the shed. The rush of warm outside air had a pungent, earthy smell. The

35

temperature outside obviously was much higher than that inside the windowless shed. The bright sunlight blinded her momentarily and she retreated a step or two.

Bo walked directly to the locked tack room, spun the tumblers on the lock, opened the room, went inside, and returned with a leather harness and a log, which he stood on end, blocking access to the door. He then sat, balancing on the log, the harness in his hand.

She had seen how quickly he could move and rejected the idea of making a run for it. She needed his help to find her way back to civilization, anyway.

Of course, in the daylight, Cappy's references to bears and pumas and wild pigs seemed exaggerated. This Bo would just have to return her to her real life.

Watching him jab a new hole and thread a wire through the leather strap, Sara knew he wasn't there in the shed to mend that harness. He must have wanted to see her again. Yes, she was pretty sure of that, despite his refusing to look at her.

Determined to take stock of her situation as quickly as possible, Sara decided she first needed to find out if she could communicate with him.

"Bo?" She hesitated. "That is your name, right?" He gave no indication he heard. "My name is Sara. Sara Loomis." Still no response. "Bo, can you hear me?"

Nothing.

"Do you hear or do you read lips?"

Raising his face, Bo fastened his dark, dark eyes on her and gave a brief nod.

"You *do* hear, then?"

Another nod.

"I don't believe you're mute. Bo, I heard you laugh out loud when the coyotes ran away. I figure that means you *can* talk."

He didn't deny it. Didn't respond at all.

Sara rubbed the palms of her hands together. "I see."

He continued patching the harness.

"Five men took me hostage in a robbery yesterday." She spoke slowly, enunciating each word carefully. "They planned to kill me. One of them, a young guy they called Cappy, was supposed to do it. He

36

brought me here instead. Tied me to the side of your cabin." Bo suddenly glanced up and gave her a hard, puzzled look. She didn't think it a good idea to tell him Cappy had promised Bo would murder her quickly and mercifully.

"Will you take me back? To a highway? Or a county road? If you'll take me to a road somewhere, I can get home on my own. Will you do that?"

Bo studied her a moment before he shook his head once, no, then turned his attention back to the harness.

"Why not?" She tried not to show her annoyance. "I'll pay you. I can pay you well." Still no response. "Please."

He wouldn't look at her, acted as if he hadn't heard.

Sara's shoulders slumped. Okay, she wouldn't press it right now. They could come back to that later. Keeping her voice even, she said, "I haven't had much to eat or drink since the day before yesterday. I'm pretty hungry, but mainly I'm thirsty. Could you give me a drink of water? Please."

His dark eyes rounded as he raised them to hers. Well, at least she had his attention.

"I cook a little. Not much from scratch, but I'll try. I don't suppose you have any TV dinners or chips or..." She paused and risked a glance into his ebony eyes. He stood. Unable to read his thoughts, she stiffened and retreated a step.

Bo hung the harness on a nail in the tack room, closed the door and reattached the combination lock before he stepped toward her. She didn't want him to sense her fear, but when he reached for her arm, she shrank. Her apprehension seemed to please him, although it was hard to read his face through the beard and all the hair spilling over his forehead.

She eased forward, slowly, voluntarily, hoping he wouldn't touch her. Bo grunted his approval and tossed his head indicating she should follow him.

He shuffled out the shed's door and to his right. Sara followed several paces behind, limping. Her left shoe still had its one-inch heel, the right one didn't. Bo stopped, looked at her pointedly, then at the outhouse and back at her.

She allowed an embarrassed smile. "I've been, thank you."

He nodded and continued on to a lean-to attached to the shed. Chickens strutted about the small fenced yard, pecking at bits of feed scattered over the dirt. Their movements seemed terribly erratic. Sara had never before been that close to live chickens. Apparently, the lean-to was a chicken house.

Bo opened the crude gate and indicated she should accompany him into the chicken yard. He latched the gate behind them.

She watched spellbound as Bo caught one of the hens and carefully, making sure Sara could see, positioned its head in his large hand. She edged back several paces. The chicken squawked and flapped as the man's grip tightened. Bo flipped the fowl's body up and down sharply, then gave it a spin, still clasping the head firmly.

Sara heard neck bones popping above the bird's deafening squawk. The chicken's body suddenly broke free, its head still firmly clasped in Bo's hand. The headless body convulsed around the yard, flapping, throwing dust each time it landed and went airborne again. Sara stood in stunned disbelief, shaking her head, trembling.

The other feathered occupants continued pecking at the feed, little disturbed at the disruption caused by the plight of their yard mate.

Sara squeezed her hands together, trying to control the trembling, lifted them to her throat, sucked both lips and felt herself quake.

The hen's body hit the ground again and again, flapping and spinning in the dust.

Finally, when it stopped, Bo picked it up and threaded its feet through the chicken wire fence. Dangling upside down, the bird's blood ran down and soaked the ground beneath it as the man seized another victim.

Sara was unable to turn away, hypnotized again by the captive bird's terror.

Instead of flipping the hen, as he had done before, Bo secured the chicken's head then attempted to hand it to Sara. She looked squarely into his face, unable to fathom what he intended, yet afraid she knew. Her hands remained limp at her sides. Her breathing became ragged.

Bo grunted the guttural sound, and shook the hen in front of her. Denying to herself that she could touch the chicken, Sara reached to take it.

The exchange was made and she had the bird's head clamped firmly in the palm of her hand. Tears filled her eyes. She gulped, gasping for air. She felt moisture and looked down. Her thumb was over one of the hen's open eyes. She trembled and raised her other hand to grip the bird's head with both hands.

The hen's body was heavy, dangling as it did. Suddenly the chicken began struggling. Flailing talons spurred Sara's arms, raking the raw, open places on her wrists.

Her human scream was as urgent as the hen's shriek as Sara released the chicken and scrambled to the gate without a plan or a thought. She fumbled with the simple latch, not able to unfasten it. Hopelessly, she crumpled into the dirt sobbing, looping her fingers through and pressing her forehead against the chicken wire.

She heard a commotion as Bo again found and captured the second chicken, wrung its neck and waited for the flapping to subside. She peeked to see him gut both birds with his knife.

Carrying the feet of both hens in one hand, Bo reached around Sara to unfasten the latch on the gate, then waited for her to stand and follow him from the chicken yard before again securing the latch. Limping along behind, swiping at the tears still trickling down her face, she followed him to the cabin and inside.

Bo took the dripping hens to a pot already boiling on the cook stove, dropped them into the water and motioned Sara to sit in one of the two rocking chairs on either side of the hearth. Both chairs were of woven wicker stretched over aged wooden braces. One of the chairs had pads of a faded floral fabric over foam rubber. Sara chose the padded chair.

Inside the cabin, Bo seemed immense, ducking his head as he shuffled. His movements were slow, methodical, as she might have expected from such a grizzled old fellow.

Light came from a kind of awning window on one wall. Coals from an earlier fire glowed in the fireplace and drew Sara's gaze. A ghastly odor filled the room as the chickens began to cook.

Sara sat, rocking, the silence marred only by the simmering water on the stove regaining its boil. Her breathing was steady except for an occasional hiccupped sob. Eventually she settled into the rocker's cushioned padding.

She couldn't remember ever having thought a chair as comfortable as this one. In fact, she seldom paid attention to chairs at all. Perhaps the comfort of the chair was related to the fact she was again exhausted and it was still early in the day. The awful smell permeated the room.

Bo stood over a hutch beside the cook stove. He appeared to be preparing food.

Ravenous, Sara realized her host hadn't washed his hands. "The first rule of cooking," her mother had repeated hundreds of times during Sara's formative years: "Wash your hands."

But when Bo handed her a thick slice of bread slathered with butter and sprinkled with sugar, Sara's reservations regarding hygiene lapsed.

He also handed her a cup of cold milk and another of coffee with milk and sugar, a little sweeter than she liked, but she needed the boost the extra sugar would provide. She drained both cups, feeling the liquids meander through her chest and down, down. Her stomach growled its appreciation.

The awful odor seemed to have diminished.

Bo sat in the other rocker and propped his feet on the small footstool fronting it. He drank his coffee black and took only butter, no sugar, on his bread.

Just as Sara had begun to relax, Bo finished eating, wiped his hands on his pant legs, stood, drew his knife and stepped in front of her. She watched in horror as he bent and picked up her left foot. With a single thrust, he whacked the heel off her one good shoe, leaving both of her expensive Cappezios heel-less. It meant no more limping. She didn't, however, feel thanks were in order as he tossed the amputated heel into the fireplace.

Bo pulled the chickens' odorous, dripping, feathered bodies from the kettle and tossed them onto the crude table. Sara gasped at the putrid smell of the steaming corpses. Bo slid into the lone straight-backed chair and patiently began plucking handfuls of feathers, tossing them onto the floor. That's when Sara realized there was no flooring in the cabin, only dirt beneath their feet. She supposed having no floor simplified housekeeping.

She glanced around, reviewing the rest of the one-room structure.

A large wooden box of a bed, neatly made up with layers of hand-sewn quilts, filled one portion of the room. Those quilts would be high-dollar items in any craft show and Sara wondered how Bo had gotten them. Perhaps he'd made them himself.

The cabin walls seemed oddly cut and Sara realized the upper halves of the walls doubled as a primitive kind of awnings which could be pushed out and propped up in warm weather to allow a breeze. Despite the morning chill, the windows on one side were open, allowing sunlight to brighten and warm the cabin.

Sara had no natural sense of direction, but bright, morning sunlight angling inside obviously came from the east. Now all she needed to know was the direction to the nearest road.

"I'll bet you can open those awnings and get a good breeze from the south and east in warm weather, right?"

Bo frowned and allowed one brusque nod, yes.

The southwest quadrant of the cabin boasted an old school teacher's oak desk and a large, heavy chair. Situated beneath the closed window on the west wall was an aged steamer trunk.

The west wall also had a shelf of books. Surprised that Bo could read, Sara couldn't help being curious about the kinds of books in his library. Maybe she could browse later.

The fireplace occupied most of the north wall and the kitchen—actually the stove and hutch/cupboard and the crude table with a single chair—took the final quadrant, the northeast.

Feeling better after they ate, Sara watched Bo pluck the first chicken. Having gotten somewhat accustomed to the hideous smell, she was tempted to help. After all, she needed to get into the man's good graces.

She scooted her rocking chair closer to the table and cautiously touched the damp feathers of the second hen: The bodies now seemed to be less those of living creatures, more something which belonged in the meat market. She supposed she could help with this part.

Tentatively, she grabbed a handful of feathers and tugged. They held.

"Damn," she whispered, sitting straighter. She was still considerably lower than the surface of the table. Bo glanced up but his eyes didn't meet hers.

She selected three feathers and pulled. They didn't budge. Exasperated, Sara stood, wrapped her hand around one feather, gritted her teeth, and yanked. The lone quill popped free, knocking her off balance. She examined the feather's end thoughtfully, pursed her mouth and set her mind to the task. Irksome, yanking one feather at a time to prepare chicken that she most certainly would not be able to eat. How could anyone eat food she had known personally when it was alive?

"I never realized how primitive this food chain business is," she muttered.

Bo didn't bother to glance up but his beard moved. Smiling or frowning? She couldn't tell. She'd like to be able to make him smile. It might help her cause.

When the feathers were plucked, Bo left the bare chickens on the table, stepped outside, dumped the water from the pot and went to a metal device in the front yard where he pumped a long handle until water ran from the large spout. He rinsed the pot, then refilled it with fresh water.

Watching from the cabin door, Sara searched the sky for jet trails, and listened for any kind of vibration—a car, a train, anything. She neither saw, nor heard, nor felt anything.

Back inside the cabin, she watched as he cut up the chickens, dropped the pieces into salted water seasoned with some kind of leaves and brought the contents to a boil. He loaded wood in the cook stove, adding more periodically to keep the water bubbling.

Late in the morning Bo peeled out of an animal skin shirt down to a cotton flannel work shirt cuffed to reveal well developed forearms. He was certainly a muscular old duffer. He picked up his gun and shells, swept two quilts off his bed, and indicated Sara should follow.

Outside, he looked up, studying the sky to the southwest. Incoming clouds rolling fast, low over their heads, veiled the sun's brightness. The air, warm early, had turned muggy.

Bo led Sara back to the shed and motioned her inside. Reluctantly, she obeyed. He handed her the quilts, slammed the door shut, and she heard the wooden beam slide into its hasps.

Discouraged, but at least fed, Sara stretched one quilt over part of the hay in her stall and left the other folded on top of the first. Then she paced, occasionally kicking at the base of a log in the wall which looked weakened by weather or water damage.

She had to escape. Once out, she had to avoid the men who wanted to kill her. She might be able to manage Cappy by himself, but Franklin and the others were dangerous. And what about Bo? Was he friend or foe?

She thought idly about Richard Nixon and his enemies list. Until yesterday, Sara had had no enemies. Now she had a full card. The big question was, who was Enemy Number One?

Bo? Yes. Maybe. Then, probably Franklin, closely followed by the other robbers she could identify.

Then there were the four-legged enemies, the hungry ones prowling the woods looking for meat. She needed a weapon, dared not break out of this shed without one.

She went to the locked tack room and peered through the seams in the board walls. There was a saddle on some kind of saw horse and the leather straps, harnesses, she supposed. There was the pitchfork, a shovel, a hoe, and a sickle. Pretty primitive stuff.

Scanning around inside the shed itself, she found the pole she'd used the night before.

Poking and prodding, she was not able to pry her way into the tack room. The pole kept breaking off in bits and pieces.

She tossed the remains aside, paced back to her stall and dropped onto the quilt pondering.

Did Bo mean to harm her? Was he part of a kidnap plot? She didn't think so. Didn't think there was a plot. Not much of a plan at all. Her kidnapping was happenstance. Franklin was a horny little gnome looking for a throw-away woman. Well, he'd picked the wrong girl this time.

She hated sitting in the gloom, needed something to do. She stood and paced again, prowling the walls until she came upon what might have once been a mop handle. She picked it up and again tried driving it into spaces between rough-hewn logs of the shed's walls.

Finally, looking at the handle, then back at the hay, she got an idea. Sorting, she found some hay was stiff, like straw—broom straw.

Sitting again, Sara gathered the stiffest, thickest pieces of hay and began fashioning them to the pole with the occasional tender reed, adding strands until her makeshift broom was thick and fairly uniform. She nodded, satisfied and hummed, "Good enough for a dirt floor."

Admiring her work, Sara felt a vibration. Machinery, a truck, maybe, rumbled over a mountain road, somewhere close. She dropped to press her ear against the ground of the shed floor to determine the direction from which the sound came or which way it was going.

It seemed to be north of her, moving west to east. If she were outside, she might be able to feel the sounds from different areas and be more sure of their direction. It would give her something to guide her when she made her escape.

Chapter Four

The marvelous smell of the cooking chicken wafted across the yard and into the shed a long time before Bo reappeared to take Sara back to the cabin.

She watched in amazement as he combined flour with salt, bacon drippings and egg, shaped the batter into balls, and dropped them into the boiling chicken broth. After all his trouble, she hated to boycott the meal. Also, her galloping hunger was a consideration. Her stomach roiled.

Sitting spellbound in the padded rocker, Sara watched the man steam stalks of broccoli and sprinkle cinnamon over apple slices. The preparations seemed natural. She marveled at his confidence in his own masculinity, assurance that allowed him to do things most men would consider woman's work.

The aroma made Sara's mouth water as she sat rocking, waiting. She wished she had brought the new broom. There were still a few errant chicken feathers. But she didn't want to appear pushy.

She looked around for the gun. It and one other hung on pegs over the door, too high for her to reach without something to stand on. And bullets? Did he keep the guns loaded? And where did he keep the extra bullets?

She forced herself to look away from the guns, not wanting to telegraph her thoughts. What else could she think about? Oh, yes, she might be boycotting the chicken—because of her earlier feeling of kinship with the hens. That was this morning. She'd eaten only the slice of bread and drunk single cups of milk and coffee in more than twenty-four hours. Her stomach groaned again, loudly.

Sara revised her plan. She would force herself to be hospitable and eat the chicken; not only that, but anything else set in front of her. It *was*, after all, common courtesy and she *did* need to find a way to get on Bo's good side.

The man put plates on the table. She needed to be cultivating him, encouraging him to like her. "Can I help?"

He regarded her oddly, his black orbs staring from behind all that hair directly into her face. He nodded once and pointed toward a drawer in the hutch.

Rummaging there, she found eating utensils, along with scissors, tape, writing paper, pens, glue, sewing notions, and other miscellaneous items. Seeing the long paper scissors, she hesitated. Bo's gaze flickered from her to the scissors and back to her face. His eyes narrowed and he shook his head almost imperceptibly. She grabbed a pen and paper and held them up, pretending to have been considering them. "Hey, here's a ballpoint and paper. You can write me notes."

He turned back to his preparations and shook his head.

"Sure. That way you can tell me things. You can draw a map, give me directions out of here."

He continued ignoring her.

Deflated, annoyed, Sara put away the pen and paper, again studying the scissors. Slowly, she withdrew two knives and forks and placed them on the crude table.

Obviously unaware of her earlier sentiment regarding the chickens, Bo served her a full plate. Spurred by hunger, she consumed every morsel, including broccoli stalks, and was mopping gravy with a dumpling before she thought again of the planned boycott.

It certainly had been a day for trashing preconceived notions. She wondered if she had progressed far enough to be able to stab this man with a pair of scissors. Wringing the necks of innocent chickens was one thing. Thrusting steel into her gentle captor's heart hardly seemed justified, was definitely not an apt way to show her appreciation for his hospitality.

She smiled wryly to herself. Sharing his food only bought a man so much. She sighed. It would take a lot to talk herself into actually sticking scissors into him unless, of course, he hurt her.

Why did he refuse to take her to a road somewhere? What could he possibly want with her, except...no, she wasn't going to think about that.

After supper, Bo settled in the second rocking chair with his pipe and slipped a thin piece of wood from his shirt pocket. It was seven or eight inches long and maybe two inches wide. He wrestled his knife from the pocket of his leather trousers, scraped it back and forth over a hand-held whetstone, settled back, and cut into the wood. Sara's eyes flitted to the drawer in the hutch as she tried to think of a way to get to those scissors.

She told herself *not* to look at the drawer, not to think of the scissors. He mustn't suspect. "What're you making?" she asked.

Ignoring her, Bo methodically chipped away at the wood, apparently satisfied with the silent project, not needing the company of another human being.

How could he live isolated like this? Alone? The poor old soul.

She sat straighter. Why should she care? She was only marking time, pretending an interest in his work, attempting a little after-dinner conversation.

With a mute?

She glowered down at her hands pressed together in her lap and rocked harder, trying to decide which of them—she or Bo—was the most addled. He obviously didn't want to share his life. Then why wouldn't he draw her a map and send her on her way?

She had to get through to him. Or she might have to resort to using the scissors. He was too big for her to threaten. She would have to injure him severely, if he tried to stop her. She'd be sorry if it came to that. He seemed harmless enough, but she was definitely leaving here, one way or another.

* * * *

Sara felt strange that night, burrowed into her nest of hay in the shed, having left the cabin without the scissors. The quilts were spread over and under her and she felt oddly safe, watched over by the man in the cabin.

She roused from a deep sleep when Bo knocked twice and flung the shed door open. Hurried strides brought him quickly over the sod floor.

Scrambling to her feet, Sara shrank from his hands as he reached for her. "No." She shook her head, peering at him, trying to read his face. He grabbed her hand. Brightness jabbed the dark, providing an instant of light followed by rolling, distant thunder.

Sara jerked free and flailed at Bo as he grabbed for her again. "No. Please. I can't." She slapped at him, stumbling backwards. "You won't enjoy it. I'm no good at it. No! Please, don't do this."

Bo hesitated, regarding her oddly in the intermittent snatches of light which were closely followed by the rumbling. It sounded as if it were getting nearer. He caught her arm but she jerked out of his grasp, lurching to the far wall.

The anger in his onyx eyes was obvious as lightning forked, illuminating the shed with another instant of strobe brightness before sending renewed groans ricocheting through the mountains. Bo made a sound that rivaled the thunder, and lunged. She skittered to one side and tried to dart past him, but again he moved more quickly than she thought possible, flung his arms around her, and unceremoniously tossed her up and over his shoulder.

She screamed, her voice muffled by mother nature's frenzied explosions, which suddenly seemed to be detonating directly overhead.

Bo jogged out of the shed. Bouncing on his shoulder, Sara kicked and screamed and pummeled his back with both fists. He didn't flinch or seem to notice. Instead, he glanced at the sky and broke into a lope.

She stopped struggling when they bypassed the cabin. Her curiosity piqued, she suddenly noticed that the air was static, hot, stifling. She glanced at the sky.

Clouds raced and lightning jabbed the darkness, followed by booming reports that filled the eerie stillness and reverberated, rolling, rumbling off through the mountains.

Bo carried her into a cave cut into the wall of the mountain immediately behind his cabin. Deep inside, amid gunnysacks and boxes of foodstuffs, he stood her on her feet. Bo then returned to the mouth of the cavern. Sara followed.

Hail suddenly pounded out of the still silence, hammering the ground beyond the cave. Pellets became marble-sized and battered the tin roofs on the cabin, the shed, and the outhouse. The din was deafening.

Sara crept closer to stare into the darkness, which was punctuated by flashes of light and the echoing ovations. Sidling close, she didn't attempt to speak, doubting that Bo could hear her words over the accelerating roar of the storm. He spared her a quick glance before turning his attention back to the tumult.

In the breathtaking brilliance of lightning strikes, she saw the shaggy clouds, tornadoes forming, dipping, teasing, then failing to take shape, popping back up into the heavens. She had watched these displays all her life and had seen, too, the devastation left in the path of these meteorological marauders. She shivered at those memories.

A small funnel descended, assumed a valid form, and appeared to gather momentum. It was east of them, moving east. Sara trembled, almost losing control before she realized the twister was moving away from them; that one, at least, no threat. But there were others.

As suddenly as it had begun, the hail stopped. The silence outside was ominous as the air again spiked with heat and grew eerily still.

Anxiously, Sara followed Bo out of the cave to look back behind, to the southwest. A dozen small funnels formed from the shaggy darkness, dipped for a moment or two, then retreated.

She recalled an old legend. The danger was over when the air cooled. But this air was electric. Sara ran back toward the cave, tripped and caught herself on her poor, sore hands. Scrambling, lurching further into the cave, she dropped to her knees in a heap, covering her head with her arms. Clenching her teeth, she muttered. "Why, are you doing this to me, God? Why bring me this far, then abandon me?"

Her lips snuffled in the dirt floor as she babbled a series of prayers and recited creeds. Terrified, weeping, she felt something, someone near. She turned her head and opened her eyes without moving any other part of her body.

Bo knelt beside her. Tentatively, gently, he placed his hand on the back of her head.

She hated to be touched when she was nervous or frightened. At the moment, however, she didn't object as his great paw of a hand patted her head. Slowly, that huge, calloused hand traced down her neck, between her shoulder blades, to her waist. It was the kind of stroke she had seen her grandfather use to quiet his bird dog, Maggie, when the high-bred bitch got overly excited.

The touch of Bo's steadying hand soothed Sara, quieted her, and she grew still, calmed, just as Maggie the pointer had been beneath her grandfather's placating stroke.

Why was Bo petting her? What were his intentions? Should she be frightened? As the large hand repeated its glide, Sara twisted her neck to peer up at him.

The man was not even looking at her. Instead, he stared toward the cave's gaping mouth, stroking Sara absently.

Reassured by his seeming lack of interest, Sara leaned into him as his hand again trailed from her head to her waist. Bo's body loomed big and strong, protecting her from the furor outside.

She heard the approaching rumble, the familiar sound of a freight train accelerating. She trembled and pulled her limbs even more tightly beneath her.

Despite the oppressive heat, Sara was glad to have Bo close, a human shield between her and the yawning mouth of the cave.

The rumbling became a deafening roar but the air in the cave remained blessedly still. Sara quivered beneath the man's continuous stroking. The roar reached a crescendo of trees being torn from the earth, of things being tossed about, then suddenly there was silence.

Moments passed. The air turned chilly, almost cold.

Bo stood as a light rain began, a gentle drizzle which seemed to be apologizing for the antics of its meteorological companions. He walked to the entrance of the cave, propped his fists at his waist, and filled his lungs.

Sara sat back on her legs, silent until Bo, staring out at the night, looked back at her, growled, and nodded for her to come there. She stood, straightened her dress, dusting it off, and padded, barefooted, to his side. He stood a head taller than she was, which made him six-foot-two or better. He seemed strong, capable, invincible, a fully mature adult male facing down the elements themselves.

The rain stopped. The stars shimmered, newly washed.

Sara had been afraid, had panicked before Bo touched her, quieted her. She risked a look at his profile.

"I'm always thanking you," she said quietly.

His eyes penetrated the semi-darkness as he looked down at her. Again he allowed only a nod of acknowledgment.

"I'm sorry...for struggling. I didn't understand what you were doing. I don't like for people to touch me...personally. You know." He looked puzzled. She felt stupid. "I'm not much of a lover." She risked a glance and an embarrassed smile, "or a fighter, either. I guess you already figured that out."

Another nod and the hint of a smile beneath the hair.

"I'm afraid of a lot of things." She grinned timidly. "Of almost everything really."

He tapped his chest with his fingers.

"Right. I'm definitely afraid of you." His frown deepened. "When you came busting in the shed, I thought you wanted me for...for sex."

She could see his eyebrows knit, the movement almost indiscernible beneath the hair tumbling down his forehead.

"You scared me to death." She straightened, glanced outside then back at him and inhaled. "I misunderstood. I'm sorry." She paused and shrugged. "Anyway, thanks for... Well, thanks."

Bo nodded, then strode from the cave. She followed, but downed tree limbs dotted the landscape, although the buildings all seemed to be intact. Barefooted, she chose her steps carefully, but yipped involuntarily when she stepped down hard on a thorned twig. Bo looked back at her, then bent and tapped his shoulder. Grudgingly, she stepped closer and draped herself over the offered shoulder, voluntarily again becoming a sack of feed.

As he straightened, he wrapped an arm around the backs of her knees and set his other hand at her ankle, steadying her. Thus, Sara humbly returned to the shed.

Inside, Bo set her on her feet.

"Thanks...again," she muttered.

He gave a nod, then stepped out to close and bar the doors.

She felt weird but safe, settling in her nest. More restless than before, she longed to go home, to sleep in her own bed.

She glowered into the darkness, uneasy. Her bed was in transit somewhere. She was in the middle of moving when she was kidnapped. She didn't know anymore exactly where *home* was.

* * * *

Day 2: Early Saturday, Bo cooked bacon, scrambled eggs, and biscuits for breakfast. Sara ate like a farm hand and made no apologies. She purposefully avoided watching him eat. His manners were all right, but food matted in his mustache and spattered into his beard. It gave her an idea.

"Would you let me trim that hair back just a little from your mouth?"

He glared at her, giving no other response.

"Food sticks to it when you eat. It's gross. Very *un*appetizing."

He pinched a lock of the hair on his head between his thumb and forefinger and eyed her suspiciously.

She smiled. "No, I won't cut any of the hair on your head, *Samson*. Why? Do you think that's where you get your strength?"

She saw a slight smile play at his narrow lips. She regarded his arms, his square shoulders and thick chest, then looked away. "I don't think your strength has anything to do with your hair, old man," she said under her breath, speaking more to herself than to him.

That afternoon, Bo picked up his gun, gathered a handful of shells from a bookshelf, and turned to her.

"You don't have to lock me up." Her eyes held his as she lowered her voice. "Bo, let me go. Point the way and let me get out of here."

Shaking his head, he grunted and motioned for her to follow.

She wrung her hands and stared down at them. "Well, can I at least borrow a couple of books?"

He took a breath before he allowed one quick nod.

She browsed through the bookshelves for several minutes.

Most of the volumes were about military campaigns or historical battles. He had a smattering of "How To" books on organic gardening, herbal medicines, design and construction of a hydroelectric plant, cooking, animal husbandry, etc.

There were only three Novels: *To Kill a Mockingbird, Rifles for Watie* and *Exodus*. She took all three.

Again confined in the shed, Sara sat cross-legged, positioning a shaft of sunlight on the pages in order to read, but she couldn't concentrate. Instead she thought of Bo.

What kind of man was this? He definitely was *not* a madman, as Cappy had said, although he was eccentric.

Organic gardening? A hydroelectric plant?

Okay, he was an oddball. Also, Cappy had said Bo was old. She was less and less sure about how old. Cappy was nineteen. Maybe any fully mature man seemed old to him.

Sara had turned the pages of a half dozen chapters and thought until

52

she couldn't think anymore by the time Bo knocked twice. He led her outside where he showed her how to dig yams.

For Sara, digging sweet potatoes was like hunting Easter eggs. She gave a rebel whoop each time she probed and triumphantly turned up one of the tubers. Bent to the task, Bo appeared to ignore her sporadic celebrations.

* * * *

After a late lunch of baked sweet potatoes, Sara casually went to the hutch drawer for the scissors. She picked them up and looked to Bo who eyed her suspiciously. Did he know what she was thinking? No, he was probably just concerned about the trim. Obviously he hadn't considered she might use them as a weapon.

Stay cool, she told herself. Keep him relaxed, off guard. "You agreed," she cajoled, smiling. His usual quick nod was less emphatic. He lowered himself to sit stiffly erect at the edge of the unpadded rocking chair.

Shoving the small footstool back with her foot, studying his beard, Sara nudged his knees apart to let her close enough to work. She tried to ignore their proximity as she tilted his chin up so the light from the open awning was on his face exposing his throat.

She tried to imagine plunging the scissors into his neck and wondered if she could endure the feel of flesh tearing under her hand.

Suddenly his eyes shot to her face, a perceptive glance indicating he was fully aware of the scissors and able to read her thoughts. Was he daring her? Her breath quickened.

She couldn't do it. She wasn't that desperate. Not yet. There had to be another way, a better way. This man had been kind. She could never live with herself if she did such a thing.

Giving up the ill-conceived notion, she snipped at the strands of hair draping his upper lip.

"Are you planning to make your own electricity for this place some day?" She asked the question innocently, as if her abhorrent thoughts had not passed between them. She bent, peering, guiding the scissors around his mouth.

He nodded slightly. She flinched. "Moving like that could cost you a lip, you know. I'm armed." She clacked the scissors open and closed in front of his face and arched her eyebrows. She caught a glint of something in the black depths of his eyes. A twinkle? Maybe. She swallowed a startled laugh.

She planned to trim a little hair away from his thin lips—a token effort brought on by forfeit of her lurid scheme—but as she worked, her excavation revealed full lips and a comely mouth hidden beneath the brush. His lips were not only generous but his mouth was broad.

Finally, nearly finished, Sara attempted to take a step back to see if the shaping looked symmetrical. As she stepped, however, her heel caught the footstool and she stumbled, reeling. Her arms flailed as she teetered backward, the scissors gripped tightly in one hand.

Reacting, Bo caught the backs of her thighs with both hands just before she toppled, steadying her.

Breathless, regaining her balance, Sara flashed a quick look at him and blushed. A gurgle—half cough and half laugh—burbled from her throat. "Sorry." The word trilled with her embarrassed laughter.

Bo grinned, his dark eyes capturing and holding hers a moment before he dropped his gaze, shaking his head in disbelief. His hands lingered, however, firmly affixed to thigh muscles running the backs of her legs.

Staring, Sara cocked her head and pursed her mouth, her reaction changing from a giddy apology to an imperious glower.

Bo lowered his hands slowly, skimming her legs, but he maintained physical contact, his fingers coming to rest at either side of her knees. He glanced up and a mischievous twinkle glinted in his eyes, this time unmistakable.

Before she actually saw them, Sara had assumed Bo's teeth would be decayed or at least yellowed by age and neglect. She stared at his mouth as it spread, his grin revealing large, white, even teeth. She felt transfixed by a peculiar warmth, which sent pleasurable pin pricks spiking up and down her back.

Rattled, unable to clear her thoughts, she tilted her head and continued studying him.

Both Bo and Sara were still, crystallized in a moment until she became aware that the pointed end of the scissors wavered close to his neck. Hot breath caught in her throat. Bo looked down, his shoulders stiffened, and the grin vanished. He removed his hands from her legs, shot a glance from her face to the scissors and back, and growled a thin warning.

She laughed lightly as she turned the scissor tips down and, this time looking behind, minced back a cautious step.

Bo tipped his head, shrouding his eyes behind the curtain of hair. Still, Sara couldn't seem to force her gaze away from his mouth. Something inside her was changing, right then, a dramatic change. Her steely fear of him became molten and reformed as...as something else, something akin to fear but more intense, a feeling which defied immediate definition. She needed to think. What was this...this peculiar excitement? She needed to interrupt these sensations, whatever they were; break this reverie.

"My, what big teeth you have, Grandma," she said, hoping that injecting humor might break the brittle edge of the moment. "That's what Little Red Riding Hood said to the wolf in her grandmother's bed."

Bo gave a series of slow nods indicating he was familiar with the story.

"Your disguise is pretty bad, if you're playing the grandma."

The grin freshened, his teeth gleamed, and he cocked an eyebrow as he eased the scissors from her hand. His hands were thick, calloused...and gentle. She retreated as he stood and returned the scissors to the utensil drawer in the hutch. She knew where to find them, if she needed them sometime later on.

* * * *

Late that afternoon Bo picked up the lantern, led Sara to the shed, and accompanied her inside. Puzzled, she trailed him to a dark corner where he handed her the light and began rummaging among boxes and crates that had seemed to be part of the wall. She stood behind him, holding the lantern high enough to allow them both to see, for, even though it was daylight outside, the corners of the shed were cloaked in shadows.

Bo pulled out a large pasteboard carton, hoisted it to his shoulder and carried it to the middle of the room. He set it down, opened the lid, took the lantern from Sara, and held it high motioning for her to look inside.

The box was full of women's apparel, dresses, jeans, shirts, sweaters—most double knits and heavy woolens.

She touched the garments gingerly at first, lifting, separating, shaking out one item at a time. The sizes were too diverse to have belonged to one woman. Styles and fabrics indicated the clothes had been put away decades before.

Sara sorted through the collection, holding items up to her from time to time. "Does all this stuff belong to someone you know?"

He shook his head. No.

Most of the garments were riddled with holes. Some were small openings, eaten by moths or crickets. Other pieces had been more extensively damaged by rats and mice.

Bo hung the lantern on a nail in the crossbeam over head. While Sara examined pieces from the box, he strode from the shed, leaving the unguarded doors open. He returned with needle and thread, a cake of soap, and the enamel dishpan filled with water. He put the items on the workbench and stood watching for a few more minutes, then, leaving the lantern swinging from the nail, he strode back to his cabin. The shed doors yawned wide.

Sara regarded the open doors. It was nearly sundown, but she could leave. Is that what he intended? Was he giving her a chance to escape?

Fine. Which way? She thought of the coyotes and of the leering Franklin.

No. Of all the dangers inherent here in the mountains—predatory animals, even more predatory humans—Sara definitely preferred Bo. She smiled thinking of his smile. There was a peculiar warmth growing between them. Before long, she would probably be able to convince him to take her back to civilization. She just needed to be patient.

Turning her attention from the open doors, grateful that Bo had left her the lantern, she picked several items out of the box. Some pieces fairly dissolved in her hands. A few she rinsed in the enamel basin, wrung them—twisting until her hands burned—and draped them over the half walls between the stalls to dry. Most items she rejected. Some she mended. Several things she folded in a stack to repair later.

* * * *

After sundown, when the air turned crisp, Sara took the lantern and scurried to the cabin, lured by the mingled smells of wood smoke and cooking meat.

They ate a kind of chili with crackers and cheddar cheese. Sara noticed as they ate that Bo avoided eye contact. She washed dishes and put away leftover food, curious as Bo carried in an oval tub that looked like a watering trough.

He placed the tub in front of the fireplace, then filled all three kettles with water and put them on to heat—two on the cook stove and one on the metal arm that swung in over the fire in the fireplace. Then he hauled two buckets of creek water, partially filling the tub. He produced another cake of soap and a length of terrycloth fabric, and handed them to Sara.

She looked from the items in her hands to the tub. "I can't take a bath here." She shook her head emphasizing the denial.

Bo offered only a contradictory nod.

"There's no lock on the door."

He narrowed his eyes, tightened his mouth, stepped toward her, and reached for the front of her dress, indicating he was fully prepared to help her disrobe.

She jerked beyond his reach. "Okay, okay. I'll do it. But I need clean clothes."

Bo nodded and offered her the lantern.

Glumly, Sara took the light and trudged to the shed where she got a shirt, a pair of worn denim jeans, and a flannel nightshirt, all items she had selected earlier from the box, rinsed and mended. The jeans still had damp spots around the pockets.

The air outside was brisk, though still in the fifties, she thought, as she shooed Bo out the cabin door.

"Please don't come back until I'm dressed. Knock first, like you do at the shed. I'm modest. Okay?"

He snorted and left. Obviously he had no interest in seeing her unclothed.

She added boiling water from the kettles to the cold water already in the trough. When the temperature seemed right, she tiptoed to the door and peeked outside.

No sign of Bo.

Hurriedly, she stripped and eased into the steaming water. It felt wonderful.

Submerging herself as much as possible, she lathered all over, using the bar soap even on her hair, then rinsed quickly. She would like to have stayed curled in the tub, to have luxuriated until the water got cold, but she was afraid Bo would return.

She grabbed the towel as she stood and wrapped it around her before she stepped out of the improvised tub. Her back was still damp as she shimmied into the flannel gown and a pair of oversized ladies' cotton panties. She pulled the shirt and denims on over the gown, pivoting in front of the fire all the while, warming as if she were on a vertical spit.

She pulled the padded rocking chair as close to the hearth as she could, with the tub in the way, and tried to towel her hair dry. She ran her fingers through her dark curls to get the tangles out as well as she could, thinking it lucky that she'd had her hair cut before leaving Oklahoma.

Finally Sara pulled the footstool close, drew a deep breath, leaned back, and rocked. Bo did not return. She didn't know how long it had been, at least half-an-hour.

Relaxing, she dozed in the chair, her feet propped on the footstool, warming as the blaze in the fireplace burned down, finally giving way to embers.

She roused but didn't move when she heard Bo's motorcycle roar to life. Where could he be going over the terrible mountain roads this late?

It was Saturday night. Maybe he had a date. After all, his beard was newly trimmed. The thought of his having a date annoyed her. Probably a big old hairy creature like him, she mused. Any woman would probably serve, if he just needed an outlet for his suppressed libido.

"After all, if Jimmy Singer's right, all women are the same in the dark." She scowled. "As if Jimmy would know."

How odd, to think of Jimmy, a city slicker who couldn't survive here in Bo's world. Her thoughts quickly darted back to Bo and his motorcycle. She hadn't known the machine still ran.

It sounded as if Bo had ridden straight to the overlook. Then, which way? She listened intently The surrounding mountains played tricks with sounds, bouncing and echoing them up and down through the hollows and valleys, leap frogging them over ridges. She needed to know which direction Bo went.

She probably should look outside, look for his headlight, but to do that, she would have to get up, walk across the sod floor in her clean bare feet and open the door, letting the cold night air into the warm cabin.

Maybe next time. He'd be back.

What if he didn't come back?

Her eyes popped wide at the thought. If she were left alone, would coyotes or wolves or mountain lions eat her or would the half-wit hillbillies get her first? Of all the terrors of this place, Bo's abandoning her suddenly seemed to be the worst. Again she fretted. She needed to make him like her, needed him for her escape. Damn!

Sometime later, sleepy and shivering, Sara made her way from the rocking chair to the bed. She pulled off the top quilt, wrapped it around her and hesitated, gazing at the bed. It would sure beat sleeping in the hay in the shed. The motorcycle would wake her. She would have plenty of warning. Did she dare sleep, even for a little while, in his bed?

Yawning, she eased onto the mound of quilts and inhaled deeply. The bed smelled like him, like leather and pine, tobacco, and safety.

Chapter Five

Sunday, Day 3: At daybreak, the roar of the motorcycle woke her. Sara leaped from the bed, scrambling to disentangle herself from the quilts. Two knocks, a pause, and the cabin door opened.

Carrying a slab of bacon, Bo glanced at Sara, who stood beside his bed, one foot on the other. She squinted. The beard trimming looked even better this morning. His long, dark straight hair was combed and had a sheen as if it were freshly washed. He looked bigger and more handsome, strapping, healthy...and young. She shivered, wondering where that renegade reevaluation came from.

He put the bacon on the hutch and turned his attention to building a fire in the cook stove.

Sara thought of asking where he'd been all night, then decided she didn't want to know. Maybe he did have a girlfriend. So what? Sara didn't know why she found that thought so irksome. Some local, mentally deficient woman, no doubt. Probably a lucky thing for Sara that he had a love interest.

Or maybe he'd been hunting all night.

No, he didn't have game to clean. It was definitely a woman. Her responding irritation puzzled her.

She smoothed the covers over the bed without speaking. Bo ignored her. Shivering, she stepped into her shoes and darted out into the mist; down to the outhouse briefly where she removed the nightshirt from under her clothes, then went to get the water buckets. A frosty bite in the air quickened her movements.

The bath water was topped with a thick layer of soap scum. While Bo cooked, she emptied the tub one pail at a time.

After breakfast, Bo hauled the nearly empty tub out and turned it upside down beside the cabin. Returning, he pulled off his boots and began unbuttoning his shirt. Regarding him nervously for a moment, Sara then scurried outside and back to the shed.

* * * *

The sunshine, promising at dawn, was short-lived, giving way to a daylong drizzle which kept Sara in the shed the rest of Sunday. Despite the fact the brace was on the ground, the brackets empty, and Sara free to come and go as she pleased, she didn't.

Working with needle and thread in the limited light from the open door, she repaired clothing from the box and wondered about the women who had worn them.

The damp air got colder through the day.

Late in the afternoon, Bo brought her a plate of hash. He knocked twice at the open door but didn't look at her as he set the food on the floor just inside and left. He seemed preoccupied. At least he didn't expect her to provide his entertainment. Obviously, he had gotten his companionship and bath elsewhere—not that she cared one whit.

Day 4: On Monday, the weather cleared and the temperature climbed to sixty. Bo built two fires in the yard, placed huge black kettles over the flames, and filled the pots with water that he carried in buckets from the stream below the cabin. Sara wondered why he didn't use the pump right there in the front yard.

"Is the well water only for drinking and cooking?"

He shook his head and indicated she should try the pump. She worked for nearly a minute before she drew any water and that only a trickle.

"It's easier and quicker to carry it up from the creek, right?" Suddenly she felt a peculiar admiration for the man. He was certainly resourceful and marvelously energetic.

He put detergent in one of the pots, added his dirty clothes, and used a wooden paddle to stir them as they simmered.

Sara marveled as she watched muscles in his forearms flex. "I don't believe I've ever seen a hand-driven agitator before."

Bo continued to ignore her.

Sara watched the ritual spellbound for several minutes before she thought and ran to get her own things. He didn't object when she tossed her denim dress and undergarments into the sudsy water with his clothes.

She located the third bucket and trudged up and down to the creek helping him carry water to refill the rinse kettle after the first became sudsy. Bo wrung as much water as he could from the clothes and Sara helped him hang them from tree branches and a wire fence strung to keep his cows out of the yard.

His laundry included underwear, eight T-shirts, countless dark woolen socks, six flannel shirts and six pairs of pants—probably two weeks worth of apparel, she decided.

When the wash was finished, they emptied both kettles. Sara was ready to rest, but Bo picked up his axe and strode off up the mountain, disappearing into the woods. A short time later, when she heard chopping in the distance, she darted into the cabin, straight to the utensil drawer, and flung it open. The scissors were gone.

She rummaged. He had even removed the knives and forks. She pivoted and glared over the door at the pegs that held the guns. The pegs were empty, the guns both gone.

"Damn!"

She looked around and spied the broom, her sole contribution to his lifestyle. She grabbed it and stripped off the hay she had so carefully tied to one end. A bare mop handle wasn't much of a weapon, but it would have to do. She was leaving. Now. She had to. She was forging a subconscious bond with this man, an emotional attachment that seemed to be getting stronger. She didn't want to feel comfortable here.

Dashing outside, Sara listened. He was still chopping. She grabbed her wet denim dress and underclothing off the fence, turned the opposite direction, and plunged into the woods.

From the sound of the motorcycle Saturday night, Sara figured Bo had driven to the ridge and then probably east. She assumed the road at the bottom of the overlook went to the little community where Cappy and Franklin lived. Not the route she wanted.

Obviously, Bo didn't care anymore whether she left or stayed, as long as she didn't take any of his belongings. She was certain he wouldn't follow.

She ran east along a footpath paralleling the ridge, away from the chopping sound.

Vines and brambles soon claimed the path, snagging her hand-me-down denim pants. Thickets of large, thorned bushes and tree branches snared her clothing, scraped her arms and legs, reached out to slap and slash at her face. She tried to beat them back, but the mop handle was no match for the tangled undergrowth.

The chopping was muffled to silence by the time Sara heard something move in the underbrush in front of her. And she smelled it, a sour, putrid stench, like a wet dog who'd rolled in dung.

The faint rustling grew louder and she heard grunting. Chilling fear stopped her. Probably nothing more than a raccoon or possum foraging.

A low tree branch shivered and the grunting grew louder. It sounded like a large animal. Tiptoeing, peering, she couldn't see anything through the undergrowth.

Then she heard a low growl. Tourists were warned not to feed the brown bears, native to the area. Sara held her breath, listening. Might be a puma, or a razorback hog, other natives famous for injuring, even killing the occasional interloper.

Sara's imagination galloped through a succession of scenarios. She retreated a step, then another and, finally, turning, dropped the broom handle and bolted, hurdling headlong through the foliage. Her lungs burned as thorned bushes and low limbs whipped and stung her.

Run! She wheezed, willing her legs to go faster and faster.

She bounded into the clearing, saw the familiar cabin, and dumped the armload of damp clothes in a heap at her feet. But she was not safe. Not yet.

Gasping, she took her bearings, and breathed deeply, getting control, embarrassed by the hysteria which had stampeded her.

Clenching her teeth, she set out again, jogging the path Bo had taken. Her body settled into a rhythm. She had one destination, the one place she would again feel safe. She would rest only when she was under Bo's dark, silent gaze.

Chapter Six

Scurrying into the high woods, Sara scarcely breathed, listening for any sound. The chopping had stopped.

Pausing to catch her breath, she put her hands on her hips, stretched and breathed deeply, inhaling a familiar scent. His pipe! She could smell his pipe. She sniffed the air and walked toward the smell of his tobacco. There was no path, only her instinct, her senses, to guide her.

The scent of him grew more pronounced as she advanced, slowed only a little by brambles snagging her legs, vines and branches reaching out to lash at her face and arms. She burst into a clearing and stopped when she saw him.

He was in his shirt sleeves, on his knees, his hair cascading to conceal his profile. He appeared to be baiting a small trap. He glanced sideways at her, then his eyes narrowed and he scanned the woods behind her before he looked back at her face. He regarded her closely for a moment longer before dismissing her and turning his attention back to his task.

She felt foolish. What had she expected? She folded her arms across her stomach and walked in a tight circle to catch her breath, glancing at him from time to time.

She wanted him to hold her, but of course, that would be too much. Seeing him had to be enough.

There were several stumps nearby, evidence of Bo's industry in producing the firewood necessary to keep him through the winter.

As she grew calmer, Sara strolled to a stump that had been left hip high, and leaned against it, pretending a nonchalance she did not feel.

She watched Bo set the trap. A skinned carcass, headless, a rabbit or squirrel, hung from a branch. Their supper, no doubt.

Still ignoring her, Bo placed the trap at the base of a tree and picked up his axe. He returned to an oak at the edge of the clearing, one which was cut nearly through. Angling his broad shoulders, he gave the trunk a dozen solid whacks. The tree still standing, he tossed the axe aside, put his hands on the trunk and shoved.

Beneath the thickness of his shirts, Sara could see muscles strain, bunching all the way down his back. His buttocks and the backs of his legs tightened with his effort. She stared, mesmerized by the man more than the tree, until the stalwart oak yielded before the man's will, as she knew it would. Scolding, its tendrils reaching out to grasp at the undergrowth on either side, the tree seemed to groan objections as it fell.

Without looking at Sara, Bo retrieved the axe and immediately began cutting branches.

A little alarmed at her own electric responses to his performance, she straightened abruptly, and walked back toward the cabin. If she needed him, she could yell. He would come and vanquish any threat. Bo's consistent indifference toward her was more reassurance than if he fawned over her.

She smiled. She liked this odd relationship: their mutual awareness, their indifference...and this unexpected, peculiar sensation of pinpricks in startling locations in her anatomy.

Had he been showing off, pushing the tree over with his bare hands? Didn't most lumberjacks cut trees all the way through with a saw or an axe? She didn't know, but she felt lighthearted. If he were showing off, it would mean he found her attractive or desirable; someone, at least, worth showing off for.

What did she care? What difference could it possibly make if he liked her? He was nothing to her, a big, hairy, old mountain man, and a mute besides.

Yet he stimulated her, made her feel she had influence over him. She felt like the beautiful girl who commanded King Kong. No one asked Kong's age. Certainly no one thought him attractive. But those things didn't matter when you were able to manipulate unplumbed power.

She stopped walking to think. In civilized society, the people with the most money or celebrity held the power. Here, Bo was undisputed king and she, Sara Loomis, held sway over him. Whether her influence was real or imagined, she liked thinking about it as she began walking again, a little swagger to her steps. She would not try to escape any more until she had a plan and a proper weapon or a guide. Maybe tomorrow.

Near a small tree laying beside the cabin, she found the handsaw Bo had abandoned there earlier. She picked it up and began cutting the spindly limbs into wood for the cook stove.

She wondered about her weird feeling of contentment, of well-being, in this place. She shook her head. That kind of thinking was ridiculous. She needed to leave. She was a city woman, accustomed to electrical appliances and potable water summoned from taps in kitchens and bathrooms. She should be desperate to escape—and she was.

Yet, in all honesty, she felt oddly satisfied here. What was wrong with her? An odd memory niggled at her. Patty Hearst, kidnapped eons ago, was accused of remaining with her captors, willingly.

But that was altogether different. For one thing, Bo had not kidnapped Sara. Truthfully, he wasn't even keeping her prisoner.

Still, she couldn't leave if Bo refused to take her, one part of her argued, recalling what had happened when she ventured into the woods alone.

Not exactly a fair test, the other part of her brain prompted. Besides, if she had all that high-powered influence over him, couldn't she just make Bo take her home? Ride her out on the motorcycle?

Sure. She'd ask him. Insist, this time.

She stood still, thinking. She had already asked and he had refused. Why did he refuse?

She could get home, if she could convince him to take her to a road. She would ask him to do that. Only that.

She put down the saw and knelt to press her ear against the ground, thinking to feel vibrations from highway or road noises or machinery working nearby, something which might provide a direction for her next attempt.

Nothing.

She gazed heavenward, as she did several times a day. High above, sporadic jet vapor trails crisscrossed the sky. The trails were there regularly enough to indicate established air traffic lanes.

Sara walked to the well. Again she had to pump a long time to get a steady flow of the icy water which she drank from her free hand cupped to receive it.

Daydreaming, pacing back to the fallen sapling, she felt a rumble resonate under her feet. She dropped and pressed her ear against the ground just as it stopped.

"Yes!" She leaped up and darted toward the overlook. "They're here. Someone's come for me."

She ran to the ridge and peered over to see the clunker pickup which had spirited her from the convenience store and brought her into the mountains. It was parked and deserted in a flat area below her vantage point.

"No," she whispered, turning, wondering if she could outrun whoever was coming – get to Bo.

She risked a final look over the cliff. Cappy was there, alone, loaded with boxes and grocery sacks, stumbling over the rubble to gain the footpath that would bring him to the ridge.

Scanning to either side of this visitor who was struggling just to reach the path, Sara relaxed. He was alone.

What was the inept little Cappy doing here? Had he come for her? He carried two bulging burlap bags, juggled two pasteboard boxes in his arms, and stopped every few feet to reconnoiter.

Not exactly the hero she'd been waiting for, but better than nothing. She could go with him, as long as none of the others was there. She would have to talk him into bypassing that community where those others lived. She didn't dare risk falling back into their clutches. But she could wheedle Cappy into helping her. He had just become her new escape plan.

Darting in and out among the boulders, Sara scurried down the footpath to the place where the rubble began.

"Cappy, let me help you with that stuff."

He froze and stared with astonishment. "You s-s-still here?"

Sara smiled, surprised that it was so good to hear another human voice. "I've been waiting for you to come rescue me."

He gazed at her with his dull eyes.

"You *are* here to rescue me, aren't you, Cappy? I'm ready. Let's go." She took his elbow and tried to turn him.

He pulled away. "I thought you was d-d-dead by n-now. Where's B-B-Bo? D'you kill Bo?"

Her smile wilted. "No, he's cutting down a tree. Here, put this stuff down and let's go back to your truck." She tried to take the sacks from him but Cappy jerked them away.

"Don't he keep you hobbled or n-n-nothin'?"

She grimaced. "No. But then he didn't know you were coming or he would have locked me up today for sure."

Cappy muttered, "Guess so."

She reached for the box and again he jerked away from her. She frowned. "What is all this stuff?"

"S-S-Stores. We bring 'em up ever' m-m-month."

"Cappy, I thought you were my hero, come to save me. I tell you, I'm scared to death. You have to help me. Take me home."

"You dang sure sh-sh-should be s-s-scart a' him."

"Come on, Cappy, put this stuff down and let's go."

Cappy looked her up and down. She wore a cotton shirt from the pasteboard box in the shed. She wasn't wearing her bra. His eyes paused at her ample breasts, well defined beneath the thin fabric. He wiped dark, crusted saliva off his mouth with the back of his hand and grinned, ogling her. His uneven teeth were outlined with tobacco juice. He spat off to one side and wiped his mouth again, this time with his sleeve. Sara cut her eyes trying to look as if she were flirting, but she felt like throwing up.

"S-S-Sure, I'll take ya." Cappy put down the box and bags as his eyes again settled on her breasts. His breath quickened and he snorted a little laugh. She pretended not to notice the stare. Most men admired her breasts. Except Bo, of course. Bo never seemed to notice her that way at all. Sara wondered, fleetingly, why not.

"Franklin told me what I ought to 'a done with you," Cappy said, interrupting her puzzling. "I told 'em I k-k-kilt you. Don't make me out a liar, will you not?"

Puzzled as to how she was supposed to do that, Sara nodded solemnly, "Okay."

Cappy was turning to lead her back to the truck when his gaze shot to the ridge. His face froze and Sara heard Bo's warning snarl above them. She bit her lips, shut her eyes, and bowed her head, hoping Cappy would notice her affectation.

Bo tramped down the path, picked one box up off the ground, and jammed it into Sara's arms. She saw Cappy's chin tremble as he picked up the other box and the tow sacks and handed them to Bo.

The box she carried was light. Sara supposed the heavy items were in the bags. Bo hoisted both sacks in one hand as if they contained feathers. He snarled at Cappy, glanced at Sara, and tossed his head, indicating she should get back to the cabin, then he began climbing.

Cappy's feet slipped and he danced nervously over the rocks before he stumbled and fell toward her. "'You s-s-sleeping in his b-b-bed?" He eyed Bo who was several yards up the path. Cappy stood and dusted himself, stalling.

"The shed," she answered in a stage whisper.

"I'll be back for ya." He risked another glance at Bo and scrambled, headlong, down the rock-strewn path.

Bo kept Sara with him the rest of the afternoon, showing her how to dig Irish potatoes and what was left of the onions. He put them in burlap bags to store in the cave behind the house.

In the nearer part of the cave, he kept sacks of pears, pecans, apples and other produce. Farther back where the air was cooler, he kept smoked meat, eggs and the milk he drew twice a day from one of the cows pastured in a gully near the cabin. The near end of the water-worn ravine was blocked by the two strands of wire, which doubled as clothesline.

Bo marked the cave's entrance as his territory by relieving himself at the opening. Sara saw him do it once when he didn't know she was watching. The crude ritual was disgusting, but it seemed to discourage thieving varmints.

Excited that Cappy was coming back for her, Sara fidgeted as the day gave way to a chilling twilight. She should have told him not to mention her whereabouts to anyone else. If he came back in the truck by himself, she could convince him to take her back to civilization. She prayed he didn't bring anyone else to complicate things.

At dusk, the sky got heavy and a peculiar quiet fell over the woods around them. Sara layered on extra clothing. The wind, out of the northwest, cut through clothes and skin, chilling her to the bone.

Lost without television or even radio weather forecasts, she studied the ominous sky and wondered. It was too early for snow. At least back home it was too early. But the air looked and felt heavy, like snow was coming.

Bo went down to the pasture to feed his livestock, as he did twice every day, morning and night.

To keep herself occupied, Sara walked to the cabin. She tried to concentrate on the how-to book on quilting. She was too nervous, excited at the prospect of her impending departure. Maybe she should start supper to keep herself occupied.

Cutting up a piece of leftover venison roast, she added potatoes, onions and carrots, covered the ingredients with water, set them on the cook stove, and stoked the fire.

Going to the hutch, she took out the biscuit bowl and measured flour by handfuls, the way she had seen Bo do it, added a pinch of salt, baking powder, soda, and drippings. Bo mixed biscuits with his hands, but Sara didn't like the idea of touching the goo. She got a spoon and had just begun stirring when Bo walked into the cabin.

As she added buttermilk, a byproduct of the butter Bo churned himself, Sara felt the man come close, closer than usual. She glanced back. He peered over her shoulder and sniffed two or three times in quick succession. She wondered if he could smell her nervousness.

In four days, he had taught her a lot, for a man who did not speak. With his nose, he seemed able to track animals, sniff out places to set traps, or find certain roots. His knowledge went beyond things learned in school. Hadn't it been Bo who knew to go to the cave to wait out the storm? Sara watched and learned. It didn't take her long to figure out things had scents of their own.

Bo's was the first she learned. After she got used to it, she easily recognized his smell, which she found not entirely unpleasant. His was not a socially acceptable fragrance of aftershave or cologne, but a mingled aroma. He smelled of pine needles and gunpowder, pipe tobacco, leather, and a man's sweat dried in the outdoors. His aroma had become synonymous with safety, important she thought, in a place where one felt threatened by animals, plants, and even the weather.

Bo's fragrance now, so near, soothed her as it did when she was restless or frightened, yet she quivered.

Adding more buttermilk, she stirred the thick dough slowly with the spoon, trying to collect the bits and pieces that clung to the edges of the bowl.

Bo's hands came from both sides of her. The front of his body pressed close against her back and his breath pulsed warm on her neck. He took the dough into his hands, kneading it, picking up the errant pieces and working them into a cohesive ball. Sara stood very still. Her face became hot. She found this closeness intimidating, and at the same time, exhilarating.

Bo put the dough down, placed his hands over hers, guided them into the mixture, then massaged both hands and dough.

There was something sensual about his large, warm hands over hers, kneading the cool, malleable mixture. She didn't know why his nearness had such a stimulating effect. Her hands trembled beneath his. Her face burned. Her breath came in gulps and her heart pounded.

She had tried to contrive these responses in the past, with suitable men, and had failed. Now, here, unbidden, she fluttered in the arms of this *un*suitable man.

What was happening? What was it about this mute mountain man that triggered these responses?

And there was something else. She felt incredibly safe enveloped by his large, powerful body, as safe as a child tucked into bed at night.

The ball of dough became elastic. Abruptly, Bo released her and backed away. Sara turned in time to see him close the door, leaving the cabin, his bearskin coat gone from the peg on the inside of the door.

What had happened in those brief, intimate moments? She hadn't a clue. She had no idea what prompted the sudden familiarity nor what brought it to such a rude end.

She shaped and cooked the biscuits, peering into the crude stove from time to time, as Bo usually did, waiting for them to turn the golden brown color.

When Bo didn't return, she ate alone while the wind whistled strangely through seams between the cabin's logs. Her first try at stew turned out better than she'd hoped.

Eventually, wrapping herself in all the clothing she possessed, Sara hurled herself out the cabin door, ran to the shed, and shut herself into the familiar darkness, slamming the doors as quickly as possible to keep the cold wind from following her inside.

Shivering, she pushed all the hay in her stall into a single pile, threw one quilt over it, rolled herself into the second quilt and burrowed, without removing either her clothing or her shoes. She heard ice tapping the metal roof. Sleet.

Would Cappy venture out on such a night, risk the steep climb to rescue her? Bo might forget to bar the shed door. She could take off on her own again. But she didn't intend to freeze to death lost in the woods in this weather.

If Cappy were coming, she could wait at the ridge. On that high ground, however, she would be exposed to the elements. She decided to remain in the shed.

Sara couldn't seem to get warm. She curled into a ball, her feet and hands like ice.

Two brisk knocks and the door of the shed swung open.

Keeping the quilts wrapped tightly, Sara struggled to her knees and peered around the stall's half wall to see the lantern and Bo's form in the doorway.

"What is it? Do we need to go to the cave?"

He strode to the stall, grabbed her wrist and jerked her to her feet, growling. Maybe he suspected something, had guessed that Cappy was coming for her.

Or was this about this afternoon? Had he experienced the same strange palpitations she felt during their moments of closeness? Was that what he wanted? Silently she pleaded, "Please, God, no."

She sparred, pulled her wrist free, and stepped away from him.

It was difficult to read his facial expressions anytime. Bo always looked angry. Perhaps it was the way his eyebrows arched or the way the hair over his forehead dived to the bridge of his nose. In the semidarkness of the shed, she could not see his face at all, was barely able to discern his form.

He lumbered forward, scooped her up, quilts and all, and slung her over his shoulder as he had the night of the storm. He carried her outside, then turned to slam and secure the shed door. Sleet peppered them.

Fighting him had not worked before, so Sara tried to remain calm, dangling from Bo's shoulder, again like a sack of feed.

He carried her inside the cabin, slammed the door against the persistent wind, crossed the room and dumped her unceremoniously onto his bed.

"No." Gathering the quilts tightly around her, she leaped off the bed and made a dash for the door. She was nearly there when he grabbed her around the middle and carried her back to deposit her again on the bed. She tried to get up. He shoved her down. His eyes narrowed and a forbidding vibration emitted from his throat. She shrank.

Watching him carefully, she secured the quilts and moved to the far side of the bed to sit cross-legged, rigid, her back straight against the log wall.

Without either looking at her or removing his coat, Bo strode to the fireplace, picked up his pipe, and filled it with tobacco, moving in his usual slow, methodical way. Noting his calm, Sara again attempted to get off the bed. Without looking at her, he growled, a low, menacing sound.

Yielding, Sara wrapped up in her quilts and curled into a ball, on her side facing the wall, on top of the bedcovers.

Bo growled again. She turned her head to glower at him. Standing at the bedside, he pulled back the covers. Obviously he intended for her to get under them.

Grudgingly, she kicked her shoes into the floor and complied, still wrapped in her own quilts, her face to the outside wall, her back to him. She heard him shuffling around the room.

He built up the fire in the fireplace until it blazed. He went in and out of the door four or five times, each time returning with armloads of wood which he deposited on the hearth.

Even with brisk air seeping through the seams in the logs, the bed was warm, much warmer than her nest in the shed, but Sara shivered, dreading what she feared might be coming.

She heard the familiar sounds as Bo removed his heavy bearskin coat. The old rocking chair creaked beneath his weight and groaned its usual objections as he began to rock.

Turning her head slightly, Sara ventured a look.

Sporadically puffing his pipe, Bo whittled. The fire in the fireplace crackled. The rocker popped and creaked. There in Bo's bed, Sara breathed the scent of safety, his scent. The familiar surroundings lulled her.

Pinpricks of cold coming through seams in the wall nipped her forehead and nose, but the rest of her was warm beneath the weight of the quilts.

A long time later, dozing, she was vaguely aware of his moving around before he snuffed the lantern. She forced her eyes open. The room remained bright, bathed in the glow from the fireplace.

There was a rustling and a delay before she felt him pull back the covers and settle his body next to hers. She clenched her teeth and her fists, ready to do battle, but he didn't attempt to touch her.

Soon his breathing became even, although not the deep inhalations of someone sound asleep. Sara remained tense. Her face was cold and her shoulder was getting stiff. She wanted to roll to her other side. Dare she risk rousing him?

Slowly, carefully, she eased onto her back and waited. He didn't stir. She turned to her left side facing him. His back was to her.

Cautiously, not wanting to touch him, she put her face closer to his back, hoping to warm her frozen nose by the heat radiating from his body. She breathed in the comforting scent of him. Drifting back to sleep, Sara hoped Cappy didn't come tonight.

She opened her eyes one last time. The firelight danced. Sleet peppered the tin roof. She breathed the comforting aromas, heard the familiar noises—the smells and sounds of safety—and she slept.

Chapter Seven

It was daylight when Sara opened her eyes. Bo sat on the side of the bed pulling up his trousers. He had peeled down to only the bottom half of his long handles and a T-shirt for sleep. Curiosity overcame modesty and Sara watched as he stood.

Under the T-shirt, his waist was narrow, his back lean and supple. He certainly carried his age well. She supposed his face, hidden by all that beard and long hair, was ancient, although his eyes appeared to be the alert, watchful eyes of a young man.

He's definitely maintained a young man's body, she decided. Probably all the exercise and manual labor.

Watching him, Sara again felt the peculiar tingling. She bit her bottom lip and was trying to quell the butterflies loose in her stomach when Bo turned and looked directly into her face.

She averted her stare quickly but not before he saw something that prompted a slight smile of, what? Surprise? Approval? In that brief glimpse, she couldn't tell.

He put on his bearskin coat and tromped out.

When he returned, Sara slid her feet into her shoes, wrapped a quilt around her and dashed for the outhouse. The sun bristled over the horizon, burning off the thin sheet of ice that shimmered on dripping branches. Despite the promise of warming later, the air was brisk. She didn't dally.

Through the morning, the mountains seemed to absorb the wind and the cold from the night and the sun shone brightly. By noon Sara was shedding outer layers of clothing.

It had been a good idea, her spending the arctic night in the cabin, in Bo's bed, but she would not make a habit of it, despite his exemplary behavior.

She'd read that on very cold nights in some parts of the world, people slept with their dogs to survive. The coldest nights were those when they needed three dogs, hence the term "Three-Dog Night."

In the Ozarks, Sara figured she had experienced a "One-Bear Night," the bear being Bo. She laughed quietly to herself.

77

Obviously, she didn't appeal to him physically. Lucky for her. She shrugged off the discomfort that idea spawned. Perhaps he preferred pioneering mountain-type women like the one she assumed he was wooing Saturday night. But if theirs was such a hot romance, why didn't his woman come around? Maybe he didn't want her to know about Sara.

Then a sudden, appalling thought. Maybe he wasn't wooing a woman at all. These days, it could be a man. Sara shook her head sadly.

All this speculation was just so much fodder, again, she told herself, making the bed for the day, as Bo always did. It did no good to speculate. She didn't have any way of knowing what was true and what was not. She fumed. She could ask. She winced. What did she care anyway?

* * * *

Everyone in Settlement knew Cappy stuttered worse when he was excited. Franklin listened intently when Gilbert told him Cappy returned from his deliveries dancing, gyrating, sputtering, unable to talk.

"Hell, Franklin, he can't string three words together at once. Queenie don't know what put him in such a state. He can't calm down enough to say. She says he'd been pacing back and forth in their trailer for more'n a' hour."

Franklin hurried to the trailer to find Cappy.

"What's happenin'?" he asked as he slid through Cappy's bedroom door, grinning like he and Cappy shared a secret.

Cappy lay across his bed on his stomach thumbing through a women's lingerie catalog. He slapped it closed and sucked back the spittle glistening at one corner of his mouth.

"Nothin'." The younger man swallowed the word, obviously trying not to stutter.

Franklin leered. "Seen your girlfriend when you was making deliveries, didn't ya?"

Cappy sat up slowly, stood, and paced down the hall to the living room, gnawing on his lower lip and snapping his fingers, stepping, gnawing, and snapping out of sync. Queenie clattered in the kitchen, whipping something with an egg beater.

Franklin studied him as he followed Cappy to the living room. "She was sure a pretty 'un." Franklin eased down, straddling a wooden chair, and propped his forearms on the back, one over the other. "Anyone could tell the way she was lookin' at you, she was gonna be your girlfriend." He hesitated. "Cappy?"

"What?" Cappy fairly shouted the word.

"That woman liked you. She wanted you. Was she smooth, Cappy? Was that peachy skin soft? Did she spread 'em for you or did you have to get strong with her?"

The younger man's face clouded. He tried to speak but he stammered, couldn't form the words or get them spoken.

Franklin grimaced. "Been diddlin' with yourself again, ain't ya, bub? They say diddlin' with hisself makes some men stutter."

Cappy shook his head, staring at the floor. "I'm tr-tr-tryin' to quit it."

"I imagine it's too late now, anyhow. The damage 'as already been did. What I wanna know is, were that gal of yours sweet? How'd she taste?"

"Didn't t-t-taste of 'er."

"You licked her tits, didn't ya, boy, while you was diddlin' her? That's practically a woman's favorite part, the tit lickin'."

Cappy frowned at the floor for a long moment, then he looked up at Franklin and his face brightened. "Maybe I ain't d-d-done with 'er yet."

"Too bad she's dead then, I s'pose." Franklin looked hard at Cappy's face. "You didn't kill 'er, did you, cuz?" Franklin kept his voice low. He didn't want Queenie to hear. "Ma give you the job to do but you let Ma down, didn't ya?"

Cappy clamped his scraggly teeth over his lower lip. He wouldn't look at Franklin. He nursed his bottom lip, sucking it gently. His dull eyes glazed over and he hummed to himself.

Franklin whispered. "Where you got 'er hid?"

"What-do-you-mean, w-w-where?" Cappy reared up, glaring at Franklin and held the pose a minute before he wilted.

"Cappy, come on, you can tell me. Ain't I your own kin?" Franklin's voice fell with feigned encouragement. "You been running back there diddlin' 'er all week, ain't ya?"

"I d-d-didn't do no such a thing."

"You didn't screw her?"

Cappy shook his head.

"You didn't kill 'er neither, did ya?"

There was a delay followed by another head shake.

Franklin crooned, coaxing. "Cap, where ya got 'er hid?"

"In the sh-sh-shed, th-th-that's where."

"Which shed would that be, Cappy?"

"For me t-t-to know and you..." He turned away coughing and choking.

Franklin shook his head in disbelief. "You sure don't want nobody findin' her now, Cappy, findin' out you let that beautiful piece of pussy lay around locked up someplace cravin' a man the way she was."

"She d-d-don't like it."

"Don't like what, Cappy?"

"D-D-Diddlin'. She can't d-d-do it. Says she d-d-don't like it."

"Cappy, Cappy, Cappy, females can't never say what they like or don't like. They don't hardly know theirselves 'til you show 'em. Once I diddle 'em, there's no gettin' 'em over it. It makes 'em crazy. They just keep wantin' it, over and over again, keep beggin' for it. At least that's the way they do with me. Ain't that the way they do with you?"

"I s-s-s'pose."

Franklin lowered his voice back to the coaxing tone. "I understand, Cap. Sometimes I have to prime 'em a little myself. With this one, it might help for someone to go first, get her ready for you. I'll do it. You can be the one to hold her for me and watch real careful, pay attention to what all goes on, or maybe I ought to say what all goes *in*." He cackled. Cappy frowned, nodding uncertainly.

"Sure," Franklin said, as if he were confirming a plan. "We'll go get her from where you got her stashed. I'll diddle her first, good and proper, get her ready, then I'll keep her steady while you take your turn. If she wants more after that, we'll do it long as we're able. Why, Cappy, me and you together, we could keep going at it probably two, three days."

Cappy grinned and rolled his eyes, panting as he listened. He licked the drool again beading at the corners of his mouth.

Franklin nodded. "Now, come on. Let's get the truck and go get her."

Cappy's grin disappeared as the color drained from his cheeks. He shook his head. "I ain't goin' up there."

"Okay, I'll go get her and bring her to you, meet you someplace. Where you got her hid?" He started to get up, then stayed where he was as Cappy shook his head and set his jaw stubbornly.

Franklin cajoled and pleaded a long time before Cappy finally came out with it. "She's up to Bo's."

"That crazy mountain man's keeping her for you?" Franklin's voice cracked. He paled and slouched in his chair.

Franklin thought about things a long while, shaking his head as he dismissed one idea after another. He mumbled, recalling Sara's face, her slender frame, the exceptional breasts. The memory tantalized his brain and titillated his body.

"He's keepin' her down to his shed, did you say?"

"Yeah."

"All time?"

"No, he l-l-let's her run l-l-loose in the d-d-daytime, not tethered or n-n-nothin'. L-L-Locks her up nights. Guess it k-k-keeps the varmints off her."

Franklin grinned and raised his eyebrows. "Yeah. He's smart, that one."

"D-D-Don't tell him I sent you to g-g-git her."

"No, Cappy, I won't be doin' that. We'll wait'll the weather breaks, then I'll just slip up there first dark night and grab her. I'll tell her I'm there to get her for you, that you asked me to bring her down so's you can rescue her."

"That'll make her come all-all-all right. And the n-n-night when you g-g-go, I'll w-w-wait at Melon's and w-w-we'll ask her d-d-does she want to-to d-d-diddle with any of us."

"Yes, sir, Cappy, that's sure what we're gonna do all right."

"And w-w-we'll s-s-share," Cappy reiterated, nodding, obviously making sure they both understood the deal.

"We'll split that girl right down the middle, old buddy." Franklin laughed at his little joke.

Cappy didn't seem to get it.

Chapter Eight

Day 5: Sara cut swatches of cotton fabric from clothes in the box that had been ruined by varmints or time and began piecing them together.

This first try wouldn't be fancy, she told herself, but making a quilt with her own hands seemed like a worthwhile way to spend evenings rocking beside the fire, waiting for Bo to change his mind, or Cappy or someone to come rescue her.

Bo concentrated on his whittling. Although she expressed a polite interest, he refused to let her see what he was making.

When she got sleepy, Sara put away her materials and Bo walked her to the shed to secure her for the night. She was alive, anyway. Her survival was primitive, but, considering the alternative, acceptable.

Day 6: As they sat piecing and whittling the second night after the sleet storm, Sara heard a wolf baying. The sound was clear, mournful, and close.

Bo stopped rocking and listened intently. He seemed to hold his breath. He closed and pocketed his knife as he stood, put on his bearskin coat, and took both guns from the pegs overhead on his way out the door.

Her interest piqued, Sara layered on extra clothes, buttoned up, and trotted out into the night to follow.

Glancing back, Bo saw, then ignored her. Apparently he had no objection to her tagging along. Neither did he wait for her. She jogged to keep up with his long strides as he tramped through the darkness. Dappled light from a full moon shimmered a path. Running warmed her in the cool, still night air.

The wolf's intermittent howls broke the silence continuously.

They had gone less than two miles up and through a gulch then downhill through a stand of pines, when she saw lights from a cabin nestled in a valley separating two low mountains. That seemed to be their destination, although the wolf's doleful wail came from beyond.

A short, stout woman with a shawl clutched around her ample frame bustled up from somewhere below the cabin. Could she be Bo's girlfriend? Sara didn't think so.

Looking beyond the woman, Sara saw reflections and heard the muffled torrent of rushing water.

The woman waved. "Bo. Thank God." She spoke breathlessly as her fat legs propelled her toward them. "It's Lutie. He rode the mule acrost..." her voice faltered as she tried to catch her breath "...to cut a tree for Deborah. Before he come back," she hesitated, catching her breath again, "the river swoll. He only got part way." The woman stopped directly in front of Bo, staring up into his face and gasping. "He's stuck out there on that dern spit. The mule come on the rest o' the way without him. The water's coming up fast. Fayette ain't got back from town yet."

Sara had a hard time following the account. She peered into Bo's face. Who was Lutie and why was this woman telling Bo all this? Was he obligated to her? Sara looked again at the dark, silent sweep of the river. What did the woman expect Bo to do?

He nodded, his calm demeanor soothing the woman momentarily, allowing her to catch her breath. Apparently he understood what she wanted. He didn't seem alarmed.

The woman glanced at Sara, said "Howdy," studied her for a moment, then looked back at Bo who handed his guns to Sara, removed his coat, and handed her that, as well. She felt honored until she realized what he must be thinking. She grabbed his shirtsleeve.

"Don't be crazy, Bo. You can't go into that water. The current's too fast."

With a look of mingled annoyance and surprise, he pulled his arm free, walked into the shadows around the cabin, and returned moments later, leading a mule. Bo had skinned out of his clothes, down to the pants of his long handles, a T-shirt, and socks. Sara bit her lips and continued shaking her head. "Please don't go. I don't want you to." As if what she wanted would influence him.

He didn't hesitate as he led the mule, but the animal balked at the water's edge. Sara hoped the mule's common sense was contagious. Bo pulled the mule's head down, took a firm hold of its sizable ear, and put his mouth close to it. It looked as if Bo bit the ear, or maybe he only whispered into it. Whatever the method, it convinced the animal to step out beside him into the black, swirling water. Sara shivered and hugged Bo's coat tightly in both arms, clutching the guns in one hand, but pointing them away from her.

They plodded in the shallows, man and mule, angling against the current.

Spellbound, Sara followed the woman in tandem down the bank to the water's edge.

"Who's Lutie?" Sara had to shout to be heard above the noise of the water ruffling over the rocks along the bank. Out in the main channel, the current flowed fast and was ominously silent.

"My boy. He's eight y'ar old," the woman shouted back. "He's already been drowned once in this fool river, the year he were six. Died right here on this bank. River was swoll that night, too. I don't look for it to turn out that good again."

Usually annoyed by poor grammar, Sara absorbed the woman's words, enjoying again the ring of another human voice.

Watching the man and the mule struggle to move against the turbulence of the racing current, Sara noticed they chose their path carefully as they negotiated what appeared to be treacherous footing.

What had the woman said? Sara turned, wondering, and shouted, "Your son drowned before?"

"This one, Lutie, the one out on the spit. He's been drowned once already. His poor little body got caught up in a tree branch last time, on its way down river. Bo was here that time too. Clumb into that evil water hisself. Swum my baby out.

"Once they was out, the boy looked to be dead. Ever' body went to wailing, except for Bo. He bent his back to the boy, breathing his own air into Lutie's innards.

"Bo worked over that baby a long time, breathin' 'im, mashing his belly. Others went to shoutin' for folks to bring blankets and a light. My man, Fayette, told me to get down there beside them two and call Lutie, tell him to get hisself back here.

"Pretty soon the boy commenced to stranglin' and coughin' up more'n one child's share of that old river."

Sara's eyes strained against the darkness, trying to see the sand bar or the child. Bo was waist deep now. She trembled, shaking all over with a sinister feeling of fear and dread.

"But he weren't right in the head that night nor a lot of nights after that one neither." The woman stopped speaking. She looked grim as she, too, strained to keep her eyes on Bo and the mule.

The water crept to Bo's chest and his shadow was swallowed in the seamless joining of night and water, disappearing and reappearing eerily, like a vapor.

"Did your boy Lutie ever get right?" Sara's fear kept her eyes on the shadowy forms bobbing toward the far bank.

"Not 'til Bo brung the pup. A wolf pup, not yet weaned. Bo learned Lutie to feed it milk from a rubber glove. It 'as dead winter by then. The boy brung the animal inside to sleep nights. Caring for that pup brung Lutie back to hisself."

The woman turned and glanced up at the mountain that seemed to be the location of the continuous howling.

"That's the one, Lutie's pup, raising all the ruckus. He's full growed now, 'course. He don't run with no pack. Never did. He's a loner. But he's always close by when Lutie's out away from the place. That's how I come to know something weren't right tonight."

Bo's head went under the water. When it bobbed up, he and the mule had shot downstream.

"Ohhh..." the woman cried. "Lost their feets."

Sara lunged forward. Her companion grabbed her arm and hung on.

"He needs help," Sara shouted, twisting to break the woman's hold. She had no idea what she could do, only that she had to help him.

The current swept faster as the water rose, dank and dangerous. Bo's head bobbed back into sight. Adrenalin shot through Sara. She was a strong swimmer, but the woman kept a staying hand on her.

The man floundered, struggling for a moment before his shoulders appeared, dipped and rose again, this time remaining visible. Bo and the mule both appeared to have stopped their headlong run as the water again coursed around their bodies.

Bo's upper body appeared part of the mist above the surface as he continued moving away. Gradually he emerged on the sandbar, the mule lumbering behind.

Sara's breathing was ragged. They still had to make the return. She couldn't see well but could make out the shapes of the man and the mule as they moved along the narrow spit—which appeared to be shrinking—working their way back upstream.

Eventually, almost directly across from Sara and the woman, they stopped. She either saw, or imagined she saw, Bo lift a slim figure onto the mule's back. He led the mule several yards further upstream then turned and appeared again to be devoured by the river.

"Oh, God," she whispered, "please bring him back to me. Please." She scarcely breathed as the man, the mule, and the boy advanced slowly toward the rough river bank some distance below where the women waited.

Sara dropped Bo's coat and guns on the ground and ran, the woman close at her back. They scrambled and scurried over rocks and down a cutaway to meet the convoy as it emerged from the chill water.

Ready to throw herself into his arms, Sara stopped instead, caught her breath, and stared. Her heart pounded as Bo lifted the boy from the mule's back and stood him on the ground.

The woman stepped in front of Sara, wrapped her shawl around the child, swung him into her arms, and bustled toward the cabin. As an afterthought, she turned.

"Come on, you two!"

Sara stood paralyzed, her eyes locked on the man. She had intended to fling her arms around him, to hold onto him and comfort him and praise him for his courage. Instead, she stood stunned, staring. The powerful man who had emerged from the water was a stranger. She retreated a step, confused, frightened.

His hair and beard were plastered back revealing a high forehead, full dark eyebrows and a strong chin. The wet clothing clung to him, outlining the swells and crevices of a strapping body, broad shoulders, muscular biceps. She could see the definition of his chest and stomach, his slim waist and narrow hips. The long underwear clung to his well-formed legs. Amazed, Sara caught her breath as her eyes trailed from his face down his long physique.

This was not the old man who had shuffled into the river. Yet this was the same man who only appeared to be old behind the whiskers and layers of clothing. Now the river had exposed the truth.

Ducking his head, Bo tried to circumvent her, leading the mule toward the barn, but Sara recovered and grabbed the reins from his stiff fingers.

He yanked the straps back.

Gently, watching his face, she touched his hand, the massive hand usually warm and gentle, now unsteady in the chill wind whipping over his soaked body.

"Please let me." Her words sounded hoarse as she gazed into the familiar depths of his black, black eyes. "I want to do this, for you. Please."

He hesitated, looked at her a moment, then opened his hand, allowing her to take the reins from his icy fingers.

The woman appeared in the cabin door and shouted. "Bo, come on in here now and get shed a' them wet clothes."

Bo flashed Sara an apologetic look. She nodded, encouraging him to go. He turned toward the cabin, detouring only enough to pick up his abandoned coat and guns.

Sara took the mule to the barn, patting the animal, praising him for saving one human life, maybe two. She was amazed at her own calm. She'd been around few horses, had never even touched a mule.

Inside, out of the wind, she tied the docile animal to an iron rung, picked up a handful of straw from the corner and began wiping the water from his coat.

She rubbed a long time, exchanging dampened straw for dry from time to time. He stood very still, obviously enjoying her rapt attention. All the time she was drying him, she murmured to him about how heroic he was for going into the racing water.

"You were wonderful. Strong. Brave. You're like that man in there, silent, and dependable, and courageous."

She stopped stroking the animal and stood still a moment, contemplating.

* * * *

After she finished drying the mule, Sara found a meager barrel of oats, fed him a portion, closed up the barn, and walked to the cabin, pondering her new insight.

She knocked once at the door and stepped inside to find Bo and the woman sitting in the main room in chairs close to the fire, drinking from mugs. She risked a quick look at Bo.

Facing the fireplace, his hair was wild, as if it had been towel dried. His eyes appeared to be closed. His bare feet protruded from beneath the quilt wrapped around him. His toes wriggled as they warmed before the fire. His under clothes hung from twine strung over the stone face of the fireplace.

Lutie, in a long nightshirt, and two other young stranglers, scampered up the ladder to what appeared to be the children's sleeping loft on a second level.

As she peeled away her outer layers of clothing, Sara heard whispers and giggles overhead and glanced up.

"They'll settle down, soon as the adventure's told," the woman said. She nodded to a steaming cup on the sideboard, then motioned Sara into a small overstuffed chair off to one side of the fire. "Bo put ye in a fair portion of the milk and sugar. Is that the way ye take it?"

Sara nodded.

The family's name was Johnson. Lafayette and Lilly had nine children. There were so many youngsters in and out, up and down the ladder to the loft, that Sara wondered if they would have missed Lutie if he had permanently drowned on either occasion.

She listened carefully as Mrs. Johnson spun stories of their life in the mountains. She was glad their hostess occupied the chair between them so Sara was not tempted to look at Bo, for when she looked at him, a strange warmth stole through her. That bonding thing again, she supposed. She scowled at the thought.

"This ain't the first time Bo's came up here to do a rescue, nor the second nor the third neither," Mrs. Johnson said, rocking and slurping her coffee noisily. "And he's only been around here what, two, three y'ar?"

Surprised, Sara leaned forward to glance at Bo.

His eyes half closed, he gazed into the fire looking detached and completely disinterested. His empty cup dangled from his index finger. Getting no response, Mrs. Johnson continued.

"Come here straight out of the United States Army, Bo did. Showed up one spring, straight and tall and clean shaved. A fine-spoke man. A educated man. He didn't talk much, of course. The man never were one for idle chat."

Bo talked? How odd. Again Sara peered at Bo, who seemed

oblivious to Mrs. Johnson's review of his history. Why was he mute now? she wondered.

"He hadn't never been around hereabouts before. Just turned up one day over in that hollow. It was warm weather. He clumb over the ridge and commenced to building him a cabin, never troubling nobody with his quiet ways. He didn't mix with nobody down at Settlement.

"Some of them troublemakers down there and on over at Turkey Gap come up one evening set for mischief. They'd done heard about his quiet ways and figured him the timid sort, one what couldn't see to hisself or his place.

"They's a bunch of them lowland, cowardly folk anyhow. Fate and me got word through our kids that the pack of 'em was coming. Fate, that's my man, got his gun and slipped over to keep an eye out, make sure they didn't do Bo no real harm."

Without interrupting the story, Bo stood. Keeping the quilt around him, he got his boots, sat back down, and pulled them on, not bothering with the soaked socks. Sara saw he was already wearing his leather trousers, which he'd left behind when he went into the water. He reached out a bare arm and gathered his clothes off the line improvised over the hearth. The clothes still dripped. Mrs. Johnson prattled on about some of the other stunts "that no 'count bunch" from Settlement had pulled.

Bo retired to a darkened corner behind the sideboard and emerged in his bearskin coat, carrying his wet clothes. He picked up his guns and motioned Sara toward the door.

She shook her head. "I want to hear this story."

Pushing the unruly hair out of his face, Bo grunted his disapproval and his eyebrows knitted a harsh V into the bridge of his nose. Sara shifted slightly but stayed where she sat.

Mrs. Johnson flapped a hand, shooing him. "Now, Bo, let us women finish our visit. I don't get the pleasure of gossiping with another growed female nearly often enough. I do appreciate you saving my child's life again, but won't you settle back now and let us finish our talk?"

Bo's eyes shot daggers at Sara before he looked back at Mrs. Johnson, took a deep breath, and tromped out, swinging the cabin door closed noisily behind him.

Sara looked back at Mrs. Johnson, waiting. "What happened when the bunch from Settlement came after Bo?"

"Well, there was five or six of them lowlanders, men and boys, that night, shouting evil threats, and waving knives and guns. Bo didn't make a sound, just held back, watching, sizing 'em up.

"Fate and the kids and me was hid, but we could see the whole layout like it was a television play right here.

"The way it turned out, I was proud my kids was there. It were a fine lesson for 'em; one man protecting his place, willing to take on a bunch of heathens like them boys."

Mrs. Johnson rocked back and took several long slurps of her coffee. Sara shifted in her chair. She had a lot of questions but thought it better to let Mrs. Johnson tell this her own way and in her own time.

"They was lickered up and yellin' and making a terrible commotion. I wasn't worried 'til I seen Bo lay his gun aside." Sara remembered Bo's leaning his gun against the tree, anticipating his encounter with the coyotes her first night in the mountains.

"They come at him all at once with a banshee yell. Bo, he picked out the biggest and loudest and drew a bead on him with his eyes. That's not the way they'd planned it, I could tell. Boys runnin' in a pack like that wants to lay back, biding their time, waiting to see if a feller needs to risk hisself or not.

"When the big one fell under a single blow—him with a knife and Bo bare fisted—the others circled Bo, darting in, worryin' him one at a time, but their hearts wasn't in it.

"When he'd laid out a couple more of 'em, the others sobered up sudden and 'peared to lose their taste for fightin'. Bo stepped back and let the ones that was able carry off the others.

"It took two to manage the big man—big red-haired fellow, he were—carrying his two arms, draggin' his feets." Sara squirmed in her chair, remembering big, red-headed Holthus, the leader of the band of robbers that had kidnapped her. "They clumb back down that mountain and, far as I know, to this day, they ain't been back, except that scrawny tetched one, Cappy, coming up to make his deliveries."

"Maybe Bo got hurt that night," Sara mused aloud. "Did he talk after that?"

"Same as always. Not much."

"When did he lose his voice altogether then?"

Mrs. Johnson looked surprised. "I didn't know he had. Fate and me figured he just decided talk weren't no 'count."

Nodding, Sara narrowed her eyes as she studied the older woman. She bit her bottom lip, stood, and donned her layers of clothing again. Now how was she going to get home?

Home? A bed of hay in a shed? What was she thinking?

Mrs. Johnson stood and regarded Sara curiously. "What's your name, child, and whereabouts d'ya come from?"

"My name is Sara Loomis, and I'm supposed to be in Overt. Cappy and Franklin and a big red-haired man named Holthus kidnapped me when they robbed a convenience store. Cappy was supposed to murder me out in the woods, but he took me to Bo thinking Bo would do the killing for him. Lucky for me, I guess."

Mrs. Johnson nodded sagely. "Well, you're a heap better off with Bo."

"Mrs. Johnson." Sara posed her request quietly. "I need your help. Can you tell me how to get to a main road from here?"

"Yes, I can, but you'd best be goin' on back over to Bo's place tonight. It's nearly six mile to the road and you never know if there'll come some civil person a drivin' over that old stretch or not, especially at night."

"I don't know the way back to Bo's place. I might just as well try for the road and get myself out of his hair."

Mrs. Johnson eyed her oddly. "He'll be waitin' for ya. He wouldn't leave ya to face the varmints or them sneaky devils at night all alone. That ain't his way."

"Please, Mrs. Johnson." Sara's voice broke. "Please tell me the way to the road."

"Child, child. You got nothin' worth crying about. You got to go back Bo's way anyhow. Ask him. He'll show ya."

Sara cleared her throat and her mind with one barked cough. "What's the closest town around here?"

"Except for Settlement, Caesar's closest."

Sara tried to steady herself. "Tell me the shortest way to Caesar, then."

"Shortest way's by boat, down river, maybe seven, eight mile, but it's too swoll. You can't go that way tonight."

Sara grimaced. She'd seen all she wanted of that river this night, but she could walk it, follow the channel on foot.

"How about the road below the ridge at Bo's? Where does it go?"

"Straight to Settlement. Cappy's ma, Queenie, runs Settlement. If she caught you, she'd give you over to one of them addled boys a' hers again, and next time you might not get off so good. Like I said, you're better off with Bo, at least for the time bein', water up the way it is."

Sara stepped out the door from the Johnson's cozy home into the wintry night. She started to her right, toward the river. She would walk, stay on the bank, follow the boiling waters back to civilization.

She heard a low whistle and looked over her shoulder. Something big and black loomed at the edge of the woods. She recognized Bo's form outlined as he stepped forward in to the night's natural light. He grunted once. She turned toward him, took a deep breath, and glanced back at the water.

It would probably be best not to attempt to make her way down river at night, especially with Bo not fifty feet away. But there would be another opportunity. He wouldn't try to hold her. Now that she knew a way out, she could slip off during the daylight, some time when he was hunting or cutting wood. But why was she so reluctant to go? Of course, she didn't want to cause some big scene, telling him good-bye.

She was annoyed by her own lame excuse. In her heart, Sara knew Bo would not make a scene, or try to make her stay. But, after tonight, she was suspicious of her own volatile emotions. It would be better for everyone if she simply walked away.

The most distressing thing about her situation was that after the glimpse she'd had of him wet, she was entertaining all kinds of strange, new thoughts about the man.

She chided herself. The bond between them was growing stronger. She definitely needed to leave, and the sooner, the better.

Chapter Nine

There seemed to be no confusion in either of their minds that night when they got back from the Johnsons. Sara went straight to the shed; Bo, to the cabin for the lantern.

He waited inside the shed while she took the lantern to the outhouse, returned, and arranged her bed. When she was ready, settled on her knees in her nest, he walked over close to her.

From his coat pocket, he produced the mysterious object he had spent so much time whittling. He held it in the full light of the lantern, then offered it to her.

"A comb?" Amazed, delighted, she smiled uncertainly, first at the gift, then into his face.

"Thanks." She took it, touched it carefully, feeling the many, oversized, uniform teeth, each perfectly smooth, without a snag or a rough place anywhere. He had made it with his own hands—spent hour after hour of his time on the gift—for her. Her chin quivered as she squinted up into his face. What was wrong with her, getting emotional over a comb? Ridiculous. She had received much nicer gifts.

But never had a gift from anyone moved her as this one did. His regard seemed crafted into each small, perfect tooth.

Turning away from him, averting her eyes, she raked the comb through her hair. It caught in the tangles accumulated in days without grooming.

She continued, slowly, cautiously, persuading the comb through her dark curls. She didn't need a mirror to comb the hair she had fussed over hundreds of times in front of one.

"Thank you, Bo." She turned to find her benefactor gone and heard the wooden plank fall into its metal braces, securing the door.

Sara did not understand the sensations fomenting inside her. She wanted to giggle, to whoop, to weep. She found herself being drawn closer and closer to him; felt a special warmth for him, even for this strange lifestyle.

"Fight it," she chided aloud. Her throat ached. She mustn't let herself feel this tenderness toward him. She was beginning to understand him and his decision to live as he did, away from fools and threats, comfortable setting his own pace, doing things his own way.

"No, no," she said aloud. "That kind of thinking is a bad thing. A very bad thing."

Sara tossed the comb into the hay, careful to note where it landed. Standing, she bit her lips, clasped her arms over her midriff and paced. She felt restless, annoyed at her situation, at herself, all over again. She was supposed to be in Overt beginning her new life, her new job, finding a posh apartment, buying new clothes. Bo, life here in the mountains, was knocking her priorities all out of whack.

She continued to pace in the dark, thinking. She needed to get out of here, needed to get her priorities straight, needed to formulate a plan.

How long would it take her to get down river, walking or floating? It was seven or eight miles, according to Mrs. Johnson. At the jogging trail in the city, Sara could walk a mile in fifteen or sixteen minutes easily, jog it in nine. She should be able to reach Caesar in less than two hours. Easy...except for trees and uneven landscape and mountain lions and Queenie's half-wit sons bumbling around.

"No excuses." Sara scolded herself, mumbling the words out loud. "You've got to get out of here before..."

Before what?

Her voice dropped to a whisper. "Before you begin to think about touching him, about him touching you.

"That crude old mountain man?" She hissed, answering herself. "Give me a break."

"Old, huh? You saw those wet clothes clinging to him. That was *not* an old man's body. That guy is one very nice piece of work."

"Stop it." She grimaced. "What are you thinking? You know how you are."

"Okay, so I don't want sex. I liked the preliminaries, didn't I?"

"Bo doesn't seem like a man who'd be satisfied with preliminaries."

She began nodding. Vigorously she took off her clothes and donned her nightshirt. She slung the quilts around her shoulders and dropped down into the hay.

It didn't matter how Bo looked, how kind he was to her or how courageous he was in helping his neighbors. She had to leave. And she needed to go before winter weather prevented it.

One thing was clear: her resolve was withering. She admired him more every day, had begun thinking of him as a man, perhaps, after tonight, even as a desirable man.

"Get real," she rumbled under her breath, scolding herself again. The grumbling came out as a growl. "Heaven help you. You're even starting to sound like him."

Suddenly she was on her knees, digging through the hay for her comb. When she found it, she ran her fingers lovingly over every tooth. She allowed herself to think of Bo; to remember how strong, how virile his body looked as he emerged from the river; his dark, probing eyes; to ponder his puzzling lack of interest in her physically. After all, they had slept side-by-side in his bed and he had not touched her.

She recalled how he did touch her, his big hands warm, gentle, even at first, despite the growls and snarling.

He had nearly stopped making all those guttural noises when they were alone, at least he had before Cappy showed up on the ridge with his delivery.

It seemed odd to her that Cappy was not a significant player in her thoughts. In fact, she had almost forgotten the prospect of being rescued by the little dolt.

She was surprised by Bo's reaction to Cappy's being at the ridge, talking to her. He was definitely angry, maybe a little jealous. She smiled at the idea, then shook her head. No, Bo didn't have to be jealous of anyone, certainly not Cappy.

Occasionally, however, she caught Bo's dark eyes studying her face, scanning her body and she recognized the look. Men and boys had admired her that same way since she was fourteen years old, the year the abundant breasts blossomed on her slender frame.

At school, boys bumped into her, brushed against her, whispered together as she moved down the hallway.

On dates, they tried to touch her. She didn't mind, even liked it.

It didn't take long to learn, however, that the more liberties she allowed, the more a boy wanted.

When the first boy unfastened her bra, she marveled at the sensation, thought the excitement might be love. It wasn't.

Sara lay back in her nest in the stall and pulled the quilts tightly around her. For the first time, she felt secure enough, remote enough, to dig up those hated memories and examine them. How odd.

When that first boy had bragged about his success—told everyone he'd gotten into Sara's bra—she felt betrayed, hated him. She later analyzed it, thinking her reaction verified the adage about there being a fine line between love and hate.

It was a long time before a boy's hands were allowed to roam into her underclothes again, but eventually, it happened.

Sara liked being fondled above the waist and rationalized that there could be nothing wrong with doing something that felt so good.

A girlfriend said Sara had a reputation as a tease because she encouraged guys, egging them on, then wouldn't let them into the inner sanctum, the area from her waist to her knees.

"You are so green," a college roommate told her.

"Spell it out for Sara," another said when girls in her dorm confided their sexual exploits. "You'll have to draw a picture or Sara won't know what we're talking about."

Finally the taunts and the chiding had Sara mad at herself. Her friends were having sex. She needed to catch up. But she was a college senior before she "went all the way."

She was a student advisor overseeing a freshman women's dormitory. Even the young girls in her dorm teased her about being nearly twenty-two years old and still a virgin.

One night that spring, she told a girlfriend she was ready. The girlfriend "set her up." Sara was to go to Wesley's apartment at three-thirty on a Tuesday afternoon.

"You're a looker," Wesley said when he opened the door, then grinned. "They tell me you've never *done it?*"

She'd been mortified.

"Don't worry. It's easier than learning to ride a bike. Can you ride a bike?"

She nodded. She thought he was kidding but she was too tense to enjoy his humor.

Wesley needed to hurry. He didn't have a lot of time. His study group would be there by four.

"We'll save the lesson on foreplay for next time," he said, grinning agreeably, and locked the apartment door. "Go ahead and take off your clothes. All of them." His tone was businesslike as he unbuttoned his shirt.

Stepping out of her sandals, Sara did exactly as he said, removing her shirt and bra first.

Wesley had just unzipped his pants when he saw her nude from the waist up. His mouth gaped open, his eyes rounded, he dropped to his knees and grinned a silly grin. He kept staring at her whispering, "Thank you, thank you..." She was embarrassed, angry, and flattered all at the same time.

Recovering a little, Wesley picked up her cast-off clothes and carried them along as he ushered her into the bedroom. He sat on the end of the bed to watch as she removed her jeans and panties. She couldn't bring herself to look at him, but assumed his heavy breathing meant he liked what he saw.

He motioned her onto the bed as he wriggled out of his underwear. He kept his undershirt and socks on. She sat staring at the floor. When she ventured a look, his penis was like the rest of him, long, and thin, and stiff.

Grudgingly, he put on a condom. She insisted. The girls in the dorm had said she would have to make him do it. Sulking then, he leaped on top of her. He kissed her hurriedly, used his hands to force her legs apart, and tried to cram the narrow shaft into her. It hurt.

Alarmed, she fought him, trying to get away. She arched her back and raised her hips in an effort to bounce him off. He stayed aboard like a rodeo cowboy astride a bucking bronco. His efforts became frantic as he rammed the shaft against the front of her over and over again.

She screamed as he finally jammed it into her, and drove it straight through the resistant membrane.

Clamping a hand over her mouth, he pumped furiously, up and down, in and out. The friction of the hard little shaft burned. She pounded him with her fists and yelled, but his hand over her mouth muffled the cry.

Frightened, miserable, she watched his small, white butt bob up and down, in and out of her line of vision. He looked ridiculous. She would have laughed except for the pain that came with each determined thrust.

Someone knocked on the outside door. She heard a key turn in the lock, then voices in the living room. Wesley finished with a noisy groan and jumped off of her.

Sara felt cold, and wet, and sick to her stomach. Barely able to roll onto her side, she tried to get her bearings and locate her clothes.

"Yuck!" Wesley said, making little effort to keep his voice down. "Look what you did."

Beneath her on the bed was a smear of bloody mucous.

"I can't believe you made me do this when you were having your period."

Mortified, Sara shook her head. "Made you?" He was obviously an imbecile. "I'm not. I don't know what that is."

"It's not normal, I can tell you that. You aren't supposed to leave a mess on the bed after. You'll have to clean that up."

She didn't answer. She wanted out of there. "Is there a fire escape out this window?"

"No. You have to use the door, like everybody else." He dressed in silence, glowering occasionally at the soiled spread, obviously angry.

Sara had not finished dressing when Wesley flung open the bedroom door and stalked into the living room, gushing greetings to his study group.

"Is that a *girl* I see there in your bedroom?" a female voice chirped.

Sara leaped to close the door. She finished dressing then, head lowered, she hurried through Wesley's classmates, feeling every eye on her as she ran outside. She hadn't attempted to clean up the mess on the bed.

Back in her dorm room, she closed the door and sat gingerly on the side of her bed. Her hands limp in her lap, her shoulders bowed, she cried.

Now she had made love. Ugh. All she knew was it hurt like heck, smelled ghastly, was messy, and joyless. She hated it.

There was no doubt. She was one of the frigid ones, coldly resistant to the greatest recreation known to men.

What should she do? What *could* she do? She shook her head hopelessly.

When her girlfriends asked how it went, Sara said everything was pretty much like she'd expected.

* * * *

Looking around the darkened shed, Sara drew a deep breath and clutched the comb tightly. She was safe from that here. Franklin wanted to force her to have sex, but he was far away. Cappy she could control. Bo wasn't interested. Here, safe, she could take out old, torturous memories and examine them without being afraid.

It was nearly three years after the episode with Wesley before Sara experienced sex again. She stiffened with the memory.

* * * *

Jimmy Singer was handsome, a popular young administrator with the university. He and Sara had graduated together. He stayed on with the school, Sara went to work on the local newspaper. Eventually Jimmy asked her out for a Coke.

They went out several times, necked and petted in his car. He didn't press for more when he took her back to her rooms over the garage at her parents' house at night. The subject of sex didn't come up until spring, when they went on the picnic to Glassic Lake.

It was warm in the sun. Couples in various stages of undress lay necking on blankets and towels all along the shoreline. Sara forced herself to relax and concentrate on breathing slowly, evenly, as Jimmy spread their blanket. He knelt and put his hand on her back. She sorted and rearranged the food in their picnic basket.

He lay down, stretched out an arm and beckoned her. She smiled, dropped down beside him and rested her head on his shoulder. Sara thought it was odd when he covered their bodies with a beach towel, leaving their arms and legs exposed. She didn't ask about it.

Jimmy kissed the side of her face. He pulled her blouse free of her shorts, unbuttoned and laid it open, her exposure hidden beneath the towel. He ran his warm hand over her stomach, unsnapped the front closure on her bra and fondled her breasts as he had done before. Dread knotted her stomach.

She lay unmoving as he unbuttoned and unzipped her shorts, something he had not done before. Trying to relax, she tensed even more.

Kissing her, distracting her, he pulled her shorts and panties down to her knees, then did the same with his own shorts and underwear. She hoped to feel some kind of joy, excitement, anything but consuming terror. She didn't.

Jimmy rolled her onto her side, facing him. There they lay chest to breast, their nakedness hidden from other people along the beach by the towel draped over them. Sara trembled, feeling exposed as he shifted beneath the towel. He put his hand on her behind and pressed her against him.

She felt his cock hard against her thigh. Jimmy was perfect, she told herself. It would never get better than this. She wanted to want him. She tried to cooperate, as he attempted to insert himself into her, but her body resisted. She took a deep breath, gritted her teeth, and braced herself.

He said, "Everything's all right, sweetheart. I'm wearing protection." She shivered. "You don't have to say anything, Sara. You can't want this any more than I do."

He had misinterpreted her shiver, but it didn't matter. She was determined to make this work.

She was dry as he entered her. Involuntarily, she clamped her legs together then clenched her teeth, trying not to resist. The torturous cock penetrated. A dozen thrusts later, Jimmy groaned with pleasure.

Watching him, wide-eyed, Sara felt no passion, no pleasure, only a morbid curiosity. Her only wonder came from having given him such consuming satisfaction while she had lain there more observer than participant.

They had sex many times that summer, always partially clothed. Sara endured each encounter, grinding her teeth against her humiliation.

Disgusted by her own inadequacy, Sara began to despise his always reliable pleasure in the sex act. Here she was, twenty-five years old, successful in her chosen profession, making her own living, in her dating prime, and she hated sex. God, she hated being frigid.

She tried to side-step circumstances which would provide them opportunities for intimacy, pretending, hiding her dread each time Jimmy began the ritual.

Modest, frequently rushed, Jimmy preferred to remain partially clothed for sex. He said it was less trouble to remove only the essential clothing, then dress quickly again, and get on with other plans. The only redeeming factor for Sara was that Jimmy's sexual satisfaction came quickly. Her misery was always blessedly brief.

Finally, one afternoon late in August, in her rooms over the family garage, Sara balked.

"I just don't want to," she said as Jimmy began the familiar preliminaries.

"Why not? We're not doing anything until three. Come on."

"I don't want to."

"Are you mad at me about something?"

She shook her head.

"You trying to punish me for looking at other girls? It's innocent, Sara, I promise. You're my girl. You know that."

"Jimmy, I don't like sex."

He snapped his head back as if recoiling from a slap in the face. "What d'you mean? Sara, sex is the one way we are totally compatible. We've had great sex all summer. What's wrong with you? Come on. What'd I do?"

She winced. "I thought we knew each other well enough by now that I could finally be honest about this."

His face flushed and twisted with annoyance. "You want to be honest? Who's asking for honesty? Not me, honey. If you think we're at a place in our relationship to start discussing each other's shortcomings, I have a few suggestions of my own."

Sara stared at him. "How could you have any complaints? We've done exactly what you wanted to do, when you wanted to do it, for the last three months."

"Yeah, and the *doing it* has been good. But you're a pouter, Sara. You sulk for absolutely no reason. I all but stand on my head to try to make you happy but nothing seems to work. We used to have fun."

"That was before we became intimate."

"What the hell is that supposed to mean?"

"I don't like sex."

"Do you mean sex with me or with anyone?"

She felt the blush wash up from her neck into her face. She averted her gaze. "I don't know."

Jimmy stared at her. "Well," he hissed finally, "we sure don't want to pester you with any more of that nasty old screwing." He stomped out.

He called three days later, apologizing, wanting to patch it up.

He went to her rooms and they talked. The conversation deteriorated to the same argument and he left angry again. They repeated the same scene again and again.

After he left for graduate school in California in September, Jimmy called. He missed her. He wanted her back. He was ready to take the plunge—they could get married, if that's what she was angling for.

* * * *

Remembering Jimmy—what a fine, handsome man he was—Sara struggled to her feet in the cool darkness and paced across the shed. She should have fallen in love with Jimmy. He was everything a woman could want in a husband. Yet she never experienced inner stirrings with him, no butterflies, no unexplained tingling, no palpitations, nothing. What was it then that caused the electrical current Bo ignited?

Just seeing Bo that afternoon in the woods felling the tree, her heart jumped, her pulse raced, and she blushed furiously. And that was when she still thought of him as old.

When he put his arms around her to knead the biscuit dough, she had all those same responses plus an odd prickling sensation in the most private parts of her body. Why was that? *What* was it?

Tonight as he walked dripping from the river, she felt a rush of heat. She had willed him to survive the river, had wanted to run to him, to feel his arms around her when the ordeal was over.

Sara was roused from her musing by a noise.

The board securing the shed's door creaked as someone outside slid it from its brackets. It wasn't Bo. He always knocked twice before coming in.

She heard the heavy beam thud as it hit the ground. She crouched in the dark and waited, frightened, curious to know who was entering the shed so stealthily.

Chapter Ten

Sara didn't recognize the outlined form of the person who stepped into the shed, closed the door, turned on a flashlight and shot it around the chamber until it illuminated her.

Covered by the worn cotton nightshirt, which extended well below her knees, she still grabbed a quilt to cover herself. Her visitor hesitated, then diverted the light beam to the floor.

"Come on," he rasped finally. "Quick, 'fore he hears."

Blinded by the light, she grabbed a handful of clothing and scrambled to follow as the figure turned, doubled over, doused the light, and disappeared out the door. This was her chance.

But who was this?

What did it matter? He was here to take her home.

She followed. "Who is it?" She fell into step behind him as they hurried to the ridge. He dropped to his knees, turned and flipped the light quickly on and off in his own face. "Franklin." She whispered the name and a tremor shivered through her.

"Shhh!" He stood, bent from the waist, and again scurried toward the ridge. Sara remained where she was. "Come on," he hissed. Still she didn't move. "Cappy sent me to fetch ya. He 'as gonna rescue ya but he 'as too scart to come git ya hisself."

"Where is he? In the truck?"

"Nah, he's waitin' for us down at Melon's Walk. Come on, now. Ya wanna get outta here or don't ya?"

She shivered. Yes, she wanted to leave, but not with Franklin. A person couldn't choose her rescuers. On the plus side, he was alone, and he wasn't much bigger than she was. Could she keep him at bay, physically, until she could outsmart him? She bit her bottom lip. That shouldn't take long. If he didn't cooperate, she'd take his truck. She'd make sure it was returned, after she was well away from there.

He mumbled. "You comin' or not?"

Ignoring her better instincts, Sara clutched the quilt and the handful of clothing to her and followed.

They scrambled over the steep terrain, slipping and skinning their

105

way to the flat area below where the truck waited, the same rattle trap which had ferried her away from civilization all those days ago.

"Get in." He spat and wiped his mouth with the back of his hand. Sara darted to the passenger door, which was partially open. She climbed in and slammed the door shut. Franklin cringed at the sound and cranked the engine. It fired on the third try. He floor-boarded the truck, squealing tires, and throwing gravel as they fishtailed around and away.

He careened down the mountain without speaking for several minutes, checking his rear view mirror every few seconds.

"He can't run this fast." Sara wanted him to slow down on the curving, narrow mountain road that quickly improved from cattle track to gravel road to asphalt.

"He's got that big black machine that'll catch this 'un in a heartbeat."

The motorcycle. "I didn't hear it start up. Where's Melon's Walk? How far is it from here?"

Franklin cut his eyes and allowed a nasty smile. "'Fore that, I'm taking you to another little place I know."

"You said we were going to Melon's Walk to meet Cappy."

"We'll get there." He licked his lips, "Cappy's awful lathered up about diddlin' ya. Not wanting ya to disappoint the boy, I thought I ought to prime ya for it first, so you'll know what's expected."

She eyed him carefully. Franklin was too excited, a little "lathered up" himself. This road was good enough. She could get herself back to civilization from here. A hairpin curve danced in the headlines. Franklin slowed the truck. Sara jerked the handle and rammed the passenger door with her shoulder.

The handle fell off in her hand. The door held fast.

Franklin smirked. "That handle don't work. There's a special way. You gotta know it."

She cranked the window lever.

"It takes two fellers to open that winder' and that when she's standin' still."

He turned off the asphalt onto a dirt trail that spiraled down, down into a canyon, a well of darkness.

Sara fought her growing panic. She had to keep her head. She could handle him. At the first opportunity, she'd steal the truck and take off.

After several minutes driving down into the gloom, Franklin stopped in the middle of a single-lane path, cut the engine but left the lights on, and turned to face her. He stretched an arm on the back of the seat.

"Come on, Missy, you think we're a bunch a' hillbillies, but we know about city women and their whoring. You take any man you can get. I seen you doin' it in the magazines, in the picture shows, and on the TV." He slanted her a crooked look. "You city gals knows tricks, things you could learn me."

Sara shook her head, stricken by his incredible stupidity. She regarded his narrow shoulders, his scarecrow arms and legs. He probably had a painful little shaft to match. She tried to shake off that thought.

Franklin slipped something out of his pants pocket. With lightning quickness, he looped a cord around her left wrist and gave it a yank.

She snatched at it with her free right hand, which he snared before he bound the two wrists round and round with the cord. The quilt slid from her shoulders as Sara jerked her hands up and threw her body against him. Stronger than he looked, he put a filthy hand in her face, shoved her back, and tied her hands off with a knot, leaving a long end of rope still coiled in the seat.

This strange little gnome had a penchant for tying her up. Her wrists had barely healed from their last encounter. Maybe it wasn't just her. The leer in his eyes told her exactly what he was thinking. That was not going to happen. She'd castrate the little idiot, if he wasn't careful. The words *desperate times, desperate measures* flitted through her mind. She would not let him rape her. She would die first.

While she pondered the unthinkable, Franklin leaped from the truck and pulled the end of the cord out with him. He yanked Sara, wrists first. She slid across the seat. Her hip bumped the steering wheel as she skimmed it. She saw the keys dangling from the ignition. When she got loose, she'd run for the truck, get in, and drive. Her mouth set in a grim line. That's exactly what she was going to do.

Both feet firmly set, Franklin grabbed Sara's arms and pulled. Her body followed. She also swept out with her the extra pieces of clothing she had brought along. They scattered, swept by the wind. Smaller

107

pieces billowed, carried aloft on updrafts.

Staggering, trying to keep her feet, Sara lunged out of the vehicle to stand teetering next to Franklin who jittered nervously, looking around. His beady little eyes stopped when he sighted a massive live oak nearby. The tree, directly in line with the headlights, had expansive limbs, some of which swept low, the shadowy ends touching the ground.

Sara took a deep breath. He was too excited. She had to be calm, try to calm him.

"Is this where we're supposed to meet Cappy?" She asked the question slowly, quietly, as if the struggle in the truck had not occurred.

"No." Franklin didn't look at her. He was regarding the oak seriously as if visualizing something. Without warning, he yanked her forward as he stomped to the tree, his short legs taking choppy little steps over the uneven trail.

He had a long body but incredibly short legs. If the length of his legs had been proportionate to his torso, he would have been well over six feet tall. To Sara, he looked as if his body were a salvage job, a mixture of cast-off parts taken from a random selection of people.

Science might come to that someday, building a human who resembled Franklin, Sara thought. Obviously, however, this man was as he had been formed in a mother's womb. No wonder he had to tie women up to get a date. Even the mountain girls weren't desperate enough to go out with him.

As he was, Franklin was five-foot-eight or nine, only slightly taller than Sara. From his narrow shoulders extended long, spindly arms and small hands. But his hands were strong—very strong. She'd bet he was sensitive about his shape.

Franklin was stupid, but sly, and treacherous. She was smart. What about the man might work to her advantage?

He had a coward's mentality; had to tie a woman to subdue her. He did it efficiently. Practice, no doubt.

He ignored her as she stepped up beside him and swelled to her full height. Suddenly, she jabbed both her fists into his face and drove her heel into his foot. He screamed and backhanded her, knocking her sideways, but he didn't release the rope. Sara stumbled, tried to catch herself but hit the ground with a jarring thud and rocked back. Her right hand slid out of the cord but her left remained secure in the loop, the tether firmly in Franklin's grip. She rolled onto her side, catching herself with the free hand, splaying it in the dirt in front of her.

"You stupid idiot." She hissed the words.

Franklin sneered, baring ugly yellow fangs dangling at either side of the empty gums in the front of his mouth. "If I'm so stupid, how come you're the one trussed up like a sow about to get her head bashed?"

He set one foot, then ground the other one into her hand braced in the dust. She groaned and tried to yank her hand free. He shifted more weight onto the grinding foot. His mouth closed behind thin, angry lips and he peered down, bullying her with his stare.

"If I smash this hand, you won't never play the piano again." He hesitated. "D'you play the piano?"

She didn't answer as a gnawing fear nibbled at her anger. He set his jaw and put more pressure on the hand. "Like that, do ya?"

"No." She yielded. "Yes. I play the piano."

"It don't matter. You ain't gonna be playin' no more no how." He put his full weight on her hand and ground it back and forth. She screamed into the night, a resounding shriek, and the sound carried, echoing through the mountain hollows.

Franklin leaped sideways off the hand. "Shuddup!"

Trembling, Sara lifted the crumpled hand. She whimpered when he grabbed it, binding her wrists again, this time more tightly.

The hand that had been under his foot was tender when she tried moving it, but it didn't feel broken.

This couldn't be happening, she told herself, following quietly as Franklin stomped to the tree, tossed the length of cord over a high branch and pulled, hoisting her arms so she could prop her hands on the top of her head. It was a ridiculous position. She felt frightened, vulnerable.

When she was secured, he returned to the truck for a bundle, which appeared to be a sleeping bag. Keeping her eyes on him and using her thumbs, she worked on the knot binding her to the overhead branch as she thought. He was much stronger than he looked. She'd underestimated him—or overestimated herself. Maybe she should forget the truck and just run.

Franklin took great pains in selecting the spot for his sleeping bag.

On his hands and knees, he smoothed away rocks and sticks, concentrating on his task. She tried to calm down—to think.

On his second trip to the truck, he turned off the headlights and returned with a bag which he placed on a rock several feet from the bedding. He produced two quart jars of what looked like moonshine whiskey. He opened one jar and took a long swig, which induced a coughing fit. He wiped his eyes and ventured a look at Sara.

Under his scrutiny, she was acutely aware of her clothing. The thin nightshirt outlined her breasts. She rounded her shoulders to conceal them as much as possible. The shirt normally hung nearly to her shins but with her arms raised, it was hiked to her knees. When Franklin turned back to his chores, she began working on the cord again, clawing frantically with her thumbs, tearing her nails, trying to ignore the swelling, injured hand.

The night air grew cold. She could see her breath in puffs, and chills covered her arms and legs. Dressed as she was, she was going to get badly chilled before dawn. She shivered and hoped by dawn, the cold was the worst of her problems. She should never have come with Franklin. How could she have been so stupid?

She worked the bindings and eyed her adversary carefully as he hummed and busied himself making camp, tippling frequently from the fruit jar, glancing up at her from time to time, freezing her thumbs mid scratch.

Her hand throbbed in the cold. She mustn't think of her weaknesses, must focus on her strengths. She was smarter than he was. She needed to take advantage, make that work for her.

"Franklin," she said in a coaxing voice. He looked up. "I'm cold. I wish we had a fire."

He studied her hard. She lowered her eyes.

"I'm sorry if I embarrassed you. I knew it was too much to ask." She pretended to be ashamed for making such a difficult request. "Campers need special equipment to build campfires. I just thought that you, being a mountain man, might know a secret. Please go on. I'm learning a lot just watching you work."

Franklin cocked his head and the naked gums reappeared, gleaming behind his toothless grin. "They ain't nothin' to buildin' a fire."

"You're being modest. No one could come out here in the

wilderness and build a campfire without the right equipment."

He scurried to gather dried grass and small sticks which he piled into a heap on flat, bare ground. He rimmed the site with rocks, then hunkered, his back to her. She heard a match snap before he ignited a small flame and turned, his grin expectant, eager for praise.

"Oh, Franklin." Sara forced herself to smile. "I never dreamed you could do it. Thank you very much."

Giggling, he knelt and bent low to blow on the flame as he added small sticks.

"You are really good at this."

He added larger pieces of wood and, finally, an armful of dead branches.

"Franklin, you're a regular Daniel Boone."

He had produced a nice blaze, one which Sara hoped might be visible against the nighttime sky, should anyone be looking.

Another swig from the jar and Franklin swaggered forward, eying Sara. She stopped working on the bindings hoping they were loose enough.

Her eyes darted from his face to the fruit jar and back. "Did you bring enough for me?" She tried to sound playful.

Holding the mouth of the container with fingers wrapped over the top, he sidled closer, stopped a few feet in front of her and took another long drink. Grinning, he let the brown liquid dribble through his scraggly beard and down his chin.

Sara struggled for control of her facial expression. She didn't want her revulsion to show. He was still out of range. The cord was so loose she was afraid it might fall off the branch before she was ready. If she could hurt him, really hurt him, she'd break for the truck. The keys were there. Make it to the truck, and she was home free.

"Come on, Franklin, I'd share with you."

He took another step and another swallow. His eyelids drooped. His dull eyes had gotten duller but the silly grin continued. Clutching the jar, fingers clamped over the lip, he reached for the neck of her shirt. She eased back as far as the cord allowed. Franklin shuffled forward.

She took one stride, planted her left foot and brought her right knee straight up, slamming it into his groin.

He let out a wild banshee shriek, dropped the jar, grabbed himself with both hands, and crumpled to his knees then onto one side, writhing in the dirt.

Before he hit the ground, Sara's right hand was free. The cord still tight around her left, slithered over the branch and coiled to the ground.

She ran for the truck, scrabbling at the cord still attached to the one wrist. She couldn't get it off. She'd leave it for now.

The keys dangled tauntingly in the ignition behind the closed window on the passenger side. She yanked the door. It held. She yanked again and kicked it before she remembered. The handle didn't work.

She glanced over her shoulder. Franklin was on his knees, holding himself with both hands, looking around in a stupor, probably trying to locate her.

She ran to the driver's side, leaped into the truck, locked the door, and turned the key. The starter ground but didn't fire.

Frantically, she pumped the gas pedal, stole another look at Franklin, and tried again.

He was on his feet, staggering, still holding himself.

The engine wouldn't turn. She smelled gasoline. She'd flooded it. Damn! She rammed the accelerator to the floor and held it as she tried again and again. The starter ground more and more slowly until, finally, it quit.

She looked for Franklin. He wasn't there.

The driver's side door flew open. She had locked it. She knew she had. Damn this damned truck anyway.

Franklin grabbed at something and she realized again that the cord was still tied around her wrist. He snatched up the line trailing out the door and gave it a savage yank.

Sara's upper body lurched sideways, following her arm. Her feet still in the floorboard, she couldn't catch herself as she skidded out and down, face first.

Chapter Eleven

Franklin caught a fistful of her hair and yanked Sara's head up. Grabbing at his hands, she clamored to her feet.

The whites of his eyes looked yellow and the pupils, red. They bulged with fury and pain.

"Don't look at me, bitch." He swung and his hand caught the side of her head. She flew sideways with the impact and hit the ground, her face again snuffling in the dirt.

He tossed the hank of her hair, shaking loose strands off his fingers, and lunged, grabbing for her again.

She ducked as he snatched another handful of hair and kneed her in the side. Her feet skittered in the dirt, spinning her as she tried to get back to her hands and knees.

He yanked the rope still tied to her left wrist, pulling her arm out from under her, and she nose-dived. Her nightshirt flapped. He kicked at her and she scrambled frantically, dodging his feet.

Squirming, slithering in the dirt, Sara avoided one well-aimed boot, then a second. Her evasions only seemed to fan his rage.

Franklin yanked the rope and pulled Sara's captive arm up over her head giving him a clear shot at the exposed rib cage as she sprawled on her side in the dirt, gasping for air.

Sneering, he drew back and landed a boot to her stomach. The blow knocked the wind out of her. She lay stunned, silent. Unable to draw a breath, she clawed at him feebly with her free hand, mutely pleading for help. He laughed.

"Not so brave now, are you, puss? You gonna die. Oh, yeah, you gonna die right here, right now. I'm gonna watch." He jigged around in a circle, high-stepping. "You not gonna breathe no more air. You gonna suffocate yourself right outta this world, eating dirt."

Sara managed to draw a whisper of air, then a gulp. She had seen high school and college football players get the wind knocked out of them. They had looked frightened, but none of them had died of it. She would get her breath. She would recover...this time. The nagging question was, could she survive the next?

Watching her, Franklin pranced on his toes and grinned, finally slowing to arch his bristly eyebrows.

"No, you not gonna die...yet." His grin got bigger and he licked his lips. "You not gonna get dead without me knowing how you taste. You got them nice woman tits. Sweetest tits I ever seen." He rubbed the fingers of one hand over the palm of his other. "I'm gonna feel of 'em, smear 'em with peanut butter and lick 'em clean." A tremor ran the length of her body. "That ain't all I'm gonna do with 'em neither."

The mousy brown patch of chin hair twitched as he looked her up and down, finally settling his gaze back on her breasts, still concealed beneath the torn shirt. "I'm gonna be real careful with the prettiest one. Then I'm gonna to cut it off with my knife. Gonna put it in my collection." He leered. "It'll be my prize one, 'til I find a better 'un."

What was he talking about? He couldn't be saying what she thought he was saying.

"Always before when I cut them tits off, the women was passed out or maybe dead. I ain't gonna be that good to you." Again he slurped back drool.

Sara pretended not to hear. She kept her eyes averted and struggled to control her involuntary trembling.

"And that cunt a' yourn be mine too." She blinked, her breathing erratic. "I'm gonna diddle ya all night long. I might diddle ya tomorrow and next day, and day after that one, too."

She flinched as he raised his eyes to hers.

He slurped repeatedly and his voice dropped to a hiss. "But you gonna have to beg me for it. 'Long as you pleasure me, you gonna live. See?" He suddenly froze and regarded her with mock sorrow.

"Cappy's little heart's gonna break wide open when I tell him about how, after me, thinkin' about that little prick of his made you jump right off that ridge yonder into this here canyon.

"But Ma and them others'll know how ya begged, how good you was to me. Oh, yeah, I'm gonna tell 'em all about how it is."

He shuffled toward her.

Staring at his boots, Sara struggled to her knees, then to her feet. She tried to stand, but couldn't seem to unbend. It felt as if her ribs were tangled together.

Franklin caught the trailing end of the rope, looped it around her free wrist, and yanked.

She stumbled but kept her feet, still doubled over.

"We'll get you straight soon enough." He shoved her.

Clamping her arms across her stomach, Sara staggered, desperate to stay on her feet, avoid any more kicking, as they walked back to his camp.

He pranced. "Man, I got a good idea now. I mean a good 'un."

Back under the tree, Franklin again tied Sara's wrists, this time with greater care. He tossed the end of the rope over an upper branch and hoisted her arms. She unfolded slowly as he pulled her arms up and up, until she was stretched as far as she could go. She teetered on the balls of her feet to keep the cord from pulling her hands off. Her stomach roiled and she thought she might heave. Her ribs still felt as if they were knitted together. She moaned and her head rocked back. Up, high above the barren tree, was serenity, a star-studded sky. She saw something flutter and tried to focus.

It was a bit of fabric floating on the wind. Strangely, it seemed to be on fire. How could that be?

Pieces of her clothing scattered over the ground must have blown into the fire and gotten caught in an updraft sweeping through the hollow. She wished she were there too, floating high above this scene, free.

She heard Franklin move and she squeezed her head back between her arms to watch him. Unable to turn her face to either side, she twisted and cut her eyes until she located him.

He backed off, leering at her. "Won't be kicking a man's balls now, will you, sweet tits? Trouble is, I were too good to you before this." He stepped forward, then scowled as he ogled her up and down.

Stretched as she was, onto her tiptoes, Sara was half-a-head taller than Franklin. Comparing their heights, his eyes filled with rage. He straightened, stretched his neck out, got as tall as possible, even bobbled up on his toes. The top of his head came only to the bridge of her nose.

Blood trickled from her wrists down her arms, meandering into her hair. Her throat ached and she wanted to cry but she didn't have the strength for tears.

With one quick movement, Franklin's hand shot like a serpent's strike and ripped the front of her nightshirt open. He leaped back, warily eying her knee.

To his obvious chagrin, her ample breasts remained concealed behind either side of the nightshirt's cotton sheeting. But the tear exposed her panties. Franklin licked the drool oozing from the corners of his mouth.

"We gonna have some good times now." He pranced on his toes, leering, pretending to ignore what she decided was his continuing vexation over the difference in their heights.

He took a step back to survey his subject, then scurried to dig in his camp sack. He produced a jar of peanut butter and continued sorting among the supplies.

Sara rocked her head back and tried to think of something, anything to give her hope.

Could she stall him?

Stall until when? Until Bo or Cappy or one of the Johnsons...until someone came. She thought of her parents, felt sorry for them, sorry their only child was about to die, murdered by a hillbilly half-wit.

She had to do something. She squeezed her head between her arms again. She didn't have many options left.

"Franklin, did you ever go out with a girl who liked you or do you always have to hog-tie your women?" Her voice rasped.

He scowled up from the sack.

"Come on," she urged, trying to ignore the blood flowing more and more freely from her wrists, "you can tell me. I can't tell anyone if I'm dead. I'm the one person with whom you can be totally honest." She cleared her throat. "Tell the truth. Have you ever had sex with a woman of her own free will?"

"'Course I have. Sure I have. Lots and lots of times."

"Name one."

He sneered. "You."

She quailed. Surely no one would believe that. "No, not me."

"Why not you? All you women want it. Why you gotta play games? I know you want what I got right here in my pants." He patted his trousers gingerly, frowned down at himself, and muttered, "If you ain't gone and ruined it. All you women want a man to pleasure 'em, diddle

116

'em proper. Here I am, willin'. What kind of female are you?"

Sara felt woozy. She tried to select her words carefully. "I'm the kind who hates sex with anybody. Not just you, Franklin, with any man."

Maybe if she stalled long enough, she would bleed to death or pass out, escape the final humiliation. The trickling blood oozed through her hair and pooled in the hollow above her collar bone. Her throat was clogged again. Come on, she thought, no longer able to see Franklin clearly. He had become a blur.

"You done had sex with that crazy Bo, I bet. You done had sex a lot, ain't you, slut, truth be told? Well, I'm the man here now. It's me you gonna be rememberin' all the way down to hell."

His voice dropped to a whine. "It's what you get for being selfish, bitch. All I wanted was to see them tits. You shoulda' just let me see 'em, let me touch 'em, and taste of 'em."

He took the lid off the peanut butter jar and hesitated, strangling for a minute on his own spittle. "You got nice tits." Not looking at her, he appeared to brighten with a new idea. "Fact is, I'm gonna have me a look at them tits, right now."

He looked uncertainly from Sara to the peanut butter. He put the jar on the ground, straightened, and sidled toward her, fondling the front of his trousers.

When Franklin's blurry form was directly in front of her, Sara summoned her last bit of strength, cleared her throat and spat. The lugie hit him directly between the eyes.

Franklin staggered backward and stumbled over a small log laying half in the fire and half out.

He wallowed on the ground, righted himself, and grabbed the piece of wood which was flaming brightly on the far end. He set his jaw and lunged, aiming the fiery brand straight at her face, perhaps at her mouth which had offended him again. She squeezed her eyes shut, hoping, praying to die quickly.

She heard something crackle in the woods to her left and her eyes popped open.

Throwing her head back, she cut her eyes and thought she saw the glint of metal hurtling through the air, red and yellow, reflecting the firelight as it flew toward Franklin.

Forcing her head forward between her arms, she couldn't see clearly but heard a loud THWACK as the metal struck the wood in Franklin's hand.

Eerily, pieces of white—bits of Franklin's fingers, she thought—arched high in the air. The burning log fell to the ground and bounced end over end away from them.

Franklin's sickening squeal of disbelief was swallowed up by an ear-shattering roar from the woods, echoing like the rage of a wounded animal.

The bits and pieces of fingers floated a moment before they plummeted into the fire that spattered and licked up the delicacies with noisy appreciation.

Franklin crammed his hand into his mouth, muffling his own shrieks. Sara watched in disbelief, cringing at his screams that were suddenly confined to the enclosed hollow of his mouth.

Hampered by her position, her blurred vision, and blood trickling over her eyes, Sara could see only a giant shadow stride out of the woods, bend to retrieve the knife, and wipe the blade on Franklin's sleeve. Her former assailant collapsed into a heap, cowering from the interloper.

Eyes rolling, Franklin offered no objections, his only sound, the tormented cries escaping around the hand in his mouth.

The shadowy form came up in front of her and cut the cord which held Sara's hands aloft. Still tied together, her arms dropped over the newcomer's head, encircling his neck. Her legs had no strength left to bear her weight.

Recognizing his scent, she clung to him as Bo lifted her. She held on tightly and buried her face in the hair that smelled of pipe tobacco...and leather...and pine.

Shifting his hold, he gathered her close. She felt a tremor pass through him. As he held her, her aching body screamed objections, but she remained silent, spent, in the safety of his embrace.

They clung to one another for a long moment. She had wished him to come, willed him there. She wanted to hold onto him until she could be certain he was real.

Finally he knelt, lowering her, and extended her gently over the ground. She held on another moment, reluctant for him to take his head

118

from the circle of her arms.

When he did, she scrubbed the palm of one bound hand over her eyes and blinked furiously, trying to see, but she had to content herself with the familiar aroma, the strength, the gentleness of the man. She needed neither eyesight nor the rumble that issued from his throat to identify the hands attending her so gently.

"Thank you," she whispered. "Oh, Bo, thank you."

Overcome, she wavered in and out of consciousness, aware of Franklin's forlorn wail somewhere away from her, his misery assuring he was no longer a threat.

Bo handled her tenderly as he cut the rope binding her arms. Coming and going, he wiped the blood from her face, washed her wrists, and wrapped them with cloth torn from pieces of the clothing he found blowing around the campsite.

She cried out when his thick fingers brushed delicately over her ribs beneath her nightshirt's thin fabric. Her stomach convulsed. Despite the pain, she rolled onto her hands and knees and retched.

Vomit splattered over her hands and the ground and even into her hair, which hung limp, matted with dried blood. One of Bo's large hands held her forehead. His other arm circled her body, that hand splaying on her stomach, steadying her.

When the heaving and gagging subsided, Bo turned her, wrapped her in Franklin's sleeping bag, picked her up, and carried her to the truck. He eased her onto the seat.

She tried to speak but her words were only a whisper. "Battery's dead."

He nodded.

"What about me?" Franklin's voice sounded far away, pathetic, pleading. Bo's body stiffened but he didn't look back. Instead, he remained outside the truck, reached inside to turn the key in the ignition and, holding the driver's side door open, pushed it to a down grade. As it crested the hill and started down, he hopped in, slammed the gear shift into low, and popped the clutch. The engine coughed and sputtered to life.

* * * *

Exhausted, Sara remembered little of the trip back to Bo's cabin, recalling only incoherent pieces of consciousness. She saw the moon, shadows, heard a hoot owl and coyotes, whose voices echoed in the distance in the chill night and sounded remarkably like Franklin's wails. She tried not to inhale too deeply, nauseated again by the odor of the sleeping bag, which smelled like filth and Franklin's spittle. She shivered.

Bo stopped the truck in the clearing below the ridge, lifted Sara out, and carried her up toward the cabin.

Despite the cold, he propped her against the water spigot in the yard. Pumping furiously, bracing her body against his legs, he coaxed out a full bucket of water. He removed the sleeping bag and tossed it away from them before he poured the icy water over her head.

She shrieked. The water stung the open abrasions all over her body, from the top of her head to her legs, which were scraped and bleeding. But she was too weak to fight him.

Twice more, Bo retrieved and mercilessly poured the chill well water over Sara's trembling, torn, and nearly naked body.

The night time temperature was dropping and the water, cold. Just as she began to spasm, Bo carried her into the cabin.

Holding her with one arm, he tossed a bearskin rug onto the floor in front of the fireplace, the only warmth radiating from dying embers.

Skeptically, he regarded the torn nightshirt, soaked with blood and vomit and well water, his eyes following to her panties visible beneath the gaping covering. He didn't attempt to remove either garment.

He secured a large piece of flannel and draped it along the floor, carefully deposited Sara on the bearskin rug beside the flannel, then walked away.

She struggled out of the soaked shirt and panties and covered herself with the flannel. Discreetly, Bo returned with an old cotton shirt, which he handed her, along with a pair of his own briefs. He picked up her discarded clothing.

She put her arms into the shirt sleeves and overlapped the sides. "Can you save my underwear?" Her voice sounded strange. Bo regarded her thoughtfully then picked up the enamel basin and tromped out again into the night.

She quaked and leaned close to glean every bit of heat she could

120

from the remnants of the fire. Still shivering, using the flannel, she dried the rest of her body, then her hair.

Inside, out of the night air and in front of the dying fire, her eyesight improved as her body temperature rose.

It took her a while, fumbling with each button, to fasten the long-tailed shirt. She was pleased that it covered and seemed to warm her. She pressed her fingers against her wrists, then gingerly felt the top of her head, her shoulders, her ribs, her stomach. She was sore, scraped, and bruised, but nothing seemed to be broken.

Afraid to attempt to stand, Sara crawled to the bed and pulled off the top quilt. She returned to the bearskin rug, wrapped the quilt around her, and lay in a fetal position facing the fireplace. She shivered with occasional spasms.

Bo returned with several items of clothing from the shed. He also brought the comb he had made for her. Avoiding her eyes, he placed the comb on the mantle over the fireplace.

He had a mixture of goo that looked like leaves and mud and that he insisted on rubbing into the open abrasions on her wrists. Sara would have objected had Bo not allowed the rest of her to remain cocooned in the quilt. The concoction smelled of mint and immediately took the burn out of her wounds.

He handed her a glass of liquid and indicated she should drink it. His warm, sure hands lifted her to a sitting position. The beverage tasted like bicarbonate of soda. She hated the taste, but he made her drink the whole glassful.

Moments later, he poured hot water in a cup, added something, and placed it in her hands, again indicating she must drink. The warm mixture trickled down her throat and soothed her.

Next, Bo produced the enamel basin, added hot water from the kettle over the fire, put the basin on the floor beside her and handed her the wash cloth.

She struggled to speak. "I'm dry, Bo. Warm. I don't want to get wet again."

He nodded and frowned, indicating she was to wash.

Grudgingly, Sara took the cloth. Bo went outside.

The warm water felt good on her face and hands as she scrubbed. She removed stubborn vestiges of scaly vomit and blood from behind her ears, her neck and hair and rinsed the cloth in the basin repeatedly.

Opening the nightshirt, she ran the warm washcloth over her throat, let it linger on her chest, then hurriedly covered herself when Bo gave his usual two-rap warning. He came in carrying an armload of firewood.

He stoked the fire to blazing, took off his heavy coat, hung it on the peg behind the door, and removed the basin and her drink cups.

From the mantle, he handed her the handcrafted comb before he tamped tobacco into the pipe and eased into his rocking chair.

Studying Sara, Bo laid the pipe in the ashtray on the table at his side and slid his chair forward, closer to her. He picked up the discarded flannel towel and beckoned her to sit while he rubbed her hair dry, working carefully around the sore places.

Eventually he tossed the flannel aside, rocked back in his chair, retrieved and lighted his pipe, and watched as she coaxed the comb through new tangles.

Finally, still wrapped in the quilt, Sara lay down in front of the fire, this time her back to it. She fixed her stare on Bo's feet in front of her, concentrated on the sound of his chair, which creaked as he rocked, and closed her eyes.

* * * *

He must have rocked a long time, for the blazing fire had settled to a warm glow before Sara opened her eyes again and looked from Bo's feet to his face.

He stared at her, his expression stoic, indifferent; revealing neither sympathy nor kindness, neither remorse nor anger. She wondered what he might say if he were able to translate his thoughts to words. She suspected it was better for her that he couldn't.

She had put herself in Franklin's hands. Her jeopardy was a result of her own stupidity. The little weasel had not forced her to go with him. If Bo thought of it, he would realize there were no signs of a struggle in the shed, nor had she cried out for his help. She doubted either of those facts had escaped his notice.

But if he blamed her, why had he come to her rescue? Why hadn't he holed up comfortably before his hearth on that chill evening and left her to her chosen fate? Certainly she was nothing to him but a constant annoyance.

She recalled how he had held her, trembling. In those brief moments, why did he shake? Was it unspent anger at Franklin? Or was it relief at having found her?

Bo could have killed Franklin there at the campsite. But he hadn't, hadn't even hit the little twit. Did Bo's restraint reflect his understanding of her contributory behavior?

No, it was simply characteristic of Bo, she thought, to use only the force necessary to turn the situation his way. Another man might have unleashed his anger, vented his frustration, might have beaten Franklin senseless. But Bo delivered no punitive blows. As soon as Franklin surrendered, Bo was content to let it end. There was no passion, no rage toward Franklin, no thought that Franklin had stolen something that Bo considered his.

Obviously, Bo felt no proprietary claim to her. That thought made her sad and suddenly she wanted to cry. Tears prickled behind her eyes. She gazed up at Bo's solemn countenance and her throat ached.

He'd taken her in, fed her, protected her, treated her gently in this primitive place where nature itself imposed constant hardships. And how had she repaid his hospitality? With hostility.

But she'd told him she didn't want to be here. The gathered tears began to spill. She wanted to be in Overt, in her new job, with a new apartment, in a new town with new people and challenges. He had no business keeping her here, forcing her to stay.

But had he actually made her stay?

No. It seemed he didn't even want her here. She could have left. But she was afraid of the animals, of being lost in the forest, of the men who had brought her here. She was being held captive by her own cowardice.

"I want to go home," she murmured into the silence of the room, choking the words out in a sob.

The fire crackled a noisy objection. As if on cue, sleet peppered the tin roof over their heads making sharp pinging noises. Bo frowned into the fire, then back at her, and pointed his thumb at the door. His face was as hard as stone. She turned her eyes from his, and struggled for control.

123

"That's why I went with him. He said he'd take me home." She choked and fought the tears. "I want to go home." Her breath caught. "I don't know the way."

When she risked a look at him, he seemed perplexed.

"I don't mean right this minute. I mean tomorrow or as soon as we can ride your motorcycle. Will you take me back then?"

He nodded, a single, definite gesture.

A sob of relief escaped her aching throat and tears overflowed her eyes. Bo averted his gaze.

Ignoring her, he removed his outer clothing down to his T-shirt and the lower half of his long underwear, blew out the lantern, turned down his bed and got into it.

Some time later, struggling to be quiet, Sara coaxed her pain-racked body to a sitting position. She wrapped her arms around her knees and stared into the fire, shivering with relief and regret. Finally she lay back—burrowing into the fur of the bear rug, tucking the ends of the quilt around her—and closed her eyes. When she did, however, her mind conjured vivid pictures of white fingers floating in the nighttime darkness.

She was aware of the fire burning low and of the staccato beat of sleet dancing over the roof. She knew she wasn't sleeping, but hovered instead in kind of a dream state. In her dreams she watched those same fingers floating in the darkness, but suddenly they weren't fingers at all, but her breasts severed from her body, white, sailing like frisbees.

A scream woke her and she sat bolt upright, straining the tender stomach muscles. The screaming came from her. Her own cries continued, interrupting her grasp of lucid thought until she willed the noise to stop. It did stop, but only when Bo's shoulder muffled her mouth.

On his knees beside her, his arms around her, Bo rocked her and made soft noises of reassurance.

"Are my boobs in here?" she mumbled into his T-shirt. He sat back and looked at her, bewildered. She reached beneath the quilt and felt her body. It was sore but whole.

Her stomach cramped. Her abdominal muscles knotted and quivered. The cold of the room intensified the muscular soreness of her overexertion to produce spasms. Her body convulsed as if she were having a seizure.

Bo lifted her out of the quilt and carried her to his bed. Sara was not alarmed. She'd slept there before, unmolested, warm, safe.

He tucked her in securely before he added wood to the fire. Squinting, she watched him, fascinated as usual by his easy grace, the coordination, the strength of his arms, his shoulders, his back. Dreamily, she admired his tight butt, then allowed her eyes to survey the muscular ripple of thighs and calves easily discernible beneath the knit underwear as he moved.

He came back and stood a moment beside the bed then, without looking at her or touching her, he took a giant step over her. Sliding beneath the covers, he stretched next to the wall where his body intercepted the snippets of breeze and even the occasional bit of sleet that found its way through the seams between the unsealed logs of the cabin wall.

Sara lay with her back to him, staring into the rekindled fire. She was going home tomorrow. Bo had agreed. It would happen. At last. She knew her parents were waiting, frantic with worry. But tomorrow it would be over.

Bo draped an arm over her. Warm, irrevocably safe, her tremors ebbed to intermittent jerks, then to an occasional flinch. She could hear or feel his heartbeat.

In her sleep, Sara was aware of Bo's moving. Rolling, shifting, she found herself face to face with him. He put one hand on the back of her head, the other he splayed in the small of her back, and pulled her tightly against him, smushing the side of her face to his chest.

Secure in his arms, unable to move, and lulled by the rhythm of his heartbeat, Sara fell into a deep, dreamless sleep.

Chapter Twelve

Day 7: There was no dawn as the sun yielded to continuing sleet and freezing rain. In the bed behind her, Sara felt Bo stir. The fire again burned low.

Nimbly, he got out from under the covers, tucking them against her before he climbed over her and out. He stretched and bent from side to side. Hunkering, he stoked the fire with the last of the logs from the night before.

Sleepily, Sara followed his every movement, enjoying the agile maneuvers of such a large lithe creature.

Bo smiled self-consciously, but didn't look at her as he pulled on his woolen trousers. He waited to button and zip them until he put a flannel shirt over the T-shirt. The delay allowed him to tuck in both shirts without having to redo his pants. Efficient, Sara thought idly, and closed her eyes, suspended somewhere between sleep and waking.

Her eyelids batted open as he tossed small pieces of wood into the cook stove, gave it a squirt of starter fluid, and put a match to it. He loaded and set the coffeepot over one burner then stepped to what Sara called the larder where he stored eggs, some meat, a gallon bottle of milk, and other items. A small door concealed the cupboard caged with hardware cloth at the back, exposing the contents to the outside temperatures, providing a kind of cold weather refrigerator, open to the cold air without making its contents available to the local wildlife.

Bo put a thick slice of ham from the larder into a black iron skillet on another burner.

As if he were there alone, completely oblivious to the woman in his bed, he sat in his rocking chair to put on his socks and boots and stood to don his bearskin coat.

Anticipating the blast of chill air, Sara pulled the covers tightly to her neck as Bo opened the door to the somber morning. He was going to the outhouse, then down to milk the cow and feed his stock. She knew his routine, the same every day, tending the animals morning and evening. How could anyone tolerate being a farmer, taking care of dumb animals out in this awful weather?

But, she thought, stricken with new insight, it's a good thing this man was bent to that kind of compassion. Certainly, she personally had reaped the benefits of his animal husbandry.

She needed to go to the bathroom but she didn't want to step out into the room, much less wend her way to the outhouse twenty yards down the path. Besides, the privy was creepy in broad daylight, a cubicle where there was neither heat nor light except that provided by the lantern carried back and forth by its itinerant occupants. On this dank, miserably chill morning, with noisy precipitation... Well, she'd put it out of her mind, at least as long as she could.

Bo obviously had no choice as to his lifestyle. What sane man would choose this deprivation as a way of life if he had any other options?

Yet, Mrs. Johnson said Bo had appeared here on his own, had carved out this place in these mountains with his two hands. But why?

Was it because of his disability? Surely, speech was not essential to living in civilized society. Sara considered his silence more an inconvenience rather than an actual handicap.

But Mrs. Johnson said Bo was able to speak when she first knew him. He no longer spoke, apparently not to anyone. How had that happened? Was his silence the result of a disease? A deteriorating condition of some sort? Maybe it was simply a conscious choice.

Living alone, except for occasional contact with people like Franklin and Cappy, conversation was superfluous. Just lying in bed watching him dress, Sara could see the man didn't indulge in wasted effort.

She stared at the ceiling, reflecting on the way Bo moved, his motion beautifully fluid, despite his size. His certainly didn't appear to be the body of a man over thirty-five.

All that hair covering his face and head was deceiving, straggling everywhere, veiling his features. Why all the camouflage?

Maybe he was a fugitive, hiding from the law. Mrs. Johnson said he arrived in military clothing. Maybe he was AWOL, a deserter.

Obviously, the man was no coward. She had seen his character tested and had heard Mrs. Johnson's stories. Bo was not the kind of a man who abandoned his responsibilities, real or imagined. She discarded the AWOL theory.

It could be that he was homely or scarred, his face terribly disfigured. Or maybe he had been ravaged in another way. Maybe he had a physical defect, a sexual limitation. Maybe he was intentionally celibate or a eunuch, castrated, or worse. Or maybe he had been abused as a child or mistreated by women and driven to become a recluse to avoid them.

Maybe.

Sara's bladder begged attention. She needed to get up, and dress, and force herself to trek down to the outhouse. Putting it off was only delaying the inevitable. Normally she was not given to procrastination; however, since she had been in the Ozarks, she had become less obsessive about things.

Once she assumed hillbillies talked and moved slowly because they had nowhere to go and little news to report when they arrived. After a week in residence, she had revised that thinking.

In the city, time dictated a person's pace, but in the mountains, time lost its dictatorial power, tamed to human whim. Those time considerations caused a peculiar, subtle difference in life styles. Without a clock dictating terms, life was more leisurely, or it seemed that way to her.

Still, she was reminded, again prodded by her needful bladder, bodily functions must have their way.

She groaned as she pulled to a sitting position. Every joint, every muscle in her body shouted obstreperous objections. The top of her head and the soles of her feet were sore. She dabbed at her hair with her fingers, trying to assess the damage to losing fistfuls of the stuff. Except for being tender, her scalp seemed to be okay. She hoped the hair would grow back.

Raising her arms to feel her head, however, Sara became fully aware of peculiar aches between her collarbones and her shoulder blades, places she never realized had muscles or nerves of their own.

Her stomach grumbled, roiling to be fed, while the outside of her midsection quivered, threatening to knot itself again.

Bo knocked twice before he entered the cabin, carrying a bucket of water, which he placed near the hearth. He filled the kettle and swung it into position over the newly resurrected fire then turned and allowed his eyes to survey the woman still in his bed.

He strode to the steamer trunk beneath the window near his desk, piquing Sara's curiosity. He lifted out a large, decorative, lidded urn.

A chamber pot?

He placed the vessel at the side of the bed, glanced at Sara, pulled his coat tightly about him, and tromped back out into the dismal day.

"I can't use that." Sara glowered at the wide-mouthed porcelain container. "It's too awful to even consider; too gross, too demeaning. What is he thinking?

"He's thinking of you," she answered herself, "thinking you don't relish the idea of going to the outhouse. He's trying to make things easier for you.

"Why?"

"Don't ask," she said, still speaking aloud.

"But what if he comes back while I'm using it?"

Still undecided, Sara gritted her teeth and eased her legs over the side of the bed, grimacing with the pain. Her stomach spasmed and she rubbed it briskly with both hands.

"Oh, I've gotta get in shape."

She lay down again, prone on her back across the bed. She gazed at the ceiling, listening to the sleet for a moment before she shimmied back under the covers. She breathed in the lingering aroma of the man, which wafted up from beneath the quilts, smiled, then gritted her teeth against her bladder's insistent appeal.

"I've got to do something," she groaned, keeping her hands on her stomach. "He'll be back."

She could wrap a quilt around her and use the chamber pot, put the lid on, then empty it herself later. Would he wait and let her dispose of the waste? She winced. She certainly hoped so.

The percolating coffee emitted comforting sounds and smells as it brewed in the old metal pot. The ham sizzled, encouraging her. Sara rolled onto her side and eased up on an elbow.

Cringing, moving very slowly, she coaxed her body out of bed, lifted the nightshirt, pulled down the briefs, squatted and relieved herself in the vessel. It was a lot easier than she thought and, despite her need, her output only covered the bottom of the container.

She smiled at how much better she felt, and at Bo's thoughtfulness as she straightened her clothing and put the lid on the pot. Gingerly, she lifted the urn by its two little handles, carried it, shuffling across the room, and placed it near the outside door.

She crept back to the fireplace and poured warm water from the kettle into the enamel basin. She washed her face and hands, scrubbed her teeth with her finger, and rinsed her mouth.

She located her hand-crafted comb on the mantle and worked it through her tangled hair carefully, repeating the effort until the dark curls tousled free.

Feeling recovered, she pulled on an old pair of denim work pants, which were only a little big on her, and quickly replaced the sleep shirt with a cotton T-shirt, also salvaged from the box in the shed.

Moving about seemed to work out some of the stiffness. Gaining confidence and freedom of movement, she sliced bread from the loaf in the larder and knifed butter over the slices.

She heard the usual rap and delay before the door opened, then closed again quickly. She looked around.

Bo was not there. Nor was the chamber pot. Drat!

He was back in a minute. Without looking at her, he placed the pot beside the fireplace, removed his coat and hung it on the peg on the door. Next he spread the oil cloth he used for cleaning game, opened the door again briefly to bring in a recently dispatched rabbit he must have left there earlier.

After breakfast, Sara refused to allow Bo to help wash up.

"Finish dressing the rabbit. Clean your gun."

He nodded with a slight smile. He cut up the rabbit, wrapped the meat and placed it in the larder, then cleaned his gun.

Resting in her rocking chair later, Sara realized that she hadn't heard a shot fired. He must have caught the rabbit in one of his snares. He hadn't used the gun, yet he was cleaning it—because she'd told him to. Was he trying to appease her? To what extent would he go to keep her emotions in check? She smiled to herself shamefacedly, opening and closing her hands to ease the soreness.

There's a lot to be said for a man who doesn't argue, doesn't complain, doesn't talk. Sara stared into the fire. Some women would probably give a lot to have a man like that around, one who was so easy to look at, too.

Plus, he warms the bed, but doesn't insist on sex. He'd be an ideal mate for some lucky...

What was she thinking?

She stopped rocking and stared into the fire.

She did enjoy watching him move. He had such natural coordination, such grace. She cast a quick glance at him as he whittled, working on a tiny item of some kind. She wouldn't ask what it was. Didn't care to know.

He has a beautiful body, she mused. She'd like to see him without clothes.

Naked?

She was horrified at even having such a thought.

Embarrassed, Sara glanced at him again. This time Bo's eyes met hers. She felt the heat of a blush and his eyebrows furrowed with unasked questions. She forced her gaze back to the fire crackling beyond the hearth. Did he guess what she was thinking?

No. He just looked up when he felt her looking at him, that's all.

Unbidden, the thought recurred. How did his naked body look, right this moment, as he rocked almost imperceptibly, his legs and hips flexing, the muscles rippling slightly. The image troubled her but she couldn't seem to banish it. She had definitely been there too long.

Still, he nearly always complied with her requests. She could ask him to take off his shirt. The next time he stoked the fire, she might. She could tell him she wanted to study his muscles.

Don't be ridiculous. She couldn't make such a wanton request. Any man would misinterpret a suggestion like that.

Would Bo?

Probably.

Therefore, she shouldn't ask.

Still, she might.

Chapter Thirteen

Sleet peppered the cabin all day long.

Sara was dejected. She'd wakened excited at the prospect of going home, not counting on the weather interfering.

"I guess we have to wait another day."

Bo nodded mute agreement.

She supposed the ordeal in Franklin's custody had left her weaker than she realized. She dozed in her chair and cat napped on the bed off and on through the dismal day. She was barely aware of Bo as he came and went like a shadow, keeping the fire stoked.

Uncertain as to what sleeping arrangements might be, Sara put the bear rug in front of the hearth when she was ready for bed that night. She knew she should return to the shed, but dreaded the prospect of trying to keep warm in the drafty little enclosure with no fire.

Bo stopped rocking and growled when he saw her spread the rug. He shook his head and pointed to his bed.

"I can't keep imposing on you, Bo. I'll be fine on the floor. It would be better if I went back to the shed but..."

He shook his head again, stood, walked to the bed, and pulled back the covers, indicating she should lie there.

"Bo, both of us sleeping in one bed isn't proper." She sounded as if she were Miss Manners lecturing a child. "It's not socially acceptable behavior."

Exaggerating, he surveyed the empty cabin and returned his gaze to her face. She smiled, feeling sheepish.

"Okay, so we have kind of a closed society here. And it's not that I don't feel safe, you understand. You've made it clear you have no interest in me, that way." She looked to him for agreement or denial but got only what appeared to be annoyed indifference.

"Don't I crowd you?"

He shook his head and flapped the corner of the covers, indicating she should get into the bed. Reluctantly, she complied.

Later, when he had banked the fire and turned out the lantern, he got his coat off the back of the door and brought it to the bed. Without undressing, he again stepped over her. Fully clothed, he remained atop the quilts and covered himself with his coat.

Sara felt a pang of conscience that she had even voiced those stupid, puritanical concerns that kept him from being comfortable in his own bed. What did it matter what anyone else thought? Who would ever know, anyway? And she had been marvelously cozy sleeping in his arms, feeling his heartbeat, clasped safely, firmly against his chest. And, with luck, this would be their last night together before he took her home.

She moved closer to him once, then again. Finally, when he was practically pinned against the wall, he draped the massive arm over her. Relaxing, she again fell into a deep, dreamless sleep.

* * * *

Another day passed with no change in the weather, as sleet and ice kept the road impassable.

Day 9: Restless, generally recovered, Sara rummaged through Bo's desk and found a manuscript of some sort. She picked up several pages, but Bo was beside her immediately, swept the sheets out of her hands, shoved them back inside the desk, closed the drawer and locked it.

"I was just looking for a piece of paper."

He unlocked the desk, gave her a blank sheet of paper and again secured the drawers and their contents with one turn of the key; then removed and dropped the key into his pants pocket.

Although Sara's curiosity was piqued, she forgot the manuscript as she concentrated on drawing a checkerboard on the piece of paper, shading alternate squares.

"We can use burned matches for one player and unburned for the other. Kings can be broken match sticks."

Bo grinned when she presented the setup and challenged him, then he proceeded to trounce her, five games in a row.

"I went to a lot of trouble to make this board and the game pieces." Her complaint was about half serious. "Have you no grace? Would it be too hard for you to let me win one time?"

With a heartless smirk and a shrug, Bo went outside to feed the stock and to bring in a new supply of firewood.

Sara strolled to the cupboard, pinched off a piece of rabbit left from breakfast, and began nibbling. It was getting late. Bo had cooked rabbit, yams and greens for breakfast. She would do ham and eggs and biscuits for supper, the second of their two meals each day, the one they took late in the afternoon.

She filled the coffee pot, put it over a burner and stoked the fire in the cookstove. She slapped a piece of ham from the larder into the iron skillet and sifted flour into the biscuit bowl, adding the other dry ingredients.

When she heard Bo coming, she popped the last bit of rabbit meat into her mouth and darted across the room to hold the door for him as he carried in an armload of wood.

He dumped the logs beside the fireplace, helter skelter, removed his coat and tossed it onto his rocking chair, then hunkered beside the wood, sorting pieces and stacking them with his usual efficiency.

Still chewing the bit of rabbit, watching him, Sara cleared her throat, uncertain if she could say what she was thinking.

"Would you take off your shirts while you're doing that?"

Had she actually said it? She thought so. She hoped she had kept her voice modulated well enough to reflect a certain indifference. She dusted her hands, pretending to ignore him.

Bo swiveled on his feet without standing, tilted his head, and, keeping his mouth concealed behind his shoulder, regarded her as if uncertain he had heard correctly.

When their eyes met, she flushed. "I sketch people sometimes." That sounded lame. "It's strictly artistic interest. When you move, I can see the tendons and muscles in your back flex and relax, but it's hard to get a good look when they're underneath your shirt and your T-shirt." Was she babbling? It sounded like it to her. "I just wanted to see exactly how they look when they're functioning. It's strictly an artist's interest." She was repeating herself. "I could see them better if your shirts were off, that's all."

He stood and turned toward her, soberly studying her face.

Had he bought that pathetic explanation? It even sounded phony to her. He might not be very astute but she didn't believe even Cappy, the dolt, would go for a line like that.

Narrowing his eyes, which were focused on her face, Bo unbuttoned

135

the flannel shirt, pulled the shirttail out of his jeans, slipped it off and tossed it on top of his coat. Averting his eyes, he grabbed the neck of his T-shirt behind his head, pulled it up and off, and discarded it as well.

Sara's breath caught.

His upper body was perfect. Except for the hair under his arms and a little trailing from his belly button into his pants, his torso was completely hairless, a stark contrast to his face and head. His shoulders and chest were still slightly bronzed, the last vestiges of a sun tan from working shirtless in the summer, she supposed. His skin was taut, his abs flat and hard. As she studied him from his shoulders to the waist of his jeans, her hands grew clammy and she developed an odd weakness inside her elbows and behind her knees. Her earlobes burned.

Looking down at his body, Bo flexed his pectoral muscles, then pumped both biceps. The muscles in his upper arms rounded. Sara risked a look, did a double-take and stared, mesmerized by his movements.

"Are you showing off?" She felt terribly self-conscious, smiling and frowning uncertainly, scarcely able to breathe, embarrassed and excited at the same time.

He turned his back to her and bent from side to side. Muscles flexed and relaxed, rippling up and down, shoulders to waist.

She rubbed the moist palms of her hands together before she clasped them tightly and frowned at him. "You know you really do brag a lot, for a guy who doesn't talk."

He snorted and turned to face her, a question in his dark eyes. She gave him a wry look. "I thought you were supposed to be an old guy. You're not old at all, are you?"

He shrugged.

"You're not over thirty-five, are you?"

He shook his head.

"Are you under thirty?"

Another head shake.

"Thirty-four?" Another shake of his head. "Thirty-three? Thirty-two? Thirty-one..." A nod. He pointed his index finger at her and nodded again.

"I'll be twenty-seven in January." She hesitated. Her smile dwindled to concern. She gazed at his bare chest, then back at his face. "Could I touch you?" Her own words surprised her.

He narrowed his eyes again and took two steps forward, placing himself squarely in front of her. He seemed to freeze in a flexed state, standing straight as if he were at attention, his arms at his sides, his hands fisted, so still she wasn't sure he was breathing. He raised his chin and looked down his nose at her, his body motionless. She inhaled the scent of him. Excitement sizzled through her like electric current.

Timidly, Sara pressed her fingers against his right forearm. The muscle tensed. Reaching up, she patted his biceps with the flat of her hand. It was like patting a rock.

"Thanks." She withdrew her hand, yielded a crooked smile, and lowered her eyes. "You can stand at ease now." Her throat felt dry; her mouth, tinny.

He continued looking at her. She glanced up and swallowed. He flexed his chest muscles again and nodded, indicating she should touch him there as well. She wanted to, but hesitated, more concerned about the effect touching him would have on her than on him.

He nodded encouragement again and shuffled forward another half step, narrowing the slight distance between them.

Sara stared hard at his bare chest, at his stomach latticed with muscle. She allowed her eyes to wander down to the fastener straining against his jeans and drew a shallow breath. She was afraid to inhale normally, fearful that their bodies might touch.

Finally, she raised her hand and, cupped it over the swell on one side of his marvelous chest. Goosebumps beaded her arm. Her heart pounded in her throat and temples. She swallowed hard and withdrew her hand.

Her face felt hot with the blush that warmed her, shoulders to scalp. Despite previous sexual experience, Sara had never before touched a man's bare chest, had never even seen one that compared with this.

When she risked a look at his face, he raised his eyebrows and motioned with his index finger from her waist to her neck. She retreated a step. The backs of her knees bumped the rocking chair.

"Me? No. No, I can't." She shook her head, surprised and alarmed. "You'd be disappointed. I don't have any muscles at all, nothing to compare with yours. It's all flab under here."

He raised his eyebrows, questioning, spread his hands, palms toward his body, then again pointed at her waist and up.

"I know you did it when I asked you to. You're a real sport. But I'm intimidated. Next to you, I'm a cream puff."

He stood motionless. Unable to read the expression on his face, she fidgeted.

"Bo, the truth is, I'm not much fun, you know, in bed...sex. Even stuck here, bored out of your gourd with nothing to do and a blizzard outside, well, it wouldn't be much fun for you and it sure wouldn't be any fun for me. I've tried. I just don't do it well. I'm uptight, unresponsive. I think the textbook term is *frigid*. I don't like sex. I wish I did."

She hesitated and lowered her voice as her eyes retraced his midsection wistfully. "I really do wish I did." She looked into his face again, eager for him to understand. "But I don't."

He held one hand, palm down, perpendicular to his waist, then raised it to his neck.

"Only our shirts? Nothing else? We leave the rest of our clothes on? Is that what you mean?"

He allowed a slight nod, his eyes trained on her face. She frowned back at him.

Bo accommodated her, provided all the essentials for survival, took good care of her. Okay, she rationalized, so he wanted to look at her, just the top of her. Big deal. He'd practically seen all of her already. Besides, it was only fair when she was standing there getting an eyeful him. She fingered the buttons on her shirt, considering.

Still sore from her struggles with Franklin, she hadn't bothered to wear a bra during her convalescence. She had not anticipated this game of strip. She should have, she supposed, since she was the one who initiated it.

She studied the floor, still thinking. Neither of them moved.

Finally, deliberately, she undid the buttons on her blouse, then hesitated. Shifting the fabric, clutching the front closed, keeping her eyes trained on the floor, she eased her arms out of their sleeves, one at a time, careful to keep her torso covered. Her eyes darted to his.

Bo didn't move, made no sound, watched without expression.

Encouraged, she stood very straight, sucked in her breath, and removed the shirt, tossing it beside his clothing on the chair.

He remained absolutely still.

Squinting, Sara forced her eyes to his face.

A slight smile played at the corners of his mouth as he regarded her with what appeared to be scientific curiosity. He held up one hand and arched his eyebrows, mutely asking permission to touch her. She had touched him, after all. Again his request seemed only fair. She drew another deep breath, braced herself and whispered, "Okay."

He placed three fingers beneath one of her breasts and lifted as if determining its weight. He seemed calm.

The coffee she had started, boiled over, the hot liquid sizzling on the metal plate. Without taking his eyes from her, Bo withdrew his hand as she moved.

Stepping around him, she hurried to the cook stove, moved the coffee pot halfway off the plate and did the same with the skillet in which the slice of ham sputtered. Water kettles simmered on the two back plates.

Ignoring Bo and the fact that they were both nude from the waist up, Sara turned her attention to the abandoned biscuit dough. She added the buttermilk and began kneading the mixture.

Moving silently to stand behind her, he slipped his arms around her, placing his warm chest against her bare back. She felt him inhale before he placed his hands over hers as she began massaging the dough.

Her breathing became erratic, the air hot in her throat and lungs. She didn't know what was happening but little gates, barriers inside her, seemed to pop open or disintegrate.

Even after the biscuit dough was the right consistency, she continued kneading it, enjoying the feel of his hands on her hands, his arms running the length of hers, the feel of him breathing in and out against her back.

The dough toughened from elastic to rubbery as his hands continued riding hers in the bowl. Beads of sweat formed along her upper lip, in spite of the winter storm raging outside.

He shifted, put his arms under hers to splay his hands on her bare midriff. His palms were warm. She felt his biceps flexing at either side of her rib cage. A tremor moved through his upper body as he acquired her breasts, one in each hand.

Scarcely able to breathe, Sara dropped the ball of dough into the bowl, rocked her head back, and allowed herself to be pulled tightly against him. She placed her hands on his as he kneaded her breasts, thumbing the sensitive nipples.

His beard tickled and she tilted her head to one side, encouraging his mouth to the nape of her neck. Groans of pleasure vibrated from his chest to her back.

Lower, she felt the dreaded cock coming to life, hard, probing at her spine. He definitely was sexually functional. So much for the eunuch theory.

Sara didn't object when his hands drifted down her stomach to her waist. She kept her hands on his, piggy backing everywhere his ventured. His touch was warm, exhilarating.

He hesitated only a moment, unfastening the closure on her jeans. Her fly flapped open and the oversized denims dropped lower on her hips.

His hands crisscrossed her abdomen, sliding slowly, tenderly, exploring, past her belly button and down inside her panties. Suddenly she flinched, returned to reality, twisting, grabbing both sides of her open jeans, frantic to escape.

He released her and retreated a step. Without looking at him, Sara refastened her jeans and grabbed her shirt from the chair. Bo caught the other end before she could slip an arm into a sleeve. Her eyes met his and his somber gaze calmed her. He shook his head slightly. His eyes remained on her face, despite the distraction of her partial nakedness directly in front of him.

Sara allowed him to take the shirt. He tossed it toward the rocker. It slid to the floor as he took her hand.

Sleet renewed its clatter on the tin roof overhead. Fires sputtering in the fireplace and the cook stove warmed the cabin. The forgotten ham and coffee wrapped the occupants in an aromatic embrace.

Bo pulled her with him as he backed up and lowered himself onto the front edge of his rocking chair. He spread his knees and coaxed her forward. She moved hesitantly until she stood squarely in front of him, between his legs.

He put his hands on either side of her waist, pulled her closer, and pressed his mouth to her stomach. His breath and his full lips were hot.

Tilting his head, he nuzzled up under a breast. His beard tickled, causing the same familiar tingling at her elbows, behind her knees, and making chills prickle and bud up and down her extremities.

Steadying her, he rubbed his hairy face against a nipple, startling and arousing her.

Her breathing became harried and shallow. She scarcely moved as he rubbed first one tender tip then the other. Then his mouth enclosed and inhaled nearly one entire breast. Sara gasped with the pleasure of his raspy tongue titillating the aching nub.

He rocked back to look at her face. Scarcely able to breathe, she stepped closer, caught the back of his head with both hands, and forced his mouth back to her breasts, directing it from one to the other and back.

She ignored his smug expression as she pressed him closer and closer, thinking to suffocate him in that mammalian mass without thinking at all.

Obliging her, he suckled each breast while his hands slid mischievously to her hips, kneading and pressing her roughly, more and more tightly to the intimacy between his legs.

Sara rolled her head back and moaned. The voice did not sound like her own but like a pagan plea coming from someone else, someone caught up in the throes of passion. She had never imagined such sounds could ever come from her.

Distracting her with his mouth, Bo again unfastened her jeans. Laying the front open, he nibbled, his warm lips inching down her stomach. His tongue skewered her belly button as he pulled her denims and underwear down over her hips, then past her thighs, below her knees and let them drop around her ankles.

Trembling, she did not open her eyes, nor did she object.

His bearded chin taunted the soft flesh of her abdomen as his mouth swept the area. She pressed herself more and more tightly against him, vaguely aware of her own sounds and movements unauthorized by her conscious will.

Trying to make herself think, Sara pushed away from him.

"All right." She sounded breathless. "Okay."

Without looking at her face, Bo pulled her back to him and

continued his siege. Her breath came in gulps. Pathetically she tried again to pull away.

"I said okay." She wheezed, gasping for air. "I'll let you. I will. But not here. Not like this. On the bed. Let's go over to the bed."

He raised his eyes to hers and she was startled, for his was not the passion-driven gape she expected, but a calculating, determined stare. He rocked his head from side to side ever so slightly. No.

She groaned. "Bo, I've never been this...this willing. Come on."

He shook his head again. She hated the smug look, the determination in his eyes.

Confused, she looked to his phallus for reassurance. It was hard, bulging against the confines of his jeans.

The muscles in his arms flexed. She couldn't restrain her fingertips, couldn't help herself as she stroked from his shoulders down, squeezing, enjoying the raw power of his straining biceps. She looked into his face, pleading with him, but he shook his head again, denying her unspoken request.

"What do you want from me?" Her voice quaked.

"Do you want me to beg? Don't be stupid. This is as good as it gets. I've never really wanted to..." She cleared her throat. This was ludicrous. Here she was standing nude in front of this man, begging him to perform that vile act. "Just know, Bo, I've never, ever been this willing to do it." She diverted her gaze, biting her lips, waiting, but he would not yield.

"Please." She whispered finally. Her eyes focused on the far wall as her fingers traced his ears and wound into his hair. "Please let's go over to the bed."

He locked his arms beneath her buttocks and stood, lifting her with him, crushing her body to his. She laced her fingers into his thick, matted hair and flutter kicked the denims and underwear off her feet as she pulled his head back. He raised his mouth and she planted her lips on his. His tongue was thick and slow as it moved across her mouth but stopped short of entering. She tried to lure him, to draw his elusive tongue inside, but he would not yield. Maybe he couldn't. Maybe he had some kind of injury that maimed his tongue and took his speech from him at the same time.

Both disappointed and pleased, she kissed him frantically, twisting, writhing high in his arms, hoping to drive him to the frenzy she was experiencing.

He carried her to the bed and carefully lowered her to sit on the side. Her feet dangled just above the floor. She kept her arms around his neck wanting to feel and taste more of him, but he was too strong and pulled out of her grasp.

As he stepped back, Sara tried to cover her breasts with her arms and crossed her hands over her lower body to hide the dark curls between her legs. Despite her effort, Bo's narrowed eyes ran up and down her body.

Stepping gingerly, he removed his boots and socks; unfastened his jeans and pushed them to the floor.

Sara's breath quickened again as she watched him step out of the jeans. Keeping his eyes on her face, he rolled his long underwear down provocatively, distracted only a moment as he worked the waffled fabric over his arousal.

The hair on the lower part of his torso was the same rich chestnut brown of his beard and the hair on his head. And nested there, she saw, not a stiff, narrow little shaft like those she had experienced before, but a magnificent penis, protracted, fully engorged.

Staring, she forgot for a moment to breathe as she glanced to his face then back at his erection. It was so pronounced that she shivered with excitement, taking some kind of perverse pride at having incited a man—particularly this man—to such a profound condition.

She gulped, shattered by a new thought. What if she couldn't accommodate such a huge appendage? It was much larger than either of those she had experienced before.

Alarmed, she looked at his face trying to read his intentions. Again her breath came in erratic gasps. Had they come too far to turn back? Would he understand when she told him they would have to stop now?

He didn't look into her face but the way his eyes swept over her, she knew he was acutely aware of every swell and hollow of her body. But could he read her thoughts? Did he know she couldn't finish this?

Crowding out her apprehension about her sexual ability was her fascination with his anatomy. He was a splendid male, tall, supple, muscular. How could she ever have thought him an elderly gentleman—she smiled a little—or even part bear.

He stood proud and straight and nude before her, allowing her to admire his man's body, every marvelous muscle flexed to its most superb state. She couldn't help a smile that came from the pleasure of realizing he was again showing off for her.

She quivered and breathed in once, twice, without exhaling. She felt light-headed, suddenly trembling with anticipation. What was happening to her? Where was the dread?

Bo knelt on the floor in front of her before she could give voice to her rapid-fire concerns.

Surprised by his benign approach, she watched, spellbound, as he took one of her feet in each hand. She giggled nervously when he ran his fingers between her toes, studying each one with tender deliberation. He lifted one foot to his mouth and kissed its instep, nuzzling, nibbling. Watching his bowed head, Sara's breath came and went in erratic bursts.

"Quit. Bo, please. I can't do this." She tried to swallow the lump in her throat, but instead gulped each breath in unsteady bursts.

Certain that she couldn't fulfill the unspoken promises of the moment, she felt obligated to let him enjoy what he could of her body, to let him find some satisfaction with her. She owed him, wanted to show her appreciation for all his patience and kindness; for rescuing her from Franklin, of course. Yes, she owed him this much and far more.

But all that was only rationale. What she was feeling at the moment was far beyond gratitude.

He continued nibbling at her feet and ankles.

And for feeding her, she thought, too, and for protecting her. She would endure his pleasure. She had endured men's pleasure before. Butterflies swarmed in her stomach. This mounting excitement was not normally part of her enduring.

"Can't we...ah..." Her voice quaked. "Can't we please just get on with it."

Ignoring her words, he touched his lips to her knees. To her surprise, her legs parted without any other prodding. Sliding forward, placing himself between them, he continued kissing and touching her, still kneeling, there on the floor.

His eyes closed, he rubbed his bearded cheek against the soft inner flesh of her thighs as he allowed his fingers to trace the backs of her legs from her heels, caress her ankles, sweep up her calves to settle at the backs of her knees, then down again.

She had to remind herself to breathe. Her legs quivered as his thick, warm lips nipped at her exposed inner thighs.

"Please." She whimpered and tried to remove his fingers prowling behind her knees. "Please quit. I can't..."

Mesmerized, inhaling as she could, Sara was sharply aware of the gooseflesh crawling up her legs ahead of and behind the imminence of his hot breath. His fingers fondling the backs of her knees, tracing up and down, sent lucid thought tumbling into some abyss, unretrievable.

She emitted a low whine as his mouth advanced. She could feel herself lubricating, creaming for him. She was aware of a terrible mix of sweet excitement and excruciating anticipation.

Fumbling, he caught both her thumbs with one hand, squeezed them together and lifted, laying her back across the bed.

Her legs trembling on either side of him, she allowed him to stretch her arms high over her head, placing her completely at his mercy; exposed, ripe, vulnerable. She writhed and moaned, trying to remember to breathe, but she didn't struggle or oppose him.

With his free hand, he stroked her abdomen, toying with her, sweeping toward the entrance to her, each caress firmer, more threatening than the last.

"Please," she begged, undulating, arching her body toward the pressure from his hand. Her voice had become hushed, reverent.

His hand brushed her pelt.

"Please stop." When he paused, she wriggled, "No, don't stop *that*. I love...your hands..." She twisted to incite the hand to continue its exploration. "Please." Then more quietly, brokenly, plaintively, she gasped, "Please." She swallowed a low sob and began babbling.

She pressed herself to the unrelenting hand as it closed on its target, more daunting with each pass. She moaned her objection each time the hand paused. She struggled halfheartedly to sit. She wanted to touch him, to encourage him. Squeezing her captive thumbs in one hand, he kept her arms high, pressed into the bed, not allowing her to interfere with his quest.

She forced her eyes open, wanting to look at him. He was perched on the edge of the bed, squinting, his eyes bare slits, watching her face. His body was still, except for his hand, which seemed to move at the behest of the deep, throaty moans slipping from her. The hand seemed alert to every murmur as she strove beneath its touch.

As the hand began to probe, Sara's pleasure bloomed. She closed her eyes, no longer concerned about her former inhibitions or the Svengali weaving this magic spell, caught up as she was in the spell itself.

Losing control of thought or physical response, she surrendered. Every image passing through her brain flitted away, fluttering free, glistening with an eerie, vanishing glow. She moved with the hand, caught up in physical desire, yielded. She became like an animal and strove in a rhythm, her whole body straining toward an elusive pinnacle which always before had taunted her from somewhere beyond.

She began to weep and her meaningless murmuring became a small voice pleading.

The pressure from his hand settled firmly over her mound, warming her, and stopped. The other hand released her thumbs but her hands remained where they lay as she moaned objections. She didn't want the accelerating pleasure to stop. Not now. Not yet.

Gradually she became aware of her own remote, now familiar voice begging. She opened her eyes only when Bo lifted her legs, pivoted her fully onto the bed, and positioned himself over her.

"Oh, yes," she whispered. "Please. Please."

He kissed the underside of her upper arm, trailing the soft skin down to her breasts.

"Kiss me—my mouth."

His lips covered hers and Sara felt his thick, marvelous tongue searching the entrance. She sucked, wanting more of him, but still he would not yield, allowing his tongue only to taunt her.

His hands swept her nakedness, touching then abandoning the soft, tender places. She groaned as he evoked one sensation, then relinquished it, only to awaken and torment another.

Eventually, he broke the vacuum between their mouths and set his warm lips back to work at her breasts, this time ruthlessly laving, stimulating the nipples until she cried out with pleasure. Only then did he allow his engorged phallus to begin its accompaniment, touching pulsating just at the entrance to her.

She babbled, no longer able to reason or to control herself. As her passion detonated, he slipped a hand under and lifted her hips.

Methodically, he increased the pressure of his penis against the entrance, advancing slowly into the moist darkness. She pressed her heels into the bed raising herself to receive him, and her groaning became frantic beneath his lips as he positioned his thick tongue at the entrance to her mouth. Both openings begged his entry.

He went into her gradually, at first allowing only the tip of his tongue and the head of his phallus to penetrate their separate entries. She sucked, urging his tongue inside as he, at the same time, entered her below.

The cock, like the tongue, was thick and filled her, contenting her for the moment, then neither seemed enough and she summoned more.

He moved with her unspoken commands, sliding the thick tongue and the engorged phallus all the way into her, then retreating, and in again, accelerating the tempo, swaying with her as she began to follow his dance.

She arched, pressing herself against him, entreating him to plunge deeper, to plumb her depths.

As he filled her more and more, she brought her legs up, cradling him, urging him deeper and deeper.

Her fingertips brushed his burgeoning arm muscles as she ran her hands up his biceps, finally burying her fingernails in the thickness of his shoulders. And her pulsating body adopted a dance of its own, movements in sync with his, but separate.

She could feel the pleasure coming, coming... But it was not merely the physical titillation of stories and songs, but a filling, a completion, more beyond more.

As her body burst in an explosion of lights and colors, Sara threw her arms around his neck and pulled her trunk hard against him. She cried out and he groaned as they erupted together, as one.

Catapulted, she knew fully, this was it then, the paradise sought but not always found. Having achieved it, she wanted to stay.

But try as she might, she couldn't sustain the euphoria. As she felt her spiraling pleasure reverse, she flexed, straining, sucking to hold onto the man's magic, to force his body to stay within hers, to hold them in paradise, forever.

Desperate, she twisted and turned beneath him, striving to wring more from him until finally, drenched with perspiration, decompressing, then finished, she clung to him, hanging on, his tongue in her throat, the other penetrating her soul.

Moments passed.

Sara began coming to herself. She could hear the sleet against the tin roof, the fire crackling in the fireplace. But she would not loosen either hold on him, trembling with the effort to keep him. She didn't want it to end. She wanted him to stay inside her...forever. She had never known such exquisite pleasure, such pure ecstasy; was terrified that she might never know it again.

At the same time, she felt reckless, daring, deliciously wicked; her only objective in life, to hold onto this moment, to make it last, regardless of consequences, of whatever condemnations might follow.

"Don't leave me," she begged, relinquishing his tongue but keeping her arms tightly around his neck as she put her mouth against his ear. "Stay as we are. Please."

She could feel his intensity ebbing and she began to weep, quietly, defeated.

He remained poised over her for several moments before she felt him withdrawing. He attempted to disengage himself, to step over and lie beside her, but she clung to him and sobbed. "Don't leave me. You're perfect. Beautiful." She felt confused, overwhelmed with a mix of sorrow and joy.

"I didn't know... How did you know how to bring me to this?" She wept quietly. She had lost herself. Eventually her terror diminished and she grew calmer.

"Is this the way it always is for you?" She opened her eyes, frightened of the answer, and stared into his face. His dark eyes were glassy. Almost imperceptibly, he shook his head.

"No?" She was alarmed. "But this is the way it's supposed to be?"

His face reflected a kind of wonder. Mutely he allowed a slight smile and nodded.

She again tightened her arms around his neck and pulled him over on top of her.

"I love you." She was shocked by her feelings and her words. "Bo.

148

I do love you. You are wonderful...and beautiful. And you make me..." her voice broke, "you make me wonderful and beautiful."

Chapter Fourteen

"Are you starving?" Sara spoke softly, staring at the tin roof high over their heads.

She turned, laying her face against the pillow. On his side, his face resting on his arm, Bo grinned vaguely, nodded, and closed his eyes. They were still naked beneath the quilts.

He seemed momentarily spent, while Sara felt exuberant, full of new vitality, energy, confidence.

She had been reluctant when Bo began a second siege. Just because he had been able to coax those responses from her once didn't mean the pleasure could be repeated.

As before, relentlessly, almost ruthlessly, he incited her to the edge of madness before he allowed himself to explode within her.

No wonder people who experienced this kind of sex called it "making love." Lying there, gazing at the man next to her, she saw him with new insight. His body was able to electrify hers, not just once but again and again, anytime he wanted—anytime *she* wanted.

He excavated deep into her soul, found a strain of enchantment, mined it, polished it, and presented it to her as a priceless gift. And he seemed able to perform that wizardry at will.

In only those brief sessions with him, she realized she had been mistaken all this time. She was *not* frigid.

But he had taken her far beyond that. She regarded his strong hand now resting possessively on her stomach, that marvelous hand which had... She bit her lips, embarrassed at recalling the intimacy of that hand.

Bo had shown her she contained a marvelous depth of passion which could produce a frenzied ecstasy, both for herself and her partner.

Puzzled, she wondered if these new talents were limited to one benefactor. She thought of Wesley and Jimmy Singer. No, no other man was capable of this...magic.

She smiled and threw the covers off her warm, satisfied body. Bo reached out, staying her. She hesitated as he pulled her back. She saw mischief in the dark, dark irises.

"You can't be serious."

He leaned up and over to put his lips on hers, pressing her back, bracing himself on his elbows propped at either side of her head. He brushed her forehead with his thumbs and laced his fingers into her hair. Her hands swept his chest and shoulders and her breath quickened.

It was a quiet kiss, easy to maintain as they remained comfortably linked. His tongue prodded. She yielded. There was no reason to be coy. He already knew he could come and go as he pleased.

His tongue grew thick, possessive, as his mouth consumed hers. She felt the excitement swelling again in him and inside herself.

As he drew away from her kiss, he put his hands on either side of her waist and rolled onto his back, setting her astride him.

She straightened and tilted her head back. Cupping her breasts in her own hands, she began to sway from side to side ever so slightly. Suddenly she peered down at him.

"And just what do you expect me to do for you from up here, big boy?"

He grinned, lifted and moved her down a little on his torso.

Amazed, she felt the limp phallus resurrect itself beneath her, perhaps without its earlier rigidity, but obviously with the same intent.

"What are you, superhuman?"

He moved, sliding, shifting until he was positioned to demonstrate his continuing capability coupled with some versatility. His eyes became glazed as he looked into her face.

"Don't look at me. I don't want you to...to see what... I lose my... You'll think I'm... Please don't watch."

The words faded as she felt the exhilaration sharpening every nerve. She clamped her teeth together hoping to maintain some kind of control, but it was already too late.

She tried to hold herself away from him with her knees but his hands were hot on her thighs, his thumbs working a familiar magic at the vortex that was positioned so that it was completely defenseless.

"You know all the right buttons..." She slurred the words, swaying to incite, then to postpone the orgasm.

* * * *

"Please let me fix some food," she pleaded as they again lay recovering. Dark had come early. She didn't know if it was still afternoon or night. He nodded, his eyes black, enigmatic slits.

She pushed his chin aside with her hand. "Will you turn over, face the wall? I have to clean up. I don't want you to watch."

Allowing a wicked little grin, he studied her face a long moment before he placed both hands on her upper arm and summarily pushed her out of the bed. She tumbled onto the floor.

"What's the big idea?" She scrambled to her feet annoyed, naked, her hands on her hips.

Laughing, he followed her out of the bed, threw his coat over his nakedness, slipped bare feet into his boots and darted out the cabin door into the cold and shrouded sunlight.

Sara glowered at the door as it closed behind him. "I didn't mean you had to go all the way outside."

She grabbed the T-shirt he had discarded earlier, slipped it on, and shivered at the warmth of the thin layer of fabric. She twirled a full turn in the middle of the floor, hugging herself and laughing.

By the time she had settled down a little, added wood to the cook stove, and repositioned the coffee pot and skillet over the front burners—the two kettles of water occupied the back ones—Bo returned with the oval trough which he placed in front of the fireplace.

"What are you doing?"

Acting as if he hadn't heard her, he again hurried outside. She was putting the overworked biscuits to cook before Bo returned with two buckets of water.

"You must have pumped your arm off to get that much."

He tossed off the coat and, posing nude, except for the unlaced boots, directed her attention to the pumping arm, and flexed.

She smiled broadly. "Big deal. You know I'm a sucker for your muscles." Her eyes dropped to the area between his legs. "Some more than others." When her eyes again met his, he winked. She smiled and blushed. "Now I suppose you'll try to tell me you never get tired."

Purposefully he stepped close to her and placed a cold hand underneath the T-shirt slipping it into the V between her legs. She gasped, startled at his bold, icy touch, and stiffened before pushing his hand away.

"Are you saying you don't ever get tired of making love?"

He shook his head emphatically, frowned and allowed both his hands to sweep up the outline of her body without touching her. He stopped with his hands poised at either side of her face.

"Never get tired of making love...with me?"

His grin was like sunshine breaking through dark clouds. His face changed from silly to serious before he kissed her. It was a long, sultry kiss. His hands were cold as he stooped, slid them up the backs of her legs beneath the shirt, and cradled her bare buttocks, lifting her against him, making her squeal.

He released her, grinning, turned, and poured the two buckets of water into the trough. He added water from the two kettles boiling on the cook stove and the one hanging over the fireplace.

She was puzzled until he retrieved and placed a clean length of flannel on the arm of one of the rockers, put a wash cloth on the side of the tub and stepped out of his boots. He laughed at what Sara supposed was her look of surprise and he nodded, indicating she should get in the tub. When she didn't move, he again stooped and put his cold hands on the backs of her knees. She fingered the bunched muscles in his shoulders and, giggling, tried to pull back, but he held her.

When she quit trying to escape, he began simultaneously fingering the backs of her knees and suckling at her nipples through the T-shirt. Her breath caught. Wheezing, she said, "You *do* know the right buttons."

He nodded, then, before she had time to react, he caught the hem of the T-shirt and flipped it up and off over her head.

He picked her up, placed her in the tub, and climbed in himself, making her yield enough space for him. The warm water had seemed shallow until two bodies displaced it.

"Getting a little sophisticated, aren't we?" Sara picked up the wash cloth and the soap.

They began by washing each other's hair and moved down from there, touching, teasing, fondling, caressing.

There was a brief interlude as the bathing provoked renewed interest, after which they rescrubbed specific parts.

"Bo, have you ever made love with your clothes on?"

He nodded but scowled.

"It would probably be warmer, not to get naked every time."

His expression softened but he shook his head, no, and allowed his fingers to caress her ear, down her throat and continue, outlining her breasts.

"You like having all our clothes off?"

He splayed a hand on her chest and nodded once.

"You don't want anything between us?"

He grinned, nodded, and grabbed the length of flannel. Standing, he offered his hand to help her to her feet. After leading her from the tub, he wrapped the towel around them. They stood wrapped together in front of the fire for several minutes, warming.

"It's bad luck to dry on the same towel."

He removed the flannel, scooped her up and strode to the bed where he bundled them together beneath the quilts. As she warmed, she dozed.

By the time they were ready to eat, the biscuits were cherry brown and tough, barely edible. They ate every one.

Later, when they were fed and dressed, Sara directed Bo to the footstool. She sat in a rocking chair directly in front of him. Patiently she combed his tangled hair and the unkempt beard.

He had perfect ears, she thought idly. His head was beautifully shaped. She studied his individual features as she worked, but she couldn't visualize what he actually looked like under all that hair.

Disentangling it took quite a while but Sara enjoyed the intimacy and toiled determinedly, wondering as she worked, about Bo's manners, his intelligence, his ambition.

She had had glimpses of his raucous humor and his temper, but, thinking about it, she didn't actually know this man very well, except physically, of course. Carnally, they were intimately acquainted.

Yet she knew quite a lot, too, she argued with herself, about his gentle spirit, his judicious soul, his depth of integrity.

* * * *

That night snow clouds rolled in again. Renewed precipitation continued to isolate the small cabin. Sara and Bo made love, slept, ate, and made love, repeating the cycle again and again.

The unseasonably early winter storm lasted three days, during which Bo braved conditions to feed and milk his cows twice a day. Other than that, and the occasional necessary trips to the outhouse, they stayed in the cabin, frequently driven back to their bed to exercise and entertain one another.

Despite Bo's silent insistence, Sara refused to use the chamber pot. After all, she explained to him, she was not sickly, to which he beamed his agreement.

"Will you let me touch you there?" she asked on the second day as they lay naked side by side. He nodded and locked his hands behind his head, indicating she could do as she liked.

Examining him, kissing him randomly, she stroked his phallus until it was rigid. His face look pained and he gritted his teeth. Preoccupied with the appendage, she said, "You know, they really should issue operators' manuals with these things."

Bo arched his eyebrows, looking surprised. Sara avoided his gaze as she continued her gentle massage, unaware of his mounting distress.

"Men should have to take lessons, be licensed before they're allowed to operate one of these, instead of just ramming them into any old body that's available."

Clenching his teeth, Bo bit back a laugh and shook his head.

"Besides that." She stopped the massage and regarded his penis with annoyance, "I think I'm jealous. First I'm really jealous of every woman you've had before." Her eyes rounded and she glared into his face. "There've been a bunch, haven't there?"

His eyes widened and he shook his head quickly from side to side, innocently, as if he didn't know what she was talking about.

"Yeah, I'll just bet. Next thing is, I can't bear to think about you sharing it with anyone else ever again. It's like this part of you doesn't belong to you by yourself anymore. Now, it's mine, too." She regarded him pitifully. "You probably noticed. I don't have one."

His grin exploded into a laugh. He rolled up over her, pinned her to the bed, straddling her, lost the grin, and nodded solemnly. He pointed to himself, then to her and arched his expressive brows.

"You don't have to make any promises."

He nodded, arguing mutely.

She shrugged and diverted her eyes. "It's easy for me. You're the only man I've ever responded to." She looked back into his face. "You're the first man I've known who's actually qualified to operate one of these things."

Poised over her, he patted his chest and pointed to her, then patted her chest and pointed to himself.

"You Tarzan, me Jane? Okay, we hereby promise not to play around with anyone but each other. We're going steady."

Day 12: Lying on their backs in bed, Sara said, "Bo, how many times do you suppose we've made love?"

He held up both fists then opened and closed his fingers several times.

She laughed. "No, not that many."

He turned his face to hers, grinned and held up two more fingers.

"A jillion and two?"

His eyes twinkling, he nodded.

She caught his hands to examine the insides of them closely. Studying his right hand, she said, "You have a second life line. Right here." She ran her index finger down his meaty palm following a line that nearly paralleled the original.

Holding the hand in hers, Sara struggled to disengage herself from the covers and sit up. Again she traced the line with her index finger. The scar split the thick part of his palm just below his thumb. "How did this happen?"

He pointed to his knife which hung in its scabbard on the wall at the side of the bed.

"You cut it?"

He nodded.

"You had stitches. I can see the little scars. Did you do it skinning game?"

He shook his head and gave a three-fingered salute.

"In boy scouts?"

He grinned and gave her staccato thumbs down.

"Younger? Cub scouts?"

He nodded and mimed the use of a manual can opener.

"You cut it opening a can?" She stared at the scar in disbelief. He nodded, then indicated she should expand the guess. "With a can opener?"

He shook his head.

"With the can?"

He gave her a wry smile and shrugged.

"You were a klutzy kid?"

He looked pained and held up eight fingers.

"Well, most of us are klutzy when we're eight. Your scout leader took you to get stitches. Someone took care of you."

He nodded again.

"Your mother?"

His grin freshened.

"Is she still around?"

Another nod.

"Most of the time it doesn't matter that you don't speak, but sometimes it's really annoying."

He looked puzzled.

"I want to know about your family, your adventures growing up, your successes, your disappointments, what you thought about things then; what you think about things now. Are both your parents still living? Are you interested in politics?"

He nodded to both. She backtracked.

"Do your parents live near here? Am I going to meet them?"

Sobering, he shrugged.

"They don't live close then, right?"

He shook his head.

"How about siblings? Do you have brothers or sisters?"

He grabbed her, tossed her onto her back and began kissing her playfully.

She was unconcerned that she was pinned beneath him. "I'd like to know a little something about your track record with women." She allowed her fingers to trace the line of his ears beneath the mass of hair. "You aren't married, are you?"

He lifted himself away, regarded her in disbelief, grinned, shook his head slowly then ducked to begin nuzzling again.

"Have you ever been married?"

Kissing derailed other questions as he gently coerced her back to the paradise they had discovered and visited often together.

When she awoke later, Sara propped up on an elbow and peered into Bo's sleepy eyes.

"Bo, why are you here?" Her curiosity had finally gotten the best of her. "Did an ex, a girlfriend, dump you? Break your heart?"

He grinned broadly.

"No, I know better than that. One dose of you and no woman could walk away."

His grin continued.

"Mrs. Johnson said you were in the military."

He pursed his lips. The smile waned with the little nod.

"Did you get drummed out?"

He shook his head.

"Did you go crazy, get the famous Section Eight psycho discharge?"

He shook his head more slowly.

"You're not AWOL, are you?"

The grin freshened.

"Did you have some kind of disability?"

He didn't respond. Instead, he climbed over her and stepped out onto the cold, hard packed floor.

"Was it a physical problem?"

No response.

She dropped her voice. "Was it a mental or an emotional problem?"

He shot a dark look at her but still refused to indicate yea or nay, leaving her wildly curious.

When they looked out, the sun had beaten back the heavy skies and warmed the morning. A forgotten thought niggled at the back of her mind. Here was the break in the weather they'd been waiting for. He could take her home, back to her old life. She should mention it. She didn't want to.

"Let's walk over to the Johnson's," she suggested instead.

* * * *

"You're lookin' fit," Mrs. Johnson observed. Bo and Lafayette, trailed by a horde of Johnson progeny, had left the women and gone to check a fence. Again Sara found herself welcoming the sounds of other human voices as the older woman continued. "Be careful or you'll wind up in the family way with a brood of youngsters of your own."

How could Mrs. Johnson tell? Sara hadn't realized her euphoria would be obvious to the casual observer.

Mrs. Johnson glanced at her and the older woman's gentle countenance grew serious. Sara frowned, thinking.

She loved the spontaneity of making love with Bo. Concerns about diseases and/or pregnancy were for promiscuous people living in civilization. They had taken no precautions.

Mrs. Johnson continued. "I hear'd he'd give up that little Jezebel down by Settlement. That was glad news. 'Kids call her his hot tamale. Them Mexican gals comin' up from down south is eager to land 'em a good American man to keep 'em here legal."

Sara turned away. She didn't want Mrs. Johnson to see that the mention of Bo's having a girlfriend was news to her, but the revelation prompted new concerns. What kind of diseases might Bo's "hot tamale" have? How healthy were the hot tamale's other suitors?

"You gonna marry him, Sara?"

Sara stopped walking. The two women had strolled to the riverbank, picking up the autumn's incidental pecans peeking out of the slush beneath their tread. Sara turned a stunned face to Mrs. Johnson, who was looking at her.

In her stricken state, Sara's mind suddenly was assailed by wild, disconnected thoughts.

Stay with Bo? Marry Bo? Sara Loomis stuck with a hairy, mute mountain man for a mate? Not a chance. She had a real life.

No. She couldn't stay with him. The idea was absurd. No, no. Her real life didn't include him. He belonged here, tramping around in the woods. If he had a backwoods girlfriend someplace, that should make it easier for Sara to leave. She could abandon him with a clear conscience, leave him to his hot tamale.

When she left...

Her breath burned in her throat.

She couldn't leave him. How could she live without him after...?

She felt a terrible, sickening despair.

So, what were her options? Could she stay with him?

She exhaled hopelessly and glared at the muddy ground.

160

What would her parents think of Bo as a live-in, a son-in-law even? If she should remain with him, her mother and dad would expect to come visit, stay at the cabin. Where would they sleep?

Her mother complained when Sara talked about taking a one-bedroom apartment with no dishwasher. What would she say about a primitive one-room cabin with an outhouse?

Her dad would ask questions about Bo. She could almost hear him. Difficult questions. Sara didn't even know Bo's last name. That probably would be one of her dad's first—one of the easy questions.

And she could hear her mother: "What does the man do, Sara?"

Well, Mom, he skins rabbits. He wrings chickens' necks skillfully. He whittles a real nice comb.

"Oh, God, what have I done?" she whispered, ignoring Mrs. Johnson, who had wandered on ahead of her.

The idea of introducing Bo to her parents was ghastly. How would she ever explain him to them? She looked at Mrs. Johnson and hurried to catch up.

Of course, she could tell her parents she'd been frigid, had never experienced the joys of sex before; that she owed him for opening a whole closed section of her, a part which had lain fallow, undiscovered until his safari into her.

She rolled her eyes heavenward. Oh yeah, she thought, sarcastically, she'd definitely be telling her mom and dad all about that.

Mrs. Johnson turned around and was looking back at her. "It'd be good to have a neighbor woman close by. I could help you birthin' your young'uns."

Lord, help me, Sara prayed silently. She visualized little mute Bo clones in bearskin coats. The image was farcical. Bo just scraped by providing for himself. How could he support a mate, much less a batch of kids? And what would their relationship be—hers and his—when the ardor cooled?

Okay, they didn't have to stay here. She could entice him back to civilization.

Swell.

What would her friends think of him, unkempt, silent? They'd be like those simpletons in Settlement, think he was some kind of mutated animal or a madman.

She could just imagine her sorority sisters' comments when she showed up for homecoming with Bo. Could he follow their glib conversations? Would he even want to, not able to contribute; if, that is, he should have the mental capacity to think up anything to contribute?

Sara was disgusted with herself. Was she really this shallow? Was she some kind of closet snob?

Except for being a dud at sex, which no one else actually knew, Sara felt well-respected, capable, bright, successful. She was popular, often invited to people's homes, to parties. She suspected that would change if the invitations had to include Bo.

Oh sure, he seemed smart enough compared to Franklin and Cappy and the Johnsons, but intelligence is a relative thing. How would Bo measure up compared to Jimmy Singer?

Bo would excel, of course, if they both paraded naked.

Bo was by far the more excellent lover, the kinder, more considerate human being, but Jimmy had a certain, enviable social appeal. Besides, except for insisting on wearing his T-shirt and socks during sex, Jimmy wore stylish clothes which looked great on his slender frame.

Bo wore flannel shirts, long handle underwear and animal skins.

Sara trudged along trailing Mrs. Johnson in morose silence.

If she bound herself to Bo, she would be sentencing herself to the life of a mountain woman, unable to reassume her old cushy existence, prematurely stooped, worn out under the burden of too many children, overwhelming responsibilities, too many hardships.

She glanced at Mrs. Johnson as the woman prattled on unheard.

Of course, Sara argued to herself, wondering what Mrs. Johnson had sacrificed, I would have a man who loved me, who would give everything he had to keep me happy, provide for my needs. He would probably insist I use the chamber pot when the weather was bad.

Tears stung her eyes. Her throat ached. She tried to keep her face from reflecting the sarcasm, the caustic, disquieting, ungrateful thoughts flitting through her mind. She swiped unwanted tears from her face.

"It's a hard life," Mrs. Johnson was saying as Sara tuned her in again. The older woman had been talking softly all the time they were walking. "But it has its rewards. We don't worry so much about our chil'ren gettin' onto drugs or joinin' gangs and such. Of course, they don't get much schoolin' neither, only such as Fate and me is able to give 'em. It's like all the rest of life. You've got to sacrifice some things for the others."

They had been walking along the riverbank for a quarter mile or more in studied silence when Sara, gazing at the ground, deep in thought, noticed an indention, a familiar shape in the mud. The track was filled with water. She stooped to trace the imprint with her finger. It was the distinctive print of a boot.

"Have your kids come down this way today?"

The older woman looked at her oddly. "No, why?"

"Here's a footprint here by the water. I just wondered."

Mrs. Johnson came back and bent to examine the track, then straightened. "None of mine's been this far since the weather turned. This step's been made recent, by a heavy man with a small foot in a new boot. We'd better find Fate. Better find him right quick."

Hurried steps returned the two women to the Johnson's home. They waved to the men and the parade of youngsters in the distance trooping back from the pasture.

Sara's breath caught and she felt a familiar warming between her legs as she watched Bo striding toward her, tall, powerful, supple, funny, sexy, courageous, caring...

"Stranger's walking here 'bouts," Mrs. Johnson told her husband after he got near enough that she could say it in a normal speaking voice. Fate looked at her with interest.

Bo turned his alert, questioning eyes from Mrs. Johnson to Sara who nodded.

Fate said, "Show me."

On the riverbank approaching the site, Mr. Johnson told the ladies and the children to stay back. Bo stepped out into the shallow water and hunkered several times to run his fingers in more tracks. Mr. Johnson spoke quietly. Bo responded with grunts and nods or shakes of his head.

They walked up river, following footprints a long way then doubled back. "There's five of 'em," Fate said, addressing no one in particular. "Four city folks and one neighbor, looks like. Could be they're looking for deer track."

Sara heaved a grateful sigh and looked at Bo. He kept his eyes averted. She looked at Mrs. Johnson who was regarding Mr. Johnson closely.

"Is that all it is, then, deer hunters looking to set up camp?" Mrs. Johnson asked.

Mr. Johnson shook his head. "Don't much believe it is. They got dogs." He glanced at Sara. "Looking for this little lady here, most likely."

She shivered. Her rescuers had come. Finally. But she'd already been rescued, in a far more significant way than she could explain.

She looked at Bo. His dark eyes were steady on her face. He motioned with his head. He wanted to leave. She went to him, slipped her hand into his, turned as he turned, and fell into step beside him.

Suddenly she remembered her manners and looked back. "Thanks, Mrs. Johnson, for everything. I look forward to visiting you again real soon."

The Johnsons called good-byes as Sara and Bo cut through the underbrush and into the woods.

Chapter Fifteen

Bo's gait quickened as they neared the cabin. Releasing Sara's hand, he went directly to the shed. She followed, watching him, beginning to feel nervous.

He removed the cover from his motorcycle. Rummaging among stores in a dark corner of the shed, he produced containers of oil and a five-gallon can of gasoline. He checked spark plugs, filters and the fuel line before filling the gas tank.

He wiped the body of the machine with a shop rag, then stepped on board, and pumped the starter. Two tries and the motorcycle roared to life. He looked both pleased and relieved.

Nerves prickled along her arms when Sara realized what he was thinking. "I'm not leaving."

His gaze was intent. He pointed to her then to himself.

"We're both leaving?"

He nodded.

"No, Bo, this is your home. You don't want to leave the life you've built here. Not for me." Turmoil bubbled inside her. She'd begged him to take her home. But now that he was willing, she wanted to stay with him, wherever it was, just until she was tired of him. Not now. Not yet.

Then another startling thought: Did he plan to go home with her? Oh, no.

As she stared at him, alarmed, his eyes caught hers and narrowed with vague understanding. Abruptly, he turned. She followed him outside. He looked south and west to determine what the approaching weather might be.

She caught his arm. "Bo, please."

He pulled away without looking at her and she trotted behind him back to the cabin. He dug a knapsack out of the steamer trunk, tossed it on the table and began grabbing things: the rifle and the shotgun, his billfold, a small leather pouch, a handful of jerky, a change of clothes. Finally he dug out a satchel which he filled with what looked to be half a ream of a typed manuscript and several volumes from his bookshelf.

It appeared that he planned to be away a long while. Did he think he was going home with her?

She wasn't ashamed of him. Not really. Not exactly.

He went back to the shed and wheeled the motorcycle to the cabin.

She paced, watching him through the open door. To be honest, she didn't want Bo to meet her parents or her friends. But how could she tell him that?

She couldn't. Not after all he'd done for her.

If he were determined to go with her, she would just have to figure a way to explain him to...to everyone.

She fingered the quilt on the bed, then pulled it up and fluffed both pillows. She wanted to stay here, just a little longer, but he seemed determined to leave. She should quit stalling and get ready.

She looked around. Except for the clothing salvaged from the box in the shed, she had few belongings. She wouldn't be needing those shabby castoffs when she got home.

She removed her hand-me-down outer garments and slipped her own denim dress on over her panties and bra.

On the straight-backed chair, she noticed her partially finished quilt, amateurish, at best. She'd leave it.

She spotted her comb in its usual place on the mantle. Slowly, she walked to the hearth, picked up the comb, and felt a rush of sadness, a feeling of finality. She took two quick breaths, then crumpled into her rocking chair, clutching her comb. Her body convulsed with sobs.

Coming inside, Bo looked at her and frowned. He watched her a moment before he walked over to kneel in front of her, peering up into her face. He ran his warm hands along her dress from her knees to her waist. Then his hands crept beneath the fabric, easing the dress up.

She didn't object as he pulled her to her feet and lifted the dress off over her head. She clung to the comb. Bo gathered her close, kissing her, caressing her as he removed her bra and panties.

Stripped, quivering, she walked to the bed on her own as he peeled out of his clothes without taking his eyes from her.

She slid under the quilts into their bed, her safe hole, the site of the most important events of her life.

They made love slowly, Sara painfully aware that this would be their last time together here in this place. But was it she alone who realized it might be their last time together anywhere?

She didn't want to think about that.

She held him so tightly, their bodies seem to meld into a single entity. They touched and fondled each other with gratitude, and patience, and a depth of pleasure even they had not plumbed before.

As she quickened and came, Sara wondered dreamily if this part of her would survive away from him. Now that she knew something of her own sexual appetite and capability, could she achieve the ecstasy without him? The prospect frightened her.

At that moment, with that understanding, Sara made a decision. She would sacrifice her pride, her old life, her old friends, maybe even her close relationship with her parents, for Bo. She had to be with him, no matter what the cost to her pride or reputation.

"Bo?" Sara whispered when she roused, frightened. His arms around her, he grunted a response. It didn't sound as if he were sleeping. "Mrs. Johnson asked if you were going to marry me." There. She'd said it, taken the step. She braced herself for whatever came.

But Bo neither moved nor made a sound. Sara turned in his arms. "Did you hear me?"

Except for a slight nod, he didn't move.

"She asked me if we would be their neighbors."

No response. Her stomach knotted. She pulled up on an elbow to see his face more clearly, but it was stoic. She couldn't tell what he was thinking. She had a sudden new insight. What if he didn't want a wife? Didn't want her?

She rolled away from him, suddenly furious. She had worried herself into a frenzy, willing herself to sacrifice friends and family for him. What woman in her right mind would tie herself to this hairy, uneducated, silent man for the rest of her life? She should be relieved that he didn't want her. His indifference just made it easier.

Didn't it?

Had they both been pretending, playing a game? Had she fooled herself, pretending he loved her? Had she been a diversion for a hermit mired in his self-imposed solitude?

He touched her shoulder and she stiffened, fighting the tears. The man had reached into her soul and extracted passion she hadn't known existed. He probably did the same with all women. She ached with her own argument.

Possibly he was not the only man who could do that for her. There were probably many men who could. Her eyes stung. Sure, she could probably enjoy sex with other men. Most women did, didn't they?

Even Franklin mentioned the promiscuous sex viewers watched every day on television. People read about it in books and magazines. And there were all kinds of stories of celebrities marrying and remarrying, cavorting from bed to bed.

Sara could join the swarms going to singles clubs, wagging home a different guy every weekend.

Then she thought of Wesley and Jimmy and their stiff, tortuous little cocks, and she groaned.

Bo threw back the covers, climbed over her, and got out of bed.

She scrambled to sit upright, pulling the quilts up to cover her nakedness. "Where are you going?"

Moving gingerly, naked in the chill cabin, he lighted a lantern and tossed two logs on the fire, which brightened the room as much as the lamp light. Watching him, she swallowed a smile. She loved the way he moved. She wished she didn't. She adored his agile body, his perfect legs with rippling muscular calves and thighs, his tight butt. His shoulders mushroomed upward from the narrow waist. The sight of his naked body stirred tingling pleasure in her nether regions and she squirmed, trying to quell the desire that was warming her again.

He opened a box of shotgun shells and removed an item before he returned to sit on the side of the bed. He presented his closed fist, fingers up.

Sara watched quietly as he slowly rolled his fingers open.

In his palm lay a small, wooden circlet, a ring hand-carved of hickory.

She regarded the ring closely before raising her eyes to his face in disbelief. Tears gathered and she sniffed.

He lifted the ring from his palm, took her left hand and started to slip the circlet onto her ring finger. She jerked her hand away, bowed her head and covered her face with both hands.

Bo stood and hesitated a long moment, watching her before he slid the ring onto his pinkie. He skimmed into his long underwear and woolen trousers.

Sara's body quaked as she fought for control. Bo eased into his

168

rocking chair as she attempted to speak.

"I don't even know you," she stammered finally without looking at him. She got out of bed and slipped the nightshirt on before she risked a look. Bo appeared bewildered. "I don't know anything about you." She cleared her throat. "I don't even know what you look like, really, under all that hair."

She sat tentatively on the edge of the padded rocker facing him and blinked several times, trying to clear her eyesight to be able to see his face, to read his reactions.

He stared back at her, shaking his head.

"It *does* matter, Bo. Oh, I don't care if you're homely or scarred. But your expressions matter to me. It's hard to read the nuances, the changes in your moods, through all that hair. I can never tell what you're thinking.

"You read me all the time. You're always watching me." She exhaled. "You enjoy looking at me. Allow me the same privilege."

Bo gave her a questioning frown.

"Yes, of course, I enjoy looking at you. Your body should be in the movies." She looked longingly at his bare chest. "It's that beautiful." She took a ragged breath. "But I want to see your face, to be able to read your thoughts in your expressions."

Shuddering, she stood and paced to the fireplace. He stood as she did.

"Bo, I don't care if your face is disfigured. I don't think it matters to me what you look like." She hesitated then lowered her voice. "Will you shave your beard and cut that awful scraggly hair? Will you do it for me? Let me see what you look like?"

He hesitated a long moment, studying her candidly, then shook his head. No.

"Surely all that hair is not more important to you than I am."

He paced the length of the cabin and sat down in the straight-backed chair in the far corner, which was shadowy in front of the bookcase, and stared down at the floor.

Sara grimaced. "Won't you even cut it if I tell you it means the difference between keeping or losing me?"

There was a long pause before his dark eyes rose to her face. Pursing his mouth, he shook his head again.

She regarded him urgently but forced herself to remain standing where she was, by the fireplace. "You can't be that repulsive. It doesn't matter, even if you are.

"Are you a fugitive? Is your face on wanted posters? Are you AWOL from the service? Are you a criminal with bounty hunters after you? What is the awful secret that brought you here?

He didn't respond.

"Do you think you're ugly? Is that it?"

She couldn't see him clearly in the darkened corner, but his posture was defiant, not that of a man defeated, or even willing to compromise.

"Bo, do you plan to keep living like this, bury yourself someplace else? Are you going to keep yourself in exile? Is it because you think it's what you deserve?"

Still he refused to respond.

She paced to the bed, their bed, that magical place where marvelous transformations occurred. She sat tentatively and lowered the tone of her voice, trying to sound less desperate.

"Look what happens to people who live like this. Look at Mrs. Johnson, Bo, trying to manage without electricity or running water or any of the conveniences that make life bearable. Do you want me to commit to sharing that? Do you want to punish me, make me old before my time washing for ten kids in kettles in the yard? Is that what you want from me?"

He didn't move.

She wrung her hands, stared at them, then folded her arms in front of her and rocked forward and back as if easing a belly ache. She groaned as she spoke.

"I have a college education, Bo. I can support myself, make a decent living. I don't have to cower in the back woods someplace, hiding from life."

She looked at him. Still, he didn't move.

She drew another deep breath. Her whole body hurt. What kind of choice was this? Living a primitive life with him, or comfortably back in the Twenty-first Century, but without him.

"Bo." Her voice was a husky whisper. "I'm willing to try to support both of us, back in civilization." She gave him a pleading look. "I'm at least willing to try to do it. Are you?"

One eyebrow arched as he held up the ring.

She felt her mouth twist as she continued struggling for control. "I can't marry you." She shuddered. Moments passed and a haunting gloom fell over the room.

Finally, gritting her teeth, she stood.

"Live however you have to, with no one to bug you—or to love you either." She squinted. "Or maybe you can go back to your hot tamale, convince her to forgive you for having a fling with me."

Bo's face remained stoic, unreadable.

Her mouth quivered. "Is that what I've been to you? A fling? A diversion from your usual fare?"

He glowered at her from beneath his dark, furrowed brows and, risking a quick glance, she saw something glistening in his eyes, something that encouraged her to strike again.

"You're a bold man physically, Bo, but I think you're a social coward. I'm not. I'm not afraid to face life head on; responsibilities, a job, people. I'm at least brave enough to face up to challenges of real life and overcome them. I certainly don't hide from them."

His jaw clenched, Bo stood. Walking casually, moving without any apparent malice, he tossed the wooden ring into the fireplace, turned, stuffed loose items into the knapsack, and secured it.

After he put on a T-shirt, he buttoned a flannel one over it, stepped into his boots, threw on his coat, picked up the guns, the knapsack and the satchel, and strode straight out the door.

Hugging her nightshirt around her, Sara darted from their bed to the fireplace peering frantically to locate the ring. It was off to one side, away from the flames.

She got a piece of stove wood and scratched at the ring, pulling it to her.

Picking it up, she blew the ashes off of it and clenched it tightly in one fist. Wrapping that fist with her other hand, she hugged both hands to her throat. She stood wide-eyed, gasping, embracing the ring, trying to think.

Finally, opening her hand, Sara studied the circlet.

Hickory was a hard, stubborn wood. It did not yield easily to a whittler's blade. How long had Bo worked on this perfect little item, polishing, smoothing it to its flawless shape, free of any nick or blemish?

She examined it then slid it tentatively onto her ring finger. It fit. How had he crafted it exactly the right size?

She removed the ring, tore the long, narrow hem from her nightshirt, ran the strip through the ring, and tied it around her neck. It would hang there, concealed under her clothing. She fingered it beneath the fabric of her nightshirt. She would wear it hidden. She alone would know it was there, a reminder that, for a brief time, someone had known her intimately, had evoked responses from her that she had not thought possible, and that that someone had loved her. It didn't matter who he was, what he looked like, how much education he had, or how well regarded he was in society, only that he loved her. She would believe that always, whether she could prove it or not.

Sara bit her lips to keep the tears at bay as she dressed.

Other than her own clothing, her comb and the ring were the only possessions she would take away from the cabin. Any other mementos she would carry in her heart.

It was early afternoon. As she stepped outside, she was startled to hear the motorcycle's engine rev to life.

She stood at the cabin door, speechless, and watched as Bo, without looking back, rode off into the woods, without her.

Chapter Sixteen

"I thought you'd left me." Sara hurried outside talking when Bo returned a short while later with neither the guns nor the knapsack—only the satchel.

She wore the clothes she'd had on when she was kidnapped, the denim dress, underthings, and the now heel-less Cappezios. Over her dress, to ward off the chill of the afternoon, she had layered an extra shirt, a flannel jacket and a wool sweater, the most decent clothing from the box. The only thing she carried was the comb. The ring dangled hidden beneath the dress, between her breasts.

Bo regarded her oddly.

"But you came back. You're taking me home. We're leaving together. Is that right?"

He shrugged. Obviously, her guess was not quite on target. He stood, still straddling the motorcycle, and beckoned her forward. When she got close, he put the helmet on her, snapped it, and motioned her onto the machine behind him. She didn't move.

"What did the ring mean, Bo?"

He glared at her.

"Was it a friendship ring?"

He didn't respond.

"An engagement ring, then?"

Still nothing.

She lowered her voice. "Were you asking me to marry you?"

He gave her one brusque nod.

"I assume by your anger, you've withdrawn the offer."

He looked at the ground and shook his head.

"You do want to marry me?"

A single nod.

"What are you offering? A life in the mountains, isolated, cut off from my family and friends and everything else that's important to me?"

His eyes shot to her face. Her chin quivered. Every word she spoke seemed to inflict injury on them both. There were no more words to say

173

anyway. Tears blistered behind her eyes and her throat ached.

Unable to guess what he was thinking, she stepped up and threw her leg over the seat behind him. It took her a moment to get situated. He showed her where to put her feet. With no more secure handle, she put her hands on his waist as the engine roared to life.

They raced along the ridge in shale and loose rock, the wind ripping. When he slowed, she removed the helmet, wrapped her arms around him, and buried her face in his bearskin coat. Breathing between his shoulder blades, she shook as she sobbed. He seemed oblivious to her grief.

Beyond the ridge, they turned onto a dirt trail, which plunged to a gravel road and fed onto an asphalt highway. The two lanes looked expansive compared to the narrow trails earlier.

Sara looked around, wondering that civilization lurked so close to Bo's rustic little homestead.

Miles later, they came to a small store and service station. A sign over the door read, "Bus Depot."

Bo pulled in. Without cutting the engine, he indicated she should get off. When she did, her legs wobbled, and he offered a hand to steady her.

Standing, straddling the motorcycle, Bo opened his coat, took out his wallet, counted out several bills, and handed them to her. She took the money, trying to read his face, but he avoided looking at her.

"Is this it then?" She fought to dismiss the heaviness in her heart.

He turned the key and the engine's murmur stopped.

The silence of the mountains swallowed all other sound. The sun dashed in and out of gathering clouds. Sara looked around before settling her eyes on his face. "Is this the end of us, of you and me? Are we finished?"

Gazing at the road ahead, he shrugged.

"Bo, I need you." Her voice broke and dropped to a husky whisper. "How will I find you?"

His dark eyes were hard when they met hers, as indifferent as they had been that first night when he fastened the shackle on her wrist and secured her to the tree.

"What if I can't live without you?" She cleared her throat. "What will I do when I need to touch you? When I have nightmares or can't sleep without you?"

She tried to control the emotional stampede inside, to hang onto some shred of dignity in the face of his cold dismissal, but her body quaked, and tears trickled over her face.

He sank onto the motorcycle seat and bowed his head. Finally he braced the bike, stepped off and opened his arms. She flung herself into his embrace and clung to him, pressing herself against him. The reserved city girl who shunned scenes tried to control herself and think. She had lived for years without him, but he had shown her a facet of herself she did not know. She owed him but, again, she realized the raw feelings were more than gratitude. She revered this man; respected his kindness; admired his patience, his strength, his courage. She loved the way he looked, the way he laughed and teased her. Most of all, she loved the way he loved her.

And the way she loved him.

She had said the words to him. The revelation should not have come as a shock, but it did. She loved this unlikely man with every beat of her heart.

He had asked her to marry him. Maybe he loved her, too. She never dreamed that mutual love could generate so much pain.

Bo brushed the hair back from her face and pressed his lips to the side of her forehead.

"I love you," she whispered. "Take me with you. We don't have to be married. I want to live with you, sleep beside you, anywhere. Nothing else matters." She hesitated. "Don't leave me." Her voice faltered. "Please." Unbidden tears continued their run down her face.

A wizened old man shuffled out of the station. "Help you, folks? You needin' some gasoline?"

Bo shook his head. Her face smushed against his chest, Sara clung to him.

A Frito-Lay truck pulled into the driveway. As the delivery man hurried to open the van's doors, the elderly attendant abandoned Bo and Sara, responding instead to the newcomer's hello.

Sara pushed herself back to look up into Bo's face. Tears trickled through his beard.

What was wrong? Why was he so sad? If he wanted her, she was his.

"You hold the keys that unlock my soul." She caught both his hands. "You hold all the joy in my life right here in these two hands." She made no sound as she peered into his eyes and again mouthed the words, "I love you."

A skeptical smile played at his lips. He looked at the delivery man who was ogling Sara. Her eyes followed Bo's. The man hoisted a plastic carrier of chips to his shoulder and grinned broadly. "Hello, there."

"No, no, no, Bo." She put her hand on Bo's face and turned it, forcing him to look at her. "There won't be anyone else. Please, Bo, please don't leave me."

He smiled grimly and shook his head.

She tried again. "If our positions were reversed, I wouldn't leave you."

His bearskin coat hung open. She slid her hands inside and wrapped her arms around his waist, pulling herself against him. "Kiss me. Give me a kiss that will make you take me with you, or one that will last until you bring us together again."

He put his hand under Sara's chin, tilted her head, and planted his mouth over hers. She pulled her body hard against him. She wanted to remind him of his need, of how she satisfied that need. She captured his tongue, that thick, elusive member, sucked it deep, and held.

He yielded, obviously warming to her. He laced his fingers into her hair and pulled her head back. She inhaled her victory. She had him, certain now he would do as she asked. He kissed her face and neck as she swayed, rubbing herself against his body, all but gloating. She had won.

Abruptly, he pushed her to arm's length. Then, before she knew what was happening, he was on the motorcycle. Stunned, she stood speechless as the machine roared to life and, in a moment, he was gone, riding back the way they had come.

* * * *

Sara stood unmoving, confused. The old man and the delivery guy seemed not to have noticed the passionate good-bye or Bo's sudden departure.

176

Abandoned, suddenly again on her own, Sara grappled for ways to console herself. She would manage, reconnoiter, rethink things, eventually recover. She would be fine. Just fine.

First? What was the first thing she should do? *Get a grip, woman,* she chided. *He's gone. You get to begin your life all over again, starting now.*

She needed answers, needed to find out where she was before she tried to go anywhere.

There were telephones in the station. But she didn't want to call her parents. Not yet. Her emotions popped like frayed nerve endings. She was too wired to answer a bunch of questions, or to withstand a deluge of unsolicited advice. Besides, she wanted to give Bo a chance to get as far as possible, in case they wanted to accuse him of...what?

The delivery man held the door for her as she entered the store. "Hey, sweet thing, where're you from?" When she didn't answer, he tried again. "Okay. Where're you headed?"

She scowled. Those were hard questions. Sara didn't attempt answers. He serviced his displays, eyeballing her periodically, and left.

Sliding into one of the three vinyl booths lining the front windows inside the store, Sara concentrated on the old man as he emptied ashtrays and refilled salt and pepper shakers.

"Where exactly are we?" she asked finally.

"South end of the Ozark National Forest, 'bout halfway between Little Rock and Fort Smith."

"How far is that from Settlement?"

"Is that in Arkansas?"

"Yes."

"Been here seven years. Never heard of it."

Apparently the proprietor was accustomed to visiting with addlepated people. He answered her questions carefully, even got a road map and patiently pointed out their location. He kept his voice to a steady, patronizing tone.

After thinking a while, staring out at the mountains, Sara made a decision. She would try to pick up her life where she'd left off. She'd go to Overt.

That seemed sensible. Yes, the plan seemed sound so far as it went. Then, if she still had a job, if she decided to stay, to live there, she'd expand on her plan. So far, so good.

How much time had passed? She'd lost track of the days. She'd been abducted on Halloween, October thirty-first.

She got up and strolled over to check a newspaper lying open on the counter. The dateline was Saturday, November ninth.

"Is this today's paper?"

The old man didn't seem surprised by the question. "No, ma'am. That's Saturday's. Should have one today, but it's a holiday, Armistice Day, Monday, November eleventh. Won't be a new paper out 'til tomorrow."

An eighteen-wheeler rumbled in, lining itself up with the outside pumps. A solemn middle-aged couple climbed down, stiff and badly wrinkled.

Had they started out lusting after one another, Sara wondered, only to wind up bumping along side-by-side, tolerating each other in the truck?

The woman said something. The man looked up, obviously surprised, and grinned, then let out a loud guffaw. The woman twittered good-naturedly and patted his shoulder as she sidled by him and into the store.

The woman thrust a thermos on the counter. "Fill it with the high octane caffeine, Omer, and remember, extra packets of cream and sugar."

The old man grinned.

The woman stuck coins in the jukebox and hit the buttons without looking at the selections, then ambled into the ladies' room.

Sara wondered about her lost days, her twelve days in the mountains. In the scheme of things, what was twelve days out of a lifetime? Not much, really. Not even two weeks.

Yet the past twelve days had been significant, perhaps the most important of her life.

The music from the juke box swelled, filling every cranny in the building with strains of "How Am I Suppose To Live Without You."

Tears gathered as she listened. "...now that I've been loving you so long..." It wasn't all that long, really. "...when all that I was living for is gone..."

178

Sara sat down and put her forehead on her arms folded on the table in front of her.

The door slammed and a man's voice called out warm hellos above the music. The attendant's voice boomed, engaging the visitor.

Looking up, Sara coughed to disguise her melancholia, pulled a paper napkin from the dispenser and blew her nose.

She stood, straightened her shabby clothing as much as possible, and drifted over to look at the chips. Corn chips, potato chips, displays just like ones she had seen a hundred times before. They hadn't changed, the same before Bo and now...after.

"What would you say if I told you, I've always wanted to hold you..." the next selection blared, again overwhelming all other sounds in the building.

Chip displays had not changed much in twelve days, Sara mused, fingering crisp little bags. She had. Bo did it. In some respects, he had actually introduced her to herself.

"...nothing would change if we made love..."

Her chin quivered.

"...so I'll be your friend, and I'll be your lover and I know in our hearts we agree, you don't have to be one or the other. We can be both to each other..."

That's the trouble with women these days, Sara thought, angrily sniffling. We're getting our philosophy from jukeboxes.

Well, if he thought he could hide from her, Bo whatever-his-name-was was seriously mistaken. She could live the rest of her life without corn chips, if she had to, but she did not plan to last another seventy years or so without sex and Bo was her teacher, her tutor, her guide. He had taken her, taught her, made her responsive. He had a responsibility to her now and she'd, by gosh, see to it that he honored that obligation. She was a damned good investigative reporter. She'd find him.

Of course, now that he had shown her the way, maybe she could enjoy sex with someone else.

But she didn't want anyone else.

She heard the approaching rumble of another large vehicle.

"Is there a bus?" she called to the attendant, her voice breaking with her effort to stifle her unsteady emotions. The juke box fell silent.

"One's coming now."

"Does it go to Overt?"

"Yes, it does."

"Can I get a ticket?"

"Fourteen dollars. He pulls in here for maybe three minutes. Just long enough to get stopped good. Get your money out."

She opened the wad Bo had given her. Fifty dollars. Why so much? He'd given her enough to go a long, long way. Well, that was just his tough luck. She wasn't going all that far.

* * * *

The bus was sparsely filled. Some passengers dozed, some read or stared straight ahead, but all of them seemed to disapprove of Sara as she climbed on board.

Okay, so she didn't look too good. Who did they think they were? Judging by their wardrobes, they hardly looked qualified to critique hers.

She peered down again. Her denim dress was badly torn and amateurishly mended. She had layered shirts over it to ward off the chill of the November afternoon. The heels were missing from her shoes, her hair hadn't been shampooed in two weeks. She had no make-up, no purse, no suitcase. She sighed. No wonder they regarded her oddly.

One by one they diverted their gazes. Obviously, no one wanted to encourage her to sit by them. Who knew what she might be carrying, fleas, lice, or communicable diseases.

Selecting a vacant seat near the back, Sara slid across to stare out the window.

She would call her parents from Overt. They would help her recover her car...her clothing...her life.

She leaned her forehead against the cool window.

No matter how kind they were, or how enthusiastic their intentions, she feared no one could help her recover the one loss that mattered. No one could help her retrieve Bo.

She began to weep, grieving quietly. Eventually a woman across the aisle handed her a wadded tissue.

Two hours and a half-a-dozen stops later, as the bus pulled into the terminal at the edge of the business district of Overt, Sara blew her nose loudly, sat up straight, and smoothed her tattered dress. She was about to reenter the real world, a place where she at least understood the rules.

Chapter Seventeen

"Sara?" Her mother's voice broke when she answered the phone at the Loomis residence in Lone Branch. "Oh, baby... Is it really you? Are you all right? " There was a click. Someone had picked up an extension at their end of the line. "Where are you? Oh, honey, it's so wonderful to hear your voice. Tell me where you are. Daddy and I'll come get you right this minute."

Sara smiled and suddenly realized she was a grown woman, autonomous, no longer dependent on her parents for her identity.

When she was allowed a word, she said, "I'm okay and I'm really glad to hear your voice, too, Mom. I'm in Overt, in the same clothes I was wearing when they kidnapped me."

As she heard her mother repeating her words to her father, another voice broke on the line.

"Ms. Loomis, this is Agent William Krisp with the Federal Bureau of Investigation. We are eager to talk to you."

"Fine." She hadn't realized the FBI would be at her parents' house. Of course, they were involved. It was a kidnapping. Their turf. She knew that from TV.

"Where in Overt are you?" he asked.

"At a drugstore, corner of Third and Lamar."

"We have an agent there in town. His name's Kevin Larchmont, that's L-a-r-c-h-m-o-n-t. Have you got that?"

"Yes, sir."

"Stay on the line. I'm going to contact him now while you visit with your parents. He'll pick you up. Be sure to check his identification. You are to go with him, do you understand?"

"Agent Krisp, I just got off a bus after twelve days in very primitive conditions. I don't need another road trip. I will meet Mr. Larchmont, but I am not *going* anywhere. I'm staying right here in Overt. If you want to talk to me, you'll have to come here."

She was a law-abiding citizen. He had no authority to make her do anything she didn't choose to do. She'd been bullied enough in the last twelve days to last her a while.

183

There was a long delay and an excited, muffled conversation in the background, then her dad's voice boomed.

"Sara, honey, do you need to see a doctor? Are you, ah...injured..."

Krisp's gruff voice interrupted in a businesslike tone. "Have you been sexually molested?"

"I'm all right, Dad. No, I don't need a doctor."

Her father exhaled quietly. "Thank heaven."

"Agent Larchmont will take you to the Homestead Motel there in Overt," Krisp said. "He'll provide whatever you need. You can clean up and have food sent in. Stay put. Your parents and I will be there in less than three hours, sooner if the weather holds and we can fly.

"Ms. Loomis," Krisp lowered his voice, "don't talk to anyone, do you understand?"

"You mean about my abduction?"

"What else?"

"I have a phone call to make. I want to talk to the managing editor at the *Gazette* about my job. Make sure your agent understands I'm not a prisoner. I'm allowed phone calls."

Krisp hesitated. When he spoke, he didn't sound pleased. "All right. I'll tell him, but nothing about the case. Do you understand?"

"Right. Daddy?"

"Yes."

She choked, cleared her throat and took a deep breath. "It's good to hear your voice."

"Me too, sugar. We're only a couple of hours away. Take it easy. We'll be there in a little while."

Sara hung up the telephone and turned to find a tall, slim young man in a dark suit and sunglasses coming through the door of the drugstore. He walked directly to her, producing a badge and identification as he approached.

The druggist and three customers, who had gotten their purchases but remained in the store, gawked at Sara and whispered to one another. Seeing they were all talking at once, Sara wondered if anyone heard anything the others said.

"I'm Larchmont," the young man said quietly, removing the mirrored shades.

"Sara Loomis."

184

He grinned, grabbed her hand and shook it. "I'm sure glad to meet you. We've been looking everywhere."

"I was there, waiting for you to find me."

His toothsome smile continued as he moved his hand to her elbow and guided her out to a late model vehicle with antennas. He put her inside.

"I'm not supposed to ask you any questions. It's pretty tough. We're all damned curious about where you've been and who you've been with. But I guess you need to hold it a little longer until Krisp and the others get here."

Sara nodded, thinking about what she would tell the investigators. She was too good a newsperson to withhold details of her story from law enforcement people; pertinent information, that is. But could she talk about Bo yet? The awful grief swept over her again. Maybe if she wrote it out first, unemotionally, objectively, as if she were doing a news story. Writing it would be therapeutic, help get her psyche back to normal.

Maybe she could give the FBI an official version, omitting some things the investigators didn't actually *need* to know. She'd see.

"Is there a Wal-Mart store here in Overt?"

Larchmont chuckled out loud. "A Wal-Mart in an Arkansas town of thirty thousand people? Are you kidding?"

"If that's a yes, I need some things."

"Today's a holiday. Everybody in the county'll be there. You'd better keep a lower profile than Wal-Mart. How about you make a list and I'll get what you need. Your picture's posted everywhere. Someone's bound to spot you in a public place."

Maybe her picture was the reason people on the bus and in the drugstore had stared. This guy was probably right.

As he checked her into the motel—Sara remained in the car—she made a list of items of apparel and sizes and a longer list of make-up and hygiene items.

Self-conscious about Larchmont purchasing the personal articles, she stammered as they reviewed the list.

He smiled. "Don't be embarrassed. You've got it down here in detail. I'll let a sales clerk do the choosing."

From her dress pocket, she scooped the currency left from her bus ticket and tried to hand it to him, but he waved it off. "I've got it. You'd better hang onto that for emergencies."

She smiled halfheartedly and he gave her an earnest stare. "You don't act like you're afraid to be left alone."

"No, I'm not afraid. No one's after me."

He nodded but seemed to be stalling. "I'm not really supposed to leave you, you know."

She snorted a disdainful little laugh. "There's no where I want to go, Agent Larchmont. If there were, I'd be there, with or without the FBI's permission. I'll bolt the door, put the chain on, not open up for anyone but you or my parents, okay?

He nodded.

"Oh, I also need a curling iron, probably one with a three-quarter-inch barrel."

"Right." He jotted the addition on the list and opened the door. "I'll be back in half an hour."

"I'll be right here." She closed the door behind him and turned to reconnoiter. She was surprised and pleased to realize that after all her blubbering on the bus, she didn't have a headache.

She found the complimentary bottle of shampoo, got a towel, and turned on the water in the bathtub, trying not to entertain the memory of the last time she'd washed her hair—in the trough in the cabin with Bo. A tiny cry caught in her throat. "Don't," she chided out loud. "Don't do this. Let him go. Think of something else."

She adjusted the water. That was nice. Water on tap. An innovation she'd scarcely noticed or appreciated, before.

She hung her head over the side of the tub to let the water cascade through her hair and tried to think of the future; her new life in this picturesque little town, if she had a job. She rinsed, soaped and rinsed again, then wrapped a towel around her head turban style. Fumbling with the phone book, she found the number and dialed the *Gazette*.

"Bruce Crownover, please."

When the managing editor answered, she hesitated.

"Hello?" the man repeated, irritation in his voice.

"Mr. Crownover?"

"Speaking."

"This is Sara Loomis. I'm here in Overt. I want to know if you still have a job for me?"

It took him a minute, then his voice softened. "The Sara Loomis who was en route to her new job on this newspaper when she was abducted?"

"The same."

"Have we got a job for you? Yes, ma'am. Have you got a story for me? I sure as hell hope so. Did you think we'd fill your job while you were kidnapped?"

"Well..."

"Generally we don't penalize people for being late for work if they've got any kind of an excuse at all."

She chuckled lightly. "Well, sir, I've got a dandy."

His laugh burbled along with hers. "When are we going to get it?"

"The FBI wants to debrief me first. They insist I spiel it for them before I get befuddled and forget or start embellishing."

"I can understand that. But you *will* write it for us before you start penning your best seller, right?"

She laughed lightly. "Right. So am I still employed?"

"Tell you what, Sara Loomis, I'm going to set it up so that you've been on payroll since one November, how does that sound? More good news. Friday's payday."

"Don't you need my social security number or something?"

"Nah. We can do all the fine tuning when you get to the office. When do you suppose that'll be?"

"I don't know for sure. If I can answer all the FBI's questions and find something to wear, maybe Wednesday."

Crownover cleared his throat, which sounded like an affirmative response. "We're all sure looking forward to meeting you, Sara Loomis. Yes, ma'am, we're sure eager to make your acquaintance."

Chapter Eighteen

Agent William Krisp was well named, Sara decided. The man was brittle; his words, terse.

Barrel chested, Krisp stood erect at five-foot-eight, eye level with Sara, and rolled a toothpick back and forth across his mouth awaiting her responses to his succinct questions.

He had allowed her only a few moments' private reunion with her parents before directing her to one of the three chairs at the small table in the sitting area of her motel room. He had brought along a male stenographer who set up his machine across from her and began clattering the keys.

Shampooed, bathed, and dressed in new slacks, sweater, and underclothes from Wal-Mart, Sara opened her account, telling them about her rest stop at the convenience store near a town she couldn't identify.

"Blimpton, Arkansas," Krisp supplied.

She detailed her abduction, a random choice by the abductor, conversations during their wild ride in the dilapidated pickup, and the scene when they stopped at the clearing in the mountains.

She recalled some of their names—Cappy, Franklin, Holthus—but she couldn't remember the other two. Then, of course, there was Ma or Queenie. Krisp nodded sagely.

"Holthus has bright red hair and beard. He should be easy to spot." Krisp nodded again

"Franklin is the one who actually kidnapped me. He should be easy to identify. He's missing parts of three fingers on his right hand." She cringed, suddenly recalling Franklin's odor. "But I'll tell you about that later."

"He's the guy..." Agent Larchmont broke in, but shut up abruptly when Krisp flashed him a withering look.

Obviously, Krisp and Larchmont knew Franklin. Were they the ones who had brought the dogs and left footprints along the riverbank near the Johnsons? She had a feeling Franklin was their guide that day, the culprit helping the law search for the red herring. How ironic.

But Sara wanted to give her account in full before she asked any questions. She spoke slowly, trying to keep events in chronological order. Krisp seldom interrupted.

When she finished hitting the high spots in her initial account, Krisp said, "Did you fear for your life at any time?" He studied her closely, making notes in his own notebook in addition to the stenographer's word-for-word account.

She thought that seemed like a silly question. "Yes."

"Did you see any weapons?"

"Weapons?" She was astonished. "Yes. There were weapons everywhere. Rifles, shotguns, bows and arrows, knives, pistols in holsters like cowboys. Those people are still living in the old west, Mr. Krisp. They don't go to the corner grocery. They shoot game for the table. Yes, I saw weapons."

He disregarded her sarcasm. "Did you see any automatic weapons?"

"No. They're proud of their shooting. They don't hunt with Uzis."

Krisp shook his head. She realized he was probably disappointed to have unearthed common criminals instead of a politically subversive group of some kind.

"Why do you think they took you, Ms. Loomis?"

She raised and lowered her shoulders. "There was a lot of confusion, people screaming, guns firing. I was in the wrong place at the wrong time. Franklin yanked me out and threw me into the truck. I told you what Holthus said later. Queenie had told them not to take any hostages or do any shooting.

"The whole gang piled into the truck on top of me—in my lap, for heaven's sake. They were in a panic. I don't think most of them knew I was there until later."

Krisp's voice droned. "Did you see these people do anything illegal?"

Sara looked at him in disbelief. "You mean other than robbing a convenience store and kidnapping me?" She thought a moment while everyone else in the room waited.

"Well, they made moonshine," she said, realizing that might be a federal offense. "But I don't think they make it to sell. Just for family. And I think they're all related. The intermarrying in that bunch has taken its toll. I doubt there's a sound mind among them."

190

Krisp nodded soberly. "Okay, they got you to their hideout, then what happened?"

"We were near a place called Settlement. I don't think Settlement is their hideout. I think it's a community whose name reflects the imagination of its residents."

The agent allowed a tolerant smile and waited for her to continue.

"Anyway, Franklin wanted the honor of killing me. He talked about other women he'd killed." From the corner of her eye, Sara tried to ignore her mother's flinch. "I don't know if he was bragging or if he'd actually murdered someone. But Cappy, the nineteen-year-old stutterer, somehow won the honor of doing me in. He marched me off into the woods."

She detailed her conversation with Cappy as well as she could recall it, particularly his speculation that Bo would kill her quickly and mercifully.

"Taking my chances with a guy Cappy said was a mute madman seemed, at the moment, my best chance, so I campaigned for that."

She recalled her terror during her first confrontation with Bo.

"What's his full name?" Krisp asked, peering over the tops of his eyeglasses.

"I don't know."

"You mean he wouldn't tell you?"

"Bo's a mute. He doesn't speak."

"Not a word?"

"No."

"Can't or won't?"

She shrugged. "I never heard him utter a word, even in emergencies." She glanced toward her parents and lowered her voice. "I don't think he's physically able to speak."

Krisp looked hard at her, allowed his glance to wander to her parents on the sofa several feet away, then he scribbled something in the margin of his notebook.

"So what *do* you know about Bo?"

"He was in the military. Mrs. Johnson told me that. He's lived there for two or three years. She gave me that, too. In fact, she's probably the one you ought to ask about him. Most of my information about Bo, I got from her."

"Describe him for our reporter here, Ms. Loomis, and we'll get a sketch artist to give us a rendering."

Sara frowned down at her hands. "Okay." But she stalled.

"Do you have reservations about giving us a description of this man?"

She cast him a side-long look. "I don't know why you want one. I get the impression you already know what Franklin and Cappy and Holthus and Queenie look like."

Krisp settled a dark stare on Sara. "Do you have a problem with describing Bo for us?"

"Yes, I do." She straightened in her chair. "Why do you want it? Franklin kidnapped me. He was the one so darn eager to kill me; said he'd like to have done a number of other things to me first. Sexual things. And he followed through on those threats every time he got the chance.

"Cappy wanted us to have sex but he didn't know how. I told him I couldn't teach him anything about that. I can give you detailed descriptions of both of those yahoos. Why do you keep asking about Bo?"

She glanced at her parents who sat tense, side-by-side on the sofa. Her dad grimaced. Her mother refused to raise her eyes, concentrating instead on her hands folded in her lap.

Krisp held his silence. Was he reeling out rope hoping she would implicate herself? In what? Her own kidnapping?

"Bo frightened me at first," she said, relenting. "He growled and grunted, shoved me around, kept me locked up."

She told about Bo's staking her out under the tree then rescuing her from the coyote attack; about his locking her in the shed, then retrieving her before the tornado; about his providing clothes, and feeding her; about his taking her into the cabin the night the weather turned cold.

She didn't mention sleeping in Bo's bed that night, certain none of them would understand. She wasn't sure she understood that either, exactly.

"Then Franklin came to *rescue* me." She glared at Krisp. He returned the look, showing no emotion, but he flashed Larchmont a warning glance. Sara saw the exchange and made a mental note to question the junior agent later, away from Krisp's squelching looks.

"When did this aborted rescue take place?"

Krisp returned Sara's scowl of disapproval. "It was not an 'aborted rescue,' Mr. Krisp. It was an attempt by Franklin to rape and murder me. He did a pretty fair job of assaulting me as it was."

"Of course, you don't know that he would have raped or murdered you, Ms. Loomis."

Sara felt her face flush. "Mr. Krisp, I thought you wanted facts." Her words hissed between clenched teeth. "If you plan to make up a story to fit some lame theory of your own, you don't need me." She tapped her index finger on the table as she spoke. "But I am a news reporter, sir. I deal in straight-up, hard news; in facts, sir."

"Now hold on just a minute, young woman..."

She raised her voice over his attempted interruption. "I intend to write this entire story exactly as it happened. I imagine your superiors will wonder if your account and mine are different. They'll probably want to know where you got yours. I lived this nightmare and I am damn sure not going to verify a bunch of fabrications."

He glared at her. "I have no intention of dealing in anything but the facts in this situation, Ms. Loomis."

"Even if they don't make the FBI look as efficient or as heroic as you'd like?"

He glanced quickly toward her parents, at Larchmont, then at the court reporter taking down each word.

Larchmont cleared his throat and looked at Krisp. "Maybe we should delete that part of the interview."

"Not a chance." Sara shot a warning glance at the reporter.

"I have to take it all down," the stenographer said. "I'm not allowed to delete anything."

Krisp nodded to Sara, prompting her to continue.

She explained about Franklin's spiriting her away to a remote spot and tying her, hanging her from a tree while he made camp; about his tippling from the fruit jar; his threats regarding her body, his attempt to molest her, their mutual assaults upon one another; about Bo's intervention, and details of the dispatching of portions of Franklin's three fingers.

Her mother squirmed and her dad covered his wife's trembling hands with both of his. Larchmont groaned. Krisp remained stoic, as if he were unmoved by any part of Sara's account. Then he mumbled to Larchmont, "We may have to exercise the escape clause in our deal with young Franklin Kindling."

Sara's eyes narrowed. "And how long have you known that family's name, Mr. Krisp? Kindling, is that it?"

Krisp flashed an embarrassed look at Larchmont and she realized the senior agent was annoyed with himself for having let that information slip.

"Of course, Ms. Loomis, Franklin Kindling may want to file assault charges against your friend Bo for amputating his fingers for him."

Sara allowed a half snort, half laugh. "I hope he does. What a hoot. Look at my wrists." She held out her hands. Both wrists still showed ugly evidence of the rope burns. "Franklin caused every bit of that. I'll be glad to show my scars and tell a judge and jury about ropes Franklin tied so tight they made me bleed; about how he hung me from a tree limb so he could attack me; about that slimy little animal ripping open my nightshirt and about..."

"What?" Krisp finally sounded surprised.

Her eyes shot toward her parents on the sofa. "I left some things out before."

"Back up then."

Lowering her gaze, Sara provided more details of the episode in the canyon, of Franklin's boasts that he collected a severed breast from each of his many female victims. She glanced at her parents before telling of her attempts to make Franklin mad enough to kill her, and of Bo's last minute appearance in the nightmare.

She told how Bo comforted her and kept her safe with him. At that, Krisp eyed her suspiciously.

Omitting any reference to their sexual exploits, she recounted Bo's thoughtful behavior: the chamber pot, the meals, clothing from the boxes in the shed, the comb he crafted for her, their visits to the Johnsons, and finally, his bringing her out on his motorcycle and giving her money for bus fare.

Krisp's eyes narrowed. "Why didn't you call your parents from the bus station?"

"I...I guess I didn't think of it. I wanted to get away from there, from

194

that bunch of crazies in Settlement, back to civilization."

"And to give Bo a chance to get clear, isn't that right?"

Sara didn't answer. The clattering of the reporter's keyboard stopped. There was a long lull. Krisp studied her face for several seconds, then glanced at her parents.

Larchmont, idly picking his fingernails, spoke. "Does this Bo have any identifying marks, birthmarks, moles, tattoos, anything?"

Sara shook her head slightly, looking at Krisp. "No."

Larchmont continued. "Maybe on his torso, places not normally visible. Something to help us verify his identity when we get him." Larchmont glanced up then back at a particularly troublesome hangnail.

The stenographer stared out the window.

Sara's parents both gazed at a magazine on the coffee table in front of them. But Krisp looked directly at Sara and she returned his stare. Almost imperceptibly, she shook her head. Krisp nodded, puckered his lips, and drew a deep breath.

"Mr. and Mrs. Loomis," he rose casually, "I think we've pretty well heard the gist of the story now. Sara is of legal age and we'd like to ask her a few technical questions privately. I'd appreciate it if you would excuse yourselves for a little while, if you don't mind."

Sara's dad gave Krisp a hard look, then his eyes traveled to Sara, who smiled assurance.

"There's a nice coffee shop up by the motel office," Krisp continued. "How about if you wait for us there?"

Sara's parents both looked to her. She smiled again. "I'll be fine."

Her father stood. "We'll be back in half an hour." He gave her mother a hand up then walked over and kissed Sara on the cheek. Her mother hugged her tightly. They left. Agents Larchmont and Krisp and the reporter stayed with Sara.

"Did you get a tag number on the motorcycle Bo was driving?" Krisp asked. Sara thought he sat straighter in his chair and watched her facial responses even more closely than he had before.

Genuinely surprised, she shook her head. "No. I never even thought about motorcycles having tags." She chided herself for not having gotten a tag number, a way for her to trace Bo later.

"Where was Bo from?"

"I don't know. He didn't have an accent, of course. He was polite, very mannerly. Mrs. Johnson said he wasn't from around there, but she didn't know where he came from either."

"Sara," Krisp used her first name and his voice became soothing, "it's not unusual for a kidnap victim to develop a dependence...a, well, shall we say a fondness...a crush, if you will, on her abductor."

Sara felt a bright flush climb from her collar to her hairline and she bit her lips. Agent Larchmont's eyes darted from Sara to Krisp and back to Sara.

She looked at her hands folded in her lap, then set her jaw and glared at her interrogator.

"Mr. Krisp, your robbers and kidnappers are right there in Settlement, just waiting for you to come sack them up. Bo was a kindly caretaker, not a criminal."

"What we suspect, Ms. Loomis, is that this recluse, this societal outcast, took advantage of you." She noticed he was again addressing her formally. "We'd seen pictures of you, of course, but they don't do you justice. You are a nice looking young woman. A horny old hermit stuck out in the boonies like this Bo probably licked his chops getting his hands on you."

Sara's temper flared. "It wasn't like that. *He* wasn't like that."

"An old coot, cut off from all other humans, suddenly falls heir to a lovely young woman..."

"He's not an old coot."

Krisp's eyebrows shot up. "How old a man is he, Sara?"

She wrung her hands. "At first I thought he was old. Cappy told me he was and I just assumed Cappy knew. He wore a bearskin coat and his face and head were covered with all this long, unkempt hair."

"And later?"

She cleared her throat. "What do you mean?"

"Well, you said at first you thought he was old. Later did you revise your thinking? If so, what changed your mind and just what age range are we talking about here?"

She squirmed, studying the table in front of her.

"The Johnsons' son, Lutie, was trapped on a sand spit in the middle of the river. The water was rising and the current was fast. Bo waded out to get him. Saved his life, probably. Mrs. Johnson said Bo had saved Lutie once before, a couple of years ago."

"So, how did that incident change your mind about the man's age?"

"When he came out of the water, his clothes—he just had on a T-shirt and the pants to his long underwear—his clothes stuck to him. The water... He was soaked through and his clothes clung to him and he had...well, he had a really nice man's body, a young man's body. I mean it belonged to a man who was considerably younger than I thought Bo was."

Larchmont shifted uncomfortably. The reporter stared indifferently at the window as his fingers continued making the keyboard clatter. Krisp's expertise at his job had become apparent.

"Sara, were you sexually attracted to Bo?" Krisp's voice was low, confidential, coaxing.

Her chin quivered and tears stung her eyes as she bit her lower lip and whispered, "Yes."

"That's very common," Krisp said softly, his demeanor and tone forgiving, understanding. "He fed you, kept you safe, rescued you from situations you perceived to be life threatening. It's perfectly understandable that you might view him as your hero, your savior."

She stiffened and gulped down her emotions. "I appreciated his help. I am not as naive as you seem to think..."

"We've interviewed Jimmy Singer, Sara."

She drew a deep breath, clenching and unclenching her fists. "Krisp, Jimmy Singer and I had sex." She strained to speak around the lump in her throat. "Bo and I..." Her face twisted with the memory and her voice became stronger. "Bo and I made love."

Krisp frowned and nodded knowingly. "I'm sure you thought so. Speaking from a man's viewpoint, I think for him it was an opportunity to get into an attractive young woman's underpants."

Sara set her mouth. "Krisp, sex with Jimmy Singer and sex with Bo was like the difference between biting a lemon and sampling cheesecake. Lemons are tart, burn your lips, leave a bitter taste in your mouth. Cheesecake is smooth, and sweet, and you can't wait for the next bite."

Larchmont cleared his throat, obviously embarrassed. Just as obviously, Krisp tried to control a smile, a reaction apparently prompted by his subordinate's discomfort. "That's very descriptive, Ms. Loomis."

197

"It's also very accurate, Mr. Krisp."

"Nevertheless, you were his prisoner."

"No, I wasn't. When I asked him to bring me back to civilization, he did."

Krisp looked skeptical. "Do you mean to say you were there of your own free will?"

"I didn't *get* there of my own free will, of course." She splayed her hands, palms down on the table. "The weather had a lot to do with my staying longer than I needed to."

"Was it during the bad weather that you and Bo became intimate?"

"Yes."

"And what interrupted this romantic interlude?"

Sara was suddenly struck dumb. She knew Krisp saw her uncertainty and was going with his instincts.

"Somehow he found out *we* were getting close. didn't he, Sara? He was happy to have your company as long as there was no threat to his freedom, but when we started closing in, he shucked you and took off, isn't that right?"

Sara glared at Krisp, hating him. "You don't know how it was between us." She inhaled two great gulps of air, angry, suddenly less certain.

Krisp shook his head sadly. "Bo sounds like a pretty fair con artist, Sara. You were naive about sex, vulnerable, frightened. He gave you food, shelter, safety. It was only natural you should be grateful. When he made overtures, you saw a way to repay him, to demonstrate your gratitude, and you did."

How could this stranger guess so close to the truth? Tears slid down her face and she swiped at them. "It wasn't like that. He cared about me." She felt for the ring dangling around her neck, hidden beneath her new sweatshirt.

"How do you know that, Sara? Did he tell you so?"

"No. You know he couldn't."

"Couldn't or wouldn't?"

"I already told you, I never heard him speak." Sara slumped back in her chair and exhaled loudly. "Krisp, I'm tired of this."

The junior agent shifted as if he were about to stand but hesitated with Krisp spoke again.

"Ms. Loomis, your *lover* aided and abetted criminals after a crime. He held onto you for well over a week, getting his jollies. Does it matter at all to you that your parents spent every hour of that time in hell?"

She winced. What had he expected her to do?

"Young woman, law enforcement people all over this country spent valuable man hours searching for you, digging up what might have been shallow graves, hoping against hope to find you alive. If Bo had returned you to Settlement, you'd probably have been home in a few days."

Sara scrubbed tears off her face with the palm of her hand. "Krisp, I know you're not stupid. Franklin wanted to kill me that night after the robbery and every night from then on. If Bo hadn't been there, he would have. I wasn't strong enough or smart enough to stop him."

Where had Krisp gotten his information? She had a pretty good idea.

"Did you make a deal with Franklin Kindling, Mr. Krisp? You wouldn't file criminal charges against him if he'd help you find and prosecute *someone else* for the kidnapping *he* did? Even his own goons were mad at him for snatching me. Good grief, man. What kind of an investigator are you?"

Krisp ran his hands over the top of his head, smoothing the already tamed strands of hair stretched over his balding pate. "We stumbled onto Settlement accidentally, Sara. Everyone accused everyone else until we got it narrowed down to Holthus, Cappy, and Franklin, and a couple of others."

She interrupted. "Are Cappy and Franklin brothers or cousins?"

"Both. Queenie's their ma. Their dads are brothers." He gave her a sheepish shrug. "Anyway, Cappy would have told us, if he could have, but he got to stammering and stuttering so bad, we couldn't get any of it. Franklin volunteered, made the deal to tell us everything in exchange for immunity from prosecution."

"But he didn't tell the truth if he blamed Bo. Does his immunity cover lies?"

Krisp shook his head. Sara stared at him.

"How'd he say he knew about my being at Bo's anyway?"

Krisp's eyes widened. "He said he'd never seen you in person, that

Cappy took groceries up to Bo one day and saw you, and promised they'd come back to help you escape."

"Didn't see fit to mention that *he* was the one who grabbed me and tied me up in the first place, or that it was Cappy who hand-delivered me all trussed up to Bo?"

Krisp shook his head, his mouth pursed. "I'd still like to talk to Bo and those Johnsons."

Sara glanced toward the draped windows. "I don't think you'll have any trouble locating the Johnsons. But they've got no use for those people in Settlement. If they know you've made a deal with Franklin, they're not likely to have any respect for you or your investigation. They are very pragmatic people, Krisp. They see things black and white."

Krisp looked at her oddly. "Are you feeling steadier now?"

She nodded.

"Then let's get back to your personal relationship with Bo. You've confirmed that you had sex with the man."

"Yes, but why is that any concern of yours or the FBI's?" She pulled her feet up to hook her heels on the front edge of her chair and wrapped her arms around her knees.

"The extent of your emotional involvement may make a difference in your selective memory, how sympathetic you are toward him, and how much credence we can give your account."

"I told you, I write the news. I gather information and pass it on with no embellishment."

Krisp inclined his head, indicating he understood. "We're all human, Sara, subject to our own interpretations of behavior. It's obvious that you *think* you had a close personal relationship with the man."

She started to object to his terminology, then let it go as he continued. "Could you take us back to the cabin? Could you find it again?"

"I doubt it. I have no sense of direction. The only chance I would have of finding it would be to start from the Johnsons.' I could probably find it from there." She hesitated then continued. "Krisp, when you were on the river looking for me, why didn't you go to the Johnsons' cabin?"

He flashed Larchmont a warning look. "We got there, eventually. We'll get one of them to take us to Bo's cabin. Would you like me to pick up anything for you while we're there?"

Lowering her eyes, Sara shook her head 'no.' Everything and everyone that mattered to her had left when she did.

"Sara," Krisp's voice was again kindly, "do you expect to see Bo again?"

Remembering their final moments at the remote bus depot, the corners of Sara's mouth quivered. "No."

"If you ever were going to see him again, where would you expect that reunion to take place?"

Her eyes locked on his, she exhaled, and her shoulders slumped as she whispered, "I don't expect to see him again. Not anywhere. Not ever."

"Does he know where to find you?"

"What difference does it make? If you're right and I was just an easy lay, why would he try to find me?" She glowered at Krisp but he sat unmoving, regarding her quietly. She relented. "I don't know how he would."

"Did you tell him where you'd be?"

"*I* didn't know. I didn't know if I'd still have a job or if I'd have the nerve to come here, to face people, to live alone. I couldn't have told him. I didn't know myself."

Regarding her solemnly, Larchmont offered her the tissue box. She took one and blew her nose. "Is that all?"

"For now. Do you realize, Sara, that our recovering you alive after twelve days beats all the statistics?"

"*You* didn't recover me, Krisp. Bo brought me back."

"All right, it's still unusual, getting you back after that length of time. Take it from me, you are one very lucky lady."

His voice dropped to a conciliatory tone. "You did what you had to do to survive, Sara. You played it smart. You may need counseling to help you get by this. As for me, I admire the hell out of you. You kept your head and came out of this deal alive. But, Sara, don't be pining away for your hillbilly. I guarantee, even as sweet and pretty as you are, he's not grieving for you."

He regarded her quietly, his expression unreadable, before he allowed a slight smile. "Well, maybe he is, but not enough to risk putting his head in a noose.

"You've helped clean out a nest of thieves and we in law enforcement, and the potential victims out there, thank you.

"You'd make a good cop, Sara Loomis. You've got an eye for detail. You're gutsy and you're strong, mentally and physically. You might want to consider a career change."

She laughed. He had to be kidding.

"I'm serious here. You let me know if you ever decide you're interested."

Did he intend that as a compliment or was he being sarcastic? She couldn't tell. "Right. Thanks."

Chapter Nineteen

"I don't know why you won't go out with me." The words had been Stanton Rezabec's theme song the four weeks Sara had been courthouse reporter for the *Gazette*.

Rezabec had the city beat. He was personable, attractive, probably forty years old, Sara guessed, and both cheerful and persistent.

Her first day on the job, Stanton asked her out to dinner, offering to show her some of the night spots around town.

Not sufficiently settled in her job, staying at the motel with her parents, looking for an apartment, and still roller-coastering emotionally, Sara declined, politely, firmly.

Libby Cook, the young society editor, lived at The Oaks, an apartment complex two miles from the *Gazette*. There were two apartments available in her building, one on the second floor and one on the third. Sara followed Libby home to see the vacant apartments, and to talk to the manager.

"The only elevator in the west wing is old and slow," Libby explained. "Take the apartment on two next door to me and save the climb."

The apartment on the second floor had only one bedroom. Sara's parents insisted she take a two-bedroom. Her dad was adamant.

"We'll pay the difference. Mother and I want to see you fairly often for a while. If you have two bedrooms, we can do that without being so much in the way. I know you understand."

Reluctantly, Sara agreed, realizing how much her abduction had frightened them. When she took the apartment, they relented and grudgingly went home, promising a return visit as soon as the movers delivered her furniture.

Libby bounced with enthusiasm that Sara at least would be in the same building.

"You can stay at my place until your furniture gets here."

Sara declined. "I don't want to do that. I don't mean to hurt your feelings, Libby, but I need privacy right now." Libby's face fell, dejected. Sara smiled. "But I'd take the mattress off your sofa bed, if you offered."

Libby brightened. "You've got it, girlfriend."

That afternoon the two women wrestled the mattress onto the elevator and up to Sara's vacant apartment, then argued good-naturedly about where to put it.

It ended up in the spare bedroom, out of the way when Sara's things arrived.

A reputed womanizer, Rezabec repeated his invitation twice more that first week then made loud objections when Sara kept turning him down.

He advertised their situation, noisily complaining, announcing her rejections to everyone in the newsroom who took time to listen. It became an inside joke with co-workers laying money on when she would cave.

Like most in the newsroom, Libby encouraged Sara. "Go out with him once, Sara, to shut him up."

His embellished accounts of her repeated refusals were hilarious, making even Sara laugh at his pathetic, soul-wrenching stories.

Stanton's high profile romances were legendary among the staff. Obviously he had only limited experience with rebuffs.

Sara's morale got another boost on Friday when her furniture arrived, and a mixed surprise Saturday when her menstrual period started. She wasn't pregnant. She insisted to herself that she hadn't been worried, but secretly she both celebrated and mourned.

She cried herself to sleep every night the first week, sick with grief and tormented by Krisp's theories of Bo's view of their relationship. Toward the end of the week, she finally admitted to herself, he might be right.

Browsing in the mall, Sara stepped into a small shop, The Humidor, to smell the tobacco and summon memories. She spent lunch hours sitting in the city park sniffing the pines and watching tame squirrels scamper. She poked around in a saddle shop enjoying the fragrance of the leather.

"Are you married?" Rezabec asked privately the second week of his campaign. "No," he said, answering his own question. "I know you're not. Married ladies don't blush as much as you do. No, obviously that's not the problem."

Rezabec took a new approach the third week with, "Don't try to tell me you don't find me attractive." He laughed boisterously at his own suggestion, prompting Sara to giggle at his audacity.

He persisted. "Women like me a lot. What's that old commercial, 'Try me, you'll like me.'"

Despite the turn-downs, Sara enjoyed Stanton's light-hearted teasing which provided temporary stints of relief, helped her overcome some of the awful, consuming grief.

"Ms. Loomis?" It was Krisp's voice on the phone her third Thursday on the job. She recognized it before he identified himself.

"Hello, Agent Krisp. How's the investigation going?"

"We've arrested and arraigned Cappy and Franklin Kindling. Their faces are covered on the surveillance tape from the convenience store, but we have a good shot of the truck and of a man we assume is Franklin forcing you inside. We'll need your testimony to finger him as the man shoving you into the vehicle. Can you identify that truck?"

"Yes. What about Bo?"

"Not a clue. We had forensics all over that cabin. The rough surfaces did not yield so much as one usable print.

"The Johnsons' description sounded so much like yours that our guys thought you people had memorized it. When we got the same description from the Kindlings, we were convinced everybody was for real.

"We've determined that he's between twenty-five and forty years old, something over six feet tall, has brown hair, and dark brown or black eyes. Finding him should be a snap." Krisp hesitated and Sara, realizing he was being facetious, gave a nervous little laugh which seemed to encourage him.

"We couldn't turn up a doctor or dentist that worked on him in any of the towns around there so we've got no medical or dental information to go on. No one got a tag number off his motorcycle. He paid cash for purchases, no credit cards or checks. We don't know where he came from and damn sure can't figure where he went. If he gets a haircut and a shave, he'll blend and be gone for good.

"It's a good thing he's not considered a fugitive because what we've found out about your friend Bo makes us look really stupid."

Sara smiled at the telephone, then her expression turned melancholy.

Watching from his desk next to hers, Stanton frowned with uncharacteristic concern.

"What's wrong, honey? Can I help?" he asked as soon as she hung up. Sara shook her head without speaking. "Which is it? Did they find your boyfriend or didn't they?"

"They didn't. And he's not my boyfriend. He's my best friend. The best friend I ever had."

"They tell me you don't even know his name."

She acknowledged the statement with a glower. "That was in my story in our newspaper, Rezabec. *They* didn't tell you that. I did." She hesitated. "You don't have to know someone's name for him to be your friend."

Rezabec lowered his voice to a confidential tone. "They say you slept with him—and I *didn't* get that from your story."

"Well, I'm sure *they* would know. Did *they* say I enjoyed it?"

Raising his eyebrows, Stanton leaned back in his swivel chair and propped his foot on the empty bottom drawer of his desk which he left open for that purpose. He locked his fingers behind his head and studied his moody co-worker.

"Okay, Loomis, I want you to tell me exactly what this guy's got that I haven't got?"

Looking into Stanton's serious face, Sara smiled crookedly before the smile dissolved into giggling and a shake of her head. He rocked upright in his chair.

"He's about six feet tall, right?" She nodded. "*I'm* about six feet tall. He's got brown hair. I've got brown hair. He's the strong, silent type. I'm pretty strong."

Sara's laughter ruptured through her tightly clasped lips. Several other people looked up. Stanton planted both feet firmly on the floor and leaned forward.

"What the hell is so funny?"

"You are."

"Oh, yeah? Well just wait until I get you alone in the dark. That's when you'll get your full enjoyment out of me, sweet pea."

She continued smiling broadly. "Is that some kind of evil threat?"

He sobered. "I really do want you to tell me about this guy. What makes him so special?"

"I don't know." She sighed and gazed wistfully at a blank wall. "Didn't it bother you that he couldn't talk?"

Sara twittered, the laughter again burbling up in her throat. "I found that refreshing. That, Rezabec, is the main difference between you and Bo. He's quiet and completely unassuming. You ain't either one."

Stanton grimaced and turned back to his own desk, bested, for the moment.

Leaving the building that afternoon, Sara smiled to herself. Stanton talked big but was invigoratingly harmless. His continuous kidding was helping her recover, luring her back to her old officious self. It felt good, being able to laugh out loud again. It had been too long. She had been too glum, had cried too much.

Slowly Sara began to accept what she'd known all along. She was going to be all right; not happy maybe, but all right. Eventually, when Krisp lost interest, got caught up in another case, she would begin her own search for Bo. She would start with military hospitals, inquiring about soldiers with vocal chord injuries or diseases, men discharged from active duty two or three years ago but who might be receiving follow-up treatment.

She would talk to Mrs. Johnson, find out the name of Bo's hot tamale, his Mexican girlfriend, see if the girl knew where he had come from or where he might have gone.

Originally, Sara had forgotten to mention the girl to Krisp. Apparently the Johnsons hadn't said anything about the hot tamale either.

Sara even prepared herself for the possibility she might find Bo with his girlfriend. If so, she could console herself that if he were happy without her, she could pursue her own happiness. Her fingers traced the shape of the hickory ring concealed beneath her sweater. Until then, she felt bound by a peculiar loyalty, like someone might feel toward a mate, she supposed.

But Bo wasn't her mate. They had taken no vows. She fingered the hand-carved hickory ring dangling from the chain around her neck. Neither had she mentioned the ring to Krisp or anyone else. She had replaced the strip of nightshirt with a thin gold chain from a piece of costume jewelry. She never removed the ring, although she was careful to keep it hidden.

* * * *

"Want to catch a burger and a movie?" Stanton whispered the Friday afternoon before Christmas. "My treat."

Cutting her eyes from the monitor, Sara flashed him a teasing smile. "And people say you're as tight as two coats of paint."

"Well, I didn't think you'd want to go if you had to buy, but I'm easy."

Sara looked hard at him a moment, then shrugged and smiled. "Why not? I've got no place to be. My Christmas shopping's done with nearly a week to spare."

"What'd you get me?" He raised and lowered his eyebrows.

"I'm going to let you feed me and treat me to a picture show. That's my Christmas gift to you, Rezabec."

Pretending to be offended, he glanced at Crownover, who was laughing behind the afternoon paper, then at Libby, and around the office to the faces of other staff members at other desks, all of whom, as if on cue, threw newspapers in front of their faces to hide their reactions.

"What's this, a put-up job? You told them, didn't you? You knew I'd ask. You told them you were going to say yes this time. And they all knew it but me." He pretended to be piqued. "It's a damned conspiracy. No wonder I'm paranoid."

Sara grimaced. "Does that mean you're canceling? And I was really looking forward to going out with you."

He sobered quickly. "No, ma'am, it does *not* mean anything of the kind. You said you'd go. They all heard you. That makes it a legitimate date." His chest swelled, and he stood, and strutted several steps.

"Persistence pays, little people," he admonished the room at large. "Do what I do. Dare to tread where I tread and you, too, will succeed at every significant endeavor."

Sporadic boos, hisses, and hoots filled the newsroom. Sara laughed out loud at Stanton's boasts. He leaned close to her ear. "I'll pick you up at seven."

"Do you know where I live?"

"Yes, I do-do."

She giggled again. "I hope you can calm down a little by then."

"Question is, can you get a little more excited about it by then. This is a date, doll. Get ready to be swept right off your size sevens."

Sara coughed and laughed at the same time. "I think it's your shy, backwoods manner that wows me, Rezabec."

"Well, I knew something about me would get to you sooner or later." He arched his eyebrows like the villain in a melodrama, "Just as I will make you mad about me sooner or later, my innocent pet."

Sara's amusement ebbed to an uncertain smile.

Seeing the change, Stanton became serious.

"Don't worry, Sara. I'm all bark and no bite. We'll have a blast. You won't be arm wrestling for your virtue this night." He raised his voice to make it easily audible around the room, "Unless you come on too strong and force me to defend myself. I don't want any of these fine people to think I can't handle a wildcat like you."

Sara's languid smile freshened and she nodded. "See you at seven."

* * * *

Stanton was on time, clean shaven, and wearing a seductive cologne. He wore his age well at night, suave, debonair, more Cary Grant than his daytime Jim Carrey.

Sara gave him an easy smile. "You smell marvelous." She beckoned him into the apartment and got her coat. "Where are we going?"

"To Chez Vernon, where they know me and treat me nice, and on to the Rhinestone Cowboy for a romp around the dance floor. Do you have a VCR?"

She nodded and handed him her coat. Smiling, he held it for her. "Then back here for 'Miracle on Thirty-fourth Street.' It always makes me cry. I want to show you my feminine side, the tender shy me I keep hidden beneath this garish facade."

"The shy you is really well concealed, you know." She turned on another lamp. He flinched at the additional brightness and she smiled. "Forewarned is forearmed."

Stanton received celebrity treatment at Chez Vernon and proved to be an able two-stepper at Cowboys. They got back to her place at ten-twenty. Sara stopped him at the door and glanced at her watch. "It's too late to start a movie now, don't you think?"

"Late, hell, woman, it's the shank of the evening. It's nine hours until sunrise. You can rest when you're old."

Smiling, Sara relented.

He set up the VCR while she warmed hot buttered rum for two. He pressed the play button as she eased onto the sofa beside him, allowing enough room for another person between them.

"Do you still miss him that much?" he asked, lowering the volume on the movie.

She thought about asking who he was talking about but she figured they both knew. "Yes."

"Call him."

She smiled bravely. "He doesn't have a phone."

"Go to him."

"I don't know where he is."

"Hasn't he contacted you?"

"No."

"Will he?"

"It doesn't look like it."

Stanton put his empty cup on the coffee table, shifted closer, and put his arm on the back of the sofa behind her. "Will I do? Pinch hit until he shows?"

She smiled. "You'll do fine."

"What do you mean?" The question had a note of urgency. "As a lover or a friend?"

"For which position are you applying?"

"Which one's open?"

"Right now, until we get through the holidays, I need Christmas cheer. You're the best guy around for stimulating laughs."

"I can stimulate a hell of a lot more than that."

"Just for now."

"And later?"

Her smile faded and she regarded him soberly. "If or when that time comes, I might need..."

"Help? What kind of help? Financial, psychological, what?"

She grinned sheepishly and looked at the floor, reluctant to pursue this.

"Come on, what kind of help do you think you'll need? I'm

available, yard work, painting, what?"

"Bo helped me, well, he helped me..." She stalled out. "Maybe we can talk about it another time."

Stanton eyed her seriously. "Sexually."

The word was not a question but a statement. Sara felt guilty. "Bo took things slowly. He seemed to know the right buttons to push and when to push them."

A rolling chuckle bubbled from Stanton's throat. "Like I said, I'm available. I'm a quick study. I work cheap. And," he lowered his voice suggestively, "with me, the customer's satisfaction is guar-an-teed. Can't beat a deal like that. I can start whenever you're ready. Just say go."

It was Sara's turn to laugh and she looked at him with new appreciation. "Thanks, I'll let you know."

They chatted along, commenting through the film. Eventually he held her hand. She started to object then didn't. He didn't press for more.

"I love a happy ending." Stanton stared at the TV as credits blipped over the screen.

"Me, too."

He settled a hand on her shoulder. "Maybe we'll have one of our own."

She shifted position, moving just beyond his reach. "Rezabec, how old are you?"

"Why? Does it matter?"

"I guess not. You've been married, haven't you?"

"Not so's you could tell."

"It didn't work out?"

He pretended to scowl. "*She* didn't work out. I was perfect."

"Of course."

He stood, picked up his overcoat, which was tossed on a chair at the dining table, and strode slowly to the door. Sara followed.

"I had a really good time, Rezabec. It was a great evening."

"I figured you'd say that, once I got you alone."

She laughed lightly.

At the door, he turned and leaned toward her, his arms at his sides. He touched his lips to hers. It was a quick, innocent kiss. Looking smug and satisfied for the moment with that, he swung around and opened the door before he allowed his eyes to rest on her again.

"Took me a hell of a long time to get you to the bargaining table. .I don't want to overwhelm you right off with my superior technique."

She nodded shyly, running the fingers of her hands between one another. "I appreciate your making it easy."

"Just keep that in mind later, when we get down to..."

She flashed him a warning look. He winced and swallowed his next word, obviously changing his mind. "...to knocking heads. That's all I was going to say."

"Right."

Chapter Twenty

Sara and Stanton went out for dinner again Saturday night. At her apartment door, he suggested he come in for coffee but she put him off.

They attended a pops concert at the college Sunday afternoon and went to the office Christmas party Tuesday evening where people twittered and raised their eyebrows, obviously discussing the twosome.

His good night kisses at the door grew more intense and Stanton seemed particularly piqued when Sara didn't invite him in after the office party.

"Attentive but not pushy," was the way Sara described his behavior when she spoke about him to Libby, who quizzed her nightly.

"Doesn't it hurt your feelings for him not to come on with you a little stronger?" Libby asked, obviously puzzled by Sara's reticence.

Sara eyed her new friend and confidante. Libby was younger than Sara. Only two years out of college, she was probably twenty-four, Sara guessed. Libby was short, on the pudgy side, blonde with bright blue eyes, and a cherubic grin which generally elicited responsive smiles.

"No. His approach is just fine. It makes it easy to hang out with him, knowing he's not in a big hurry to hop into my bed."

Libby wrinkled her nose and gave Sara a sidelong look. "Oh, yeah, well that's not how he got his reputation. Mr. Rezabec has left broken hearts in his wake all over the great southwest. Just watch out, sweetie. We don't want yours to be one of them."

Sara smiled knowingly. "I don't see that happening. I'm holding out for someone special."

"Like *Bo?*" Libby wrinkled her nose again, this time to display her distaste.

Sara smiled a secretive little smile. "Like I told Stanton, Bo knew the right buttons to push. Don't knock it 'til you've tried it. Meanwhile, what's going on with you? Who's the man of the moment?"

"What makes you think there is one?"

"Libby, you change men when the Emporium announces its flavor of the week."

It was Libby's turn to flash a secretive smile. "Not this week. A new

213

hunk's in town and I am into week three for this sweet baboo."

Sara chuckled. "Oh, yeah? Where'd you find him?"

"Right here in our own building. Moved in two weeks ago yesterday. Right next door to me, in two-twelve, the apartment you snubbed. Thank heaven." Libby stood and twirled in the middle of the room. "Sara, he is gorgeous. His eyes are so dark, you feel like you're looking into midnight. Those eyes are wicked. He's real tall and built like the proverbial brick outhouse."

Eying Libby's five-foot stature, Sara sputtered. "Libby, everybody's tall to you. Where's he taken you? Why didn't you bring him to the office party?"

Libby shook her head, her puzzled expression matching Sara's. "He's shy." She raised her eyebrows up and down for emphasis. "I think he's a sleeper, laying behind a log, waiting to jump my bones."

"What's he waiting for?"

"I'm not sure. I met him in the laundry room. He asked me a lot of stuff about myself. I even told him a little about you. Not too much, you know. This is *my* find.

"I took him chicken enchiladas Saturday. Wanted to get inside his place, check him out. He does *not* have one female's picture in his whole apartment. Not even his mother's. Is that good news?"

Sara laughed lightly and went to the kitchen to heat some water for tea. "Sounds like it is. You don't think he might be in the closet, do you?"

"No, he is definitely hetero."

"Maybe he's on the rebound."

Libby rubbed her hands together and grinned suggestively. "That's the way I like 'em best. Injured." She slurred the word for emphasis then dropped her voice to a whine. "Looking for comfort? I provide a great shoulder-to-cry-on."

"Is he buying it?"

"Not yet, but he is very mannerly, very appreciative, said he'd return my dish in a day or two."

"But he didn't come on with you?"

Libby looked puzzled. "Nah. That was a shocker."

Sara nodded her understanding. "Most guys do hustle you, don't they?"

"Me? In a man's apartment, alone, practically salivating? Indeed they do." Libby screwed up her face, obviously baffled. "But he made it clear he wasn't ready—yet. Did I tell you he's tall? And he has this Greek god's bod." She shrugged. "I think I may have mentioned that."

Sara nodded as Libby bopped into the kitchen and leaned on her elbows to watch Sara dunk tea bags in both cups at once.

"Okay," Libby sniffed at the tea, "so maybe he's not into small, blonde, angelic types, but I'm not worried. He'll learn. Especially with me right next door to run off any predatory females who might try to stalk him." Libby paced back into the living room, still talking. "Sara, I cannot describe what those eyes do to me. Chills race little fingers up and down my spine. Oh, lord, it's like he's looking right through my clothes." She sighed. "I promise you, x-ray vision isn't necessary. I'd have taken my clothes off for him in a heartbeat. But," she collapsed onto the sofa and slouched against the pillow back, "he didn't make a move. Didn't even say anything suggestive. I'd have given ten bucks for one slightly off-color joke."

Sara allowed a cautious laugh as she stirred sugar into both cups. "Do you always take your welcome-to-the-neighborhood offerings in a returnable container?"

"When it's a guy as good looking as this one? Damn straight. It gives them a legitimate excuse to see me again; convenient for them if they need one, and for me, if they don't. Slick, huh?

"Also, taking these guys supper makes them feel obligated. Usually they don't cook so they ask me out for dinner instead. As you can see, it's a well-thought-out routine."

Sara poured cream in both cups, stirred them, and carried one to Libby before stepping out of her shoes and nudging them under her chair. Curling her legs under her, she settled, balancing her cup. "What's this guy's name?"

Libby gazed at the ceiling and pretended a swoon. "Alex. Isn't that just the most perfect name you ever heard? Alex Cadence. Can't you just hear it, Mrs. Alex Cadence. Elizabeth Cadence. Sound sophisticated? Or simply Libby Cadence to my friends. What a name. What a man."

Suddenly Libby's face darkened and she turned to face Sara squarely. "Sara, I don't like having to say this to you, in your weakened/just-recovering condition and all, but keep your mitts off this guy. You're on the rebound too, and he's terribly, terribly attractive. If he speaks to you in the hall, in the parking lot, anywhere, pretend you don't hear him. Don't speak to him. Don't smile. He's mine. Do I make myself clear?"

Pretending to be intimidated, Sara opened her eyes wide, adopted a somber tone, and said, "Crystal."

It appeared that the cherubic Libby could be a tigress, and territorial, too. Sara chuckled at the observation.

Libby left early, saying she wanted to get home in case Alex returned the casserole dish or called.

When the phone rang a short while later, Sara grinned thinking it was Libby calling to gloat about her ploy working. But it was a man's voice.

"Ms. Loomis?"

"Yes."

"I don't know if you'll remember me. This is Kevin Larchmont."

It took her a minute. "*Agent* Larchmont. Sure I remember you. How are you?"

"Fine, thanks. Listen, I wanted to ask, well..."

"Is this information you need for Agent Krisp?"

"No, ma'am, it's not."

"Have you found Bo?"

"No, ma'am, we haven't."

She hesitated. Obviously not able to guess correctly the reason for his call, she would wait for him to tell her.

"Ms. Loomis?"

"Yes." They seemed to be starting this conversation from the beginning again.

"Well, ma'am, I wondered if you might consider..." he hesitated, then finished the sentence in a rush, "would you consider going out with me sometime? On a date?"

It was Sara's turn to hesitate, dumbfounded. She didn't want to react too quickly. Meanwhile, he continued. "You see I had to wait until we got the all-clear on you, but I've been thinking about you a lot and wondering how you were doing. You seemed like a sensitive kind of lady and one I'd like to get to know. I thought if you could see your way clear..."

An easy lay? Was that what he was thinking? He'd heard the details of her relationship with Bo. And he knew Bo wasn't her first.

"Thank you, Mr. Larchmont," she interrupted. He seemed so ill-at-ease, she wanted to let him off the hook. "That's a very nice gesture, not to mention awfully good public relations for the bureau..."

"Oh, no, Ms. Loomis, this has nothing to do with work or anything. This is strictly personal."

She cleared her throat, another stall. She had questions she'd like to ask young Agent Larchmont. His interest might make that easy. "Well, sure, then, I'd be glad to go out with you sometime. I'm going to my parents' for Christmas but I'll be back Saturday."

"How about Saturday night?"

Sara thought about Stanton Rezabec. She didn't want to hurt his feelings, but he would understand. Larchmont wasn't a real date. He was more of a business opportunity.

"Okay. What should I wear?"

"Nothing... Oh, I didn't mean 'nothing,' I meant you didn't have to get real dressed up or anything. What I meant to say was *nothing special*. We'll just take in a movie or something. Or we can have dinner, if you'd rather. Or both. Both would be perfectly fine with me. Well, anyway, what do you think you'd like to do?"

"A movie's good."

"What time?"

"Say seven-ish."

"Great!"

"I'll look forward to it, Mr..."

"Call me Kevin. I'll be off duty. No more Ms. Loomis and Agent Larchmont. We'll just be Sara and Kevin. Sounds good, doesn't it?"

"Yes, it certainly does. Kevin, you're asking me out, well, does this mean Krisp has finished his investigation?"

He paused a moment, maybe a moment too long. "Yes. You are correct about that." Then he lowered his voice. "He's prepping the case we've got on the Kindlings. The D.A.'s filing state charges against them, too."

"Has Krisp given up on finding Bo What's-his-name?"

Kevin's voice rose to normal volume as he answered. "That's correct."

"Are you at the office?"

"Affirmative."

"Are there other people listening?"

"That is correct."

"Isn't it kind of late for everyone to be working?"

"Yes, it is."

She hesitated. "I'll see you Saturday night for a movie, a regular date. And thanks, Kevin, for calling."

"You're welcome. And thank you."

Sara paced her living room, to the window overlooking the street and back. What was going on? Something. Had Larchmont been assigned to keep an eye on her, unofficially? A possibility. Krisp was pretty cagey. She'd been patient this long. She'd wait a little longer. No point in leading them straight to Bo, assuming she could find him.

* * * *

"What have we got on this weekend?" Rezabec asked Wednesday morning, Christmas Eve, as he strutted to his desk in the cubicle he and Sara shared. "I've gotta escort our congresswoman to this political bash Friday but I'll be free Saturday night and ready to yowl."

Sara turned away from her monitor, surprised. "Oh, Stanton," she began, genuinely disappointed, "this FBI guy asked me to go to the show Saturday night. I think he's probably supposed to keep me under surveillance, on the q.t. I tried to make it easy for him. He doesn't act like he gets out much. I figured you wouldn't mind."

Rezabec's face clouded. "What are you saying?"

She started to laugh, thinking his exaggerated show of disappointment was a ruse, and spun her chair around. She realized, almost too late, that he was serious and she sobered. "Stanton, this is no big deal. I'm going out with this FBI guy, Larchmont, Saturday night."

"The hell you say. Listen, honey, I've got a fair chunk of change in you now. I'm about ready to draw a little return on my investment."

Sara froze, trying to get a better read of Rezabec's face.

"Investment? You've been priming me? What for?"

"What for? Don't give me that innocent little look. I've spent four hundred and seventy-eight bucks on you in the last ten days. Why do you think I've done that?"

She felt anger ooze through her. "Got that all jotted down in a ledger somewhere, have you?"

He frowned. "I'm a good steward of my bounty. That's Bible. I don't squander my hard-earned moolah."

"No. You invest in futures that look promising, then wait for the profits to come rolling in—or maybe I should say *rolling over*—is that right?"

"Well, I might not have put it quite that crudely."

"Oh, yeah? How would you have put it?"

He began back-pedaling, obviously her responses were prompting a change of attitude. "Like any prudent investor, I expect a return, even if it's only a modest one."

She glared at him, nodding. "And now and then you make a killing?"

His grin was uncertain. "Now and then."

"And you thought I was going to roll over for you pretty soon now, right?"

"Well, we get along. You need someone. I'm someone."

"Forget it, Rezabec. You're no one."

Stanton frowned, obviously in the throes of a change of heart. "Now hold on, Sara. We're just having a conversation here. We're not setting precedents or making policy. We're just talking."

"No, Stanton, we're drawing lines in the sand. Now, you stay on your side and I'll keep to mine."

"That's not what I meant and you know it."

"You take this like a man, Rezabec, and I'll see that you recover part of your investment, so you'll have some operating capital for new speculations."

"Honey, forget the cracks about the money."

"Oh," she tried to sound surprised, "I wasn't going to pay for *your* meals and show tickets. You don't get the whole four hundred and seventy-eight bucks out of me. Only my half. I'll pay you back two hundred thirty-nine dollars. You'll just have to chin your half. Chalk it up to experience. I know I'm going to."

"Sara, be reasonable. I was only joking. I wouldn't think of letting you pay me back half."

"Half is a reasonable as I get, Stan. You'll have to sue me to get the rest."

"Sue you? Come on, Loomis. Be fair. You're trying to misunderstand this whole conversation. Come on. We've come a long way, baby."

"But this is as far as I go, bucko. You'll have to tag all the bases and score your home run with someone else."

Stanton pursed his lips, then clamped them between his teeth before he slammed his computer to shut down, and stormed out of the newsroom, oblivious to the curious eyes monitoring his departure.

Sara took a deep breath, shook her head, and shuddered.

* * * *

Kevin Larchmont was on time, his hair meticulously combed, his clothes immaculately coordinated, his shoes polished to a high sheen.

"Hey, Kevin," Sara greeted. "I'm almost ready. What show did you want to see?"

He cleared his throat. "I wasn't exactly sure."

She hesitated, then smoothly motioned him toward the sofa, grabbed the newspaper from the coffee table, folded it to the entertainment section, and handed it to him. "Let me fix you something to drink."

He grimaced. "I'm allergic to alcohol."

"How about a cola? Regular? Diet? Or I've got tea or lemonade that will just take a minute."

"No, thanks." He buried his head in the paper.

They discussed, then settled on a movie but the next feature started at eight forty-five. Their decision was followed by an awkward silence.

"How late's the library open?" Sara ventured.

"Closes at four on Saturdays."

"I knew you'd know."

"Are you hungry?" he asked.

"A little. I didn't have time for supper."

"Where do you want to go?" His question was tentative and, after

220

bickering with Rezabec over his financial investment in their dates, Sara was reluctant to suggest any place.

"How about a homemade BLT, that's bacon, lettuce, and tomato." Kevin brightened. "Good idea. Where can we get one?"

He seemed a little slow on the uptake. "Right here. I'll make them and we can talk without getting interrupted."

Before the sandwiches were ready, Sara had coaxed Kevin out of his blazer and made lemonade, in spite of his objections that it was too much trouble.

As they munched side-by-side at the bar between her kitchen and dining area, Sara approached the subject that haunted her night and day—Bo.

"Kevin, what did you think of that creep Franklin when you first met him?"

"You mean when we arrested him?" The bacon crunched as he bit carefully into his sandwich.

"No, when he took you guys on the wild goose chase down the river." She wanted verification that Franklin had been the FBI's guide.

Kevin shook his head and dabbed his mouth with his napkin. "He was a jerk. That's what we all thought. First he told us he'd never laid eyes on you, then Krisp got to working on him and he let something slip about you wearing funny shoes." He took a drink of lemonade and wiped his mouth again.

"He weaseled around but couldn't squirm out of it. Then he tried to tell us he was a poor unwilling participant in the robbery, that the other guys forced him to go along to help 'em. Off by ourselves, we got a hoot out of that.

"Later he told one of our guys you'd come on to him, begged him to...ah...well, to have sex with you. Of course, none of us had met you, but we had your picture. There was no way a girl like you'd be hustling something like him." He inhaled another bite of sandwich while she nibbled a potato chip.

"But when he told you Bo had kidnapped me, you believed him."

"Some did, but not Krisp. No, Krisp had Franklin and this whole thing nailed from the start. Krisp is a very cool guy. Very slick. On those interviews? He went really easy with you compared to the way he worked Franklin over."

She attempted a smile. "Of course, Franklin was probably a suspect and I wasn't, right?"

"Sure, that's why he interviewed you in the motel, with your folks there and all, making you as comfortable as he could, after what you'd been through."

"I wondered about that." She paused. "Anyway, go on."

"Well, what we finally pieced together, from Franklin's lies mixed with a little truth, was pretty much the story you told, especially about how Franklin happened to lose parts of his fingers. Of course, he said Bo tied him down and whacked 'em off, but other people had better opinions of Bo than that. And they thought a whole lot less of Franklin than he thinks of himself." Swinging his long legs, Larchmont swiveled his barstool to look at Sara.

"Let me ask you one thing. When Franklin showed up and took you out of the shed, did you go with him voluntarily?"

Sara toyed with her half-eaten sandwich. "That was the stupidest thing I did, and it was almost fatal. If it hadn't been for Bo..."

"Is that why you slept with him, out of appreciation, like Krisp said?"

"No."

"That's what Krisp thinks."

"I know."

Kevin frowned. "Krisp really likes you. When he likes a person, he likes them to have lofty reasons for doing things he doesn't think they should have done. Of course, what really bothered him is you not calling someone as soon as Bo let you off at that country bus stop."

Sara nodded. "He guessed right. I wanted to give Bo a chance to get away. I didn't tell Krisp, but I'd asked Bo to take me with him. He wouldn't do it. I was upset. Plus, I had no idea where I was. I had to try to get my head on straight before I faced my parents, much less any law enforcement people."

"Do you know now where you were?"

"No."

"I could take you back there, if you want to go."

"No thanks. There's nothing there I want to see."

"Have you heard from him?"

The question was innocent enough, but her chest ached with the pain of loss as she framed her answer. She raised her eyes to look squarely into his. "No, I haven't."

"Sara," Larchmont's voice was quiet, "how do you feel about Bo now?"

She didn't want Kevin or anyone else to see how deep her feelings ran. She answered cautiously. "I'd like to see him again, but I might not recognize him shaved, in regular clothes." That was enough. "Kevin, I honestly don't expect him to look me up. If he wanted to see me, I think he'd have made a move by now, don't you?"

His eyes swept her as he grimaced, then shrugged.

"I hate to admit it," she continued, feeling the familiar sting behind her eyes, "but Krisp could be right about Bo. I was there, available, too easy to pass up."

Kevin drew a deep breath, dabbed at his mouth with his napkin again, and leaned back in the bar chair. "You really didn't think about getting a tag number then, off the motorcycle, I mean?"

"No, and I wish I had." That wasn't exactly true. "My story would be stronger if Bo were found, don't you think?"

Kevin grinned, his face awash with relief.

After the show, they went for ice cream and a ride, cruising Main like teenagers.

At the door Kevin asked if he could kiss her good night. She offered him her cheek. The kiss was tepid. There was no tingle.

* * * *

"Have a good time with the FBI?" Libby asked Sara as they sipped their tea Sunday night.

"It was okay."

"Not as much fun as Rezabec?"

"No, but definitely less challenging. How're you coming with the guy in two-twelve?"

Libby's expression darkened to a scowl. "Slow."

"Well, my money's on you. Like the FBI, you always get your man."

Libby's sudden musical giggle prodded Sara to continue.

"Persist, persist, persist. And you don't give up, either."

Libby sobered again. "Give up? You jest. Obviously you haven't

223

seen Alex Cadence. He is absolutely the finest cut of beefcake I have ever met." Libby's eyes narrowed. "I will have him, one way or the other."

Laughing at her diminutive friend's determination, Sara sipped some tea. "Maybe you can skulk around, catch him some dark night in a weakened condition."

"No, no, I'm not talking one night here. I want this one for keeps."

Staring, Sara put down her cup. "Are you seriously talking about the Big M here, girl? You've seen this guy in the hall a couple of times and you're thinking marriage?"

"Sara, you haven't looked into those eyes or been caressed by that sexy croon." Suddenly Libby straightened and her voice dropped to a threatening tone. "You haven't, have you?"

Sara giggled. "I wouldn't dare. You'd never let an amateur hustle your man out from under your nose. I wouldn't try to get by you, Eagle Eye. No, I haven't seen him."

Libby put her cup down and leaped to her feet. "I've gotta go."

"You're pretty sure he'll call?"

"Hope so, but I need to get some sack time. I'm covering the Business and Professional Women's breakfast at seven in the a.m."

Libby ambled toward the door. "I'm not kidding, Sara, Of course, an overnight with him would be a memory to carry the rest of your life, one you could take out and relive again and again. He is magnificent."

Standing, a drop of tea dripped from Sara's lip to her chest. She brushed it with her fingers and laughed. "Look, you've got me drooling. I've gotta have a peek at this guy. I can honestly say I've never seen anyone this good."

"No, no, no." Libby stopped to confront her. "I thought I'd made myself excruciatingly clear about that."

"Well, can I at least sneak a peek?"

Libby rubbed her chin, pretending to consider the request. "I guess that'd be all right, but don't get close. He wears a very unusual musk which boggles the mind. Just thinking of it gets me all hot and bothered."

"You sound like you're seeing him pretty regularly."

"The garbage drop, the mail box, close encounters of the casual kind."

"Okay, so he hasn't asked you out. Why haven't you asked him?"

Libby pivoted on one foot. "I've tried everything I can think of, invited him for supper, plied him with free passes to a basketball game. He's real polite when he turns me down, but he just keeps turning me down."

"Does he say why?"

Libby gave a thoughtful pout. "No. He just says 'No thanks.' I tried to pry reasons out of him, in my own charming, inimitable way, but he won't budge. Something better break soon or I'll be looking to Stanton for consolation. Rezabec's always good for a morale-boosting overnight."

Sara frowned, sobering as they reached the door. "Libby, I didn't know you'd dated Rezabec."

"That's the kind of thing a girl likes to keep quiet, especially around the office."

"You never mentioned keeping it hush-hush when I was going out with him."

Libby shrugged. "That's because you didn't have to worry about your reputation. After living with the crazy mountain man, you didn't have any reputation left to sully."

"Thanks a lot."

Libby looked up, all innocence. "Well, surely you knew what people were saying."

"No," Sara said, "I didn't."

Chapter Twenty-one

On Monday morning Sara's car engine wouldn't turn over, much less fire. The weather was sunny but the brightness was a decoy, luring people out into a stiff north wind with temperatures wavering up during moments of intermittent sunlight, plunging to single digits when clouds rolled through.

Grudgingly she got out of the car, walked to the front, and raised the hood. She had no idea what to look for, a wire hanging loose, a lid unscrewed, something. Nothing seemed out of place. In fact, the whole area looked spectacularly clean, for a car engine.

She was about to close the hood when a shadow loomed beside her. "Need some help?" The male voice was a rich baritone.

His back was to the sun, blindingly bright as it broke between clouds, framing him in silhouette. He was tall, apparently hatless, wore sunglasses, and was bundled in a cashmere overcoat and kid gloves.

She frowned, directing his attention to the area under the hood. "Do you know anything about engines?"

"No," he said. "Sorry. Can I call someone for you?"

She bit her bottom lip and shook her head. She needed to hurry. It was a quarter of eight. "No thanks."

She glanced around to see if Libby's car was still in the lot. Gone. The BPW breakfast. Darn. She slammed the hood wondering about a city bus.

"How can I help?" the stranger prodded, reminding her he was still there.

She looked at him again, but couldn't see his face clearly with the dazzling sunlight still at his back. He motioned toward a sports utility vehicle parked on the street. "Can I give you a lift?"

She fidgeted and thought out loud. "I can call someone, but waiting'll make me late to work." She peered up at him again. "Which way are you going?"

"I have to stop by the *Gazette*, then I'm going out to the college, but I'm not on any schedule. I can take you wherever you need to go."

Trying to make out his face, she took a couple of quick side steps to get a clearer view.

He seemed vaguely familiar, somber, handsome in a rugged way, maybe thirty, six-foot or better, clean-cut with dark, close-cropped hair, and a generous mouth which sported a pleasant little smirk of a smile that didn't show his teeth. She smiled back and was surprised to feel her pulse quicken.

"I'm Sara Loomis, courthouse reporter for the *Gazette*."

"Alex Cadence."

Where had she heard that name? Oh...sure...Libby's guy. The untouchable. "Oh, you're..." She swallowed the words she had nearly blurted, recovering just in time. "You're new at The Oaks. West wing, right?"

"Right. Two-twelve. You're upstairs, in three-twenty. I've seen you around."

Surprised, she started to ask, then realized Libby had probably mentioned her apartment number. She said, "Libby Cook's a friend of mine."

He raised a gloved hand to rub his mouth as if he were smothering a laugh. "Mine, too."

"And you're going to the *Gazette*?" she asked. He answered with a nod that made the hair bristle on the back of her neck. "Good. Yes, I'll take you up on that ride."

He turned and she trailed him across the street to the SUV parked at the curb. Leaning in the passenger door, he cleared books and loose papers, tossing them into the rear seat, then stepped back and indicated she could get in.

"Why are you going to the newspaper office?" she asked, as he pulled into the traffic lane.

"I'm new at the college. History department. The dean asked me to drop off a news release and a mug shot. I guess they run articles on new faculty people."

Sara glanced at his profile, then couldn't pry her eyes from the high forehead and hawkish nose, the strong jaw line and pronounced chin. He actually did resemble some Greek god. She chided herself for thinking like a school girl...or like Libby...and smiled at the thought. "What kind of history?"

"Military mostly. Some American."

She would bet an inordinate number of women would be taking military history classes this fall, once word got around. And she'd bet a week's salary, word about him spread among the coeds on campus in a hurry.

He stopped for a traffic light and turned toward her. She wished he'd remove those darn sunglasses. She would like to see his fabled eyes. But the morning glare was too strong to suggest he take them off.

As they drove, she pointed out the coffee shop downtown where political types gathered mid morning; the second story club where jazz jam sessions were free on week nights, and Bloomers, a strip joint that invited college girls for amateur night once a month.

He chuckled, rubbing a hand over his mouth before he looked the other way. "Sounds like you're well settled. Been here long enough to know where the action is."

Something about the gesture and the statement made her uneasy, as if he knew she hadn't been in town long. How would he know that?

She winced as she solved the mystery. Libby again. Of course She'd have to speak to Libby. It was not a good idea to hustle a man by telling him too much about your girlfriends.

He shot her a cursory glance. "I was going to stop for coffee and a breakfast biscuit. Do you have time or should I wait until after I drop you?"

"No, please, I'd love a cup of coffee."

"No biscuit?"

"No, thanks. I don't get ready for food until mid-morning or so."

"Do you get to eat breakfast late?"

She laughed. "No, I just get hungry and wish I could. I assure you, no one who knows about my breakfast fetish offers to buy my lunch."

He turned his head to laugh, a rolling, infectious sound. She smiled and stretched. The car was warm, the traffic not too heavy, and he, an easy companion. She had a peculiar feeling of well-being.

He pulled into the drive-through at McDonald's near the shopping center and ordered a breakfast biscuit, one milk and two coffees with extra cream and sugar.

They got the coffee first, small ones. Still wearing the gloves, he juggled her cup and the handful of cream and sugar packets.

"Do you want some of these?" she asked, sorting them.

"No, I take mine black."

She scrutinized him suspiciously. "Why did you get extra cream and sugar?"

He looked surprised. "Didn't you tell me to?"

"No. You didn't ask."

He shrugged, regarding her soberly through the glasses. "Well, I guess you just look like a woman who takes extra cream and sugar."

"Thanks a lot."

When the clerk handed the sack through the window, Alex pulled the car over and parked long enough to bolt the biscuit in four quick bites.

Sara watched in awe. "Is one enough for you?"

He smiled self-consciously, again turning his head away from her. "I was holding back. Didn't want you to think I was a glutton."

She dumped three sugars and two creams into the coffee and stirred, reluctant to meet his gaze which she felt suddenly focused on her. With her silence, she defied him to comment on being right about the cream and sugar.

Who was this guy? Another FBI agent? No. He was too flashy for a G-man. Not really stodgy enough for a college professor either...yet.

He was maneuvering through traffic again before she allowed herself another look. Libby was right. This guy was a hunk in anyone's dictionary. She needed to stop admiring him. She'd promised Libby. Hands off. He was reserved. Libby had warned her not to smile or say hello. She was probably going to be in big trouble for riding downtown with him.

"You can pull around to the lot and we'll go though the back," she suggested when they neared the *Gazette*. "Rumors that you can find parking on the street are a cruel hoax."

Smirking, he followed her directions. She wondered why he kept squelching his smile. Maybe something was wrong with his teeth. Libby hadn't mentioned it...or any other flaw, for that matter.

Sara got out of the car and waited for him to sort through some of the displaced papers in the back seat before he turned up a file folder.

They walked to the building side by side in silence. He was a big one, all right, but Sara felt comfortable in his company, even without the cover of running dialogue.

When he stepped up to open the door, she felt an involuntary tingle at their proximity. Catching a whiff of his aftershave, she inhaled vigorously.

What was wrong with her? Where did the silly tingling come from? A hand-me-down from Libby? Probably.

Inside the building, she led him up the back stairs to the newsroom where she introduced him to Bruce Crownover, the managing editor.

"Sara, Libby was supposed to take Professor Cadence's information," Crownover said, "but she's out. Can you do it?"

"Sure."

She offered to take his coat but Alex declined. The lenses in his sunglasses were becoming lighter. She hoped they'd clear enough eventually to allow her a good look at the eyes Libby had made off limits.

He removed his overcoat but kept it, folding it over his arm. She motioned him into a side chair by her desk.

Sara hung her coat on the rack on the other side of the newsroom, jamming her gloves and cap in the pockets, then darted to the break room for two normal size cups of coffee.

"All right, let me see the press release." She took it and settled into her desk chair, swiveled to face him, opened a notebook, and grabbed a ballpoint.

Cadence stood and moved his chair from the side of the desk to spot it squarely front of her so that they were face to face, their knees almost touching. Again Sara found their proximity disconcerting as his lenses continued to clear. His dark eyes looked even more familiar as they became more visible.

He handed her the sheet of paper. "Public relations did it from my resume. There's a mug shot, too, of course, which is preferable to the picture on my driver's license, but not nearly as fetching as ones my mother has lining a hallway back home."

Was he flirting with her? Sara smiled politely without looking up, trying to concentrate on the release. She needed to keep this interview strictly business, in spite of the feeling of warmth that seemed to be intensifying. Was he feeling it, too?

"This work history has a thirty-month glitch," she said. "I guess you need to update your resume. Where were you employed immediately before coming here, Mr. Cadence?"

He raised his chin and the polite smile faded. "Research. Working on my dissertation."

"Oh? You already have your master's then?"

"As a matter of fact, I just finished a tome for my Ph.D."

"Oh, yeah?" She peered at him. "What's the title?" She lowered her eyes quickly, focusing on her hieroglyphic-mix shorthand.

"*The Psychological Effects of Deprivation on a Professional Soldier.*"

"And you've finished it?"

"Yes. I took my orals the week after Thanksgiving."

"And?" Again she lifted her gaze to his.

His mouth bowed. "I think *Doctor* Cadence sounds a bit pompous, don't you?"

Sara laughed lightly. "Congratulations. But doesn't a doctorate make you over-qualified for our little two-year community college?"

"Maybe, but the school here's got a solid reputation. Time here will look good on my resume when I'm ready to move."

"But why Booker?"

"Because it's important to me—for personal reasons—to be in Overt right now." He gave her a significant look, as if she should know what he was talking about.

Studying his face, his eyes, his demeanor, Sara felt repeated twinges. Something about Alex Cadence was eerily familiar.

"Something wrong?" he asked.

She shook her head but continued frowning. "Have we met before? Something about you seems awfully familiar."

"Maybe it's my voice. People think I sound like Clint Black or one of those other country and western singers."

Sara's mouth puckered into a rosebud. Alex laughed at the change in her expression, ducking his head and again covering his mouth with a gloved hand.

He certainly seemed self-conscious about his mouth or his teeth or something. Funny, Libby hadn't mentioned any defects.

"No," she said, "that's not it. I'm usually pretty good at accents. You're not from around here, are you?"

"No, I'm Oklahoma born and bred. How about you?" As he asked, he shifted to the front edge of his chair, so close to her that their knees bumped.

She could feel him peering into her face, saw the movement as he rocked forward and put his elbows on his knees before he began removing his gloves, slowly, deliberately.

Feeling his breath, she glanced up. His face was so close that she inched back, stiffening. Why did he seem so familiar? Despite his denial, he seemed to feel it too.

"What exactly do you mean by 'Deprivation'?" she asked.

He smiled into her face, allowing her first glimpse of his perfect teeth. No reason to be self-conscious about those.

Her heart leaped into her throat.

She'd seen those teeth, close up, before.

She knew this guy.

Her mouth tasted tinny and her breathing quickened as his voice droned. "Adjusting to major changes in lifestyle. Doing without everyday comforts. Scratching a living from the land to survive."

Sara struggled to maintain her professional demeanor, to fend off the barrage of breathless memories as she stared at his eyes—twin wells of darkness.

She glanced down and did a double take when she saw his hands, free of the gloves—big hands, but the hair on them was dark, no longer sun-bleached, as she remembered.

Rattled, she frowned, at first scarcely noticing as his hands carefully, almost weightlessly settled on her knees.

He was speaking in low, hypnotic tones, droning on about trapping small animals, killing, and cleaning, and cooking them. His voice resonated, soothing her as she watched his fingers walk down the outsides of her knees and slither beneath to the sensitive, sensuous undersides.

Tears stung and she swiped the back of her hand over her eyes trying to clear them. In spite of her blurred vision, things were suddenly coming clear as a random thought wobbled through her mind: *Bo knows all the right buttons.*

Her own words sauntered dreamily around in her brain while a little, mindless whine escaped from between her own tightly clenched lips.

Stanton Rezabec, bellowing like an injured bull, stormed into the work area he and Sara shared.

"What the hell's going on here?"

Chapter Twenty-two

Sara frowned at Rezabec, but didn't move, not wanting to interrupt the professor's rhythmic words. Cadence straightened in his chair, removing his hands from her knees. He flashed Rezabec a polite dismissive smile, turned his attention back to Sara, and removed his glasses.

Gazing into his eyes, Sara inhaled abruptly, unable to force her attention back to the blustering Rezabec.

Apparently annoyed at Sara's cool reception, Stanton slapped his notebook on his desk and stalked out of the cubicle, his tread audible as he tromped to the break room.

"Dr. Cadence," Sara asked in a hollow voice, "do you have a middle initial?"

His dark eyes shimmered. "B."

"What does the B stand for?"

He grinned broadly, apparently pleased with the question. His eyes didn't release hers. "I was a big baby. A ten pounder. My dad's been in Oklahoma a lot of years, but he hearkens back to his small town Arkansas beginnings. Dad has a favorite term. When he considers something to be outstanding, he calls it *bodacious*.

"Mom wouldn't let it be my first name. It's my second. Officially, my name's Alex B. Cadence. Everyone who knows me well—family, friends, teachers, coaches—call me 'Bo.' Always have."

Sara drew another shivering breath, nodding and staring at him.

There was no disfigurement. His features were strong. Perfect. She had assumed the unruly beard, all that hair, masked scars, imperfections. She'd never even dreamed...

Again aware of Rezabec, Sara noticed that her co-worker had stopped to give Crownover an animated report of something, during which the managing editor glanced toward Sara and the man she was interviewing.

Her breathing became erratic. "Could I see the inside of your right hand?"

Slowly Cadence turned his hand and presented it for her inspection.

There it was. The second lifeline.

"How'd you get that scar?" Her words sounded tactless.

His eyes narrowed, but he continued looking at her, into her, holding her gaze with his own. "I cut it opening a can of beans at scout camp when I was eight."

Sara's eyes brimmed with tears as she recoiled, sitting back in her chair. "Were you a klutzy kid, then?"

"A lot of kids are klutzy when they're eight."

She looked around the room, wild-eyed, feeling suddenly disoriented, biting her lips to hold in the gathering explosion.

"Sara?" Crownover's voice boomed at her shoulder. "Are you all right?"

She bobbed her head up and down, unable to breathe regularly, much less form an appropriate response.

Alex stood. "I don't think she's feeling well." He ignored Rezabec who was again pacing in and out of the cubicle. "Ms. Loomis and I live in the same building. She had car trouble this morning. I gave her a lift to work. I think maybe I'd better take her home."

Crownover nodded. "Yeah, she's flushed. Looks like she might be getting sick. Could be contagious." He grinned and nodded at her. "Probably better get her out of here before she gives me something."

"I'll take her," Rezabec offered too loudly.

Crownover, Cadence, and Sara all chorused, "No."

Alex slipped into his coat as he walked over to retrieve Sara's wrap from the coat rack. He had to pick up a glove and the stocking cap, which dropped from her pocket as he crossed the room. He held her coat as she put her hands into the sleeves, then put an arm around her shoulders to guide her toward the back stairwell.

"Hey!" Crownover called, stopping them at the bottom of the stairs.

Alex turned to look up at him.

"What about this story, the one about your new job?"

"There's no hurry. We've got plenty of time for that. Right now, I think we need to see about getting Sara home to bed."

* * * *

"See about getting Sara home to bed?" Sara repeated as they wound through traffic down the thoroughfare back to The Oaks. "I don't like what you're thinking."

Alex grinned. "I don't think you want to know what I'm thinking, given your condition and all."

"My condition?"

"You know, flushed, feverish, a little unsteady on your feet. Crownover's right. It may be contagious. I'm feeling a little lightheaded myself."

Sara gave him a hard stare. "Is this really you?"

He returned her serious look and gave her one brief, significant nod.

She shuddered. "I didn't recognize your voice, but I'd know that nod anywhere."

He reached for her hand. She pulled it away from him. When he tried again, she allowed her cold hand to be enveloped in his warm one and asked, "How long have you been in Overt?"

"Two or three weeks."

"Why here?"

He looked as if she were kidding. "You know good and well why. It's where you are."

"But you didn't come for me first thing."

"No, I had to lay a little groundwork first, take care of some business."

"More important than finding me?"

He lost the smile. "No. I've known where you were all the time. When I came to stay, you were the reason I took the apartment at The Oaks.

"I spooked around at first, afraid you might recognize me. But you didn't seem to see me or, apparently, any other guys. You obviously were not looking for any action.

"After our paths crossed a couple of times and you acted like I was invisible, I tried to get your attention. Meanwhile, I had to get this job nailed down."

"What business did you have to take care of?"

"Well," he grinned, "I did some shopping, stopped by the courthouse, checked on some things."

"The courthouse? That reminds me, the FBI is still looking for you."

"For whom?"

"For Bo."

"What's the charge?"

She started to speak, then hesitated. "I see what you mean. There's no charge." She gazed out at the traffic. "Alex...Bo? It's strange to talk to you...at least, your talking back is strange." She hesitated, getting her bearings. "Can it ever be the same for us? Can we be those people here?"

He regarded her tenderly. "If we can't, we'll go back there. Those days with you at the cabin got me on track. I'd been free falling for years—no goals, no interest in anything, until you."

He pulled up at a stoplight. "You came waltzing into my life and did a quick spit and polish on my soul. You ignited things in me, feelings other people described that I thought I'd never experience."

He smiled at her as if he were trying to convey meaning and appreciation and more, before he reached for her knee. She shifted to avoid his touch while attempting a smile.

The light changed. He pressed the accelerator and continued talking. "I had to be with you. That need drove me. I finished my dissertation, prepped for orals, and got this job all in less than two months. Thoughts of you propelled me like rocket fuel. I went nearly crazy at first, wanting to see your face, to touch you." He changed to the slow lane, studying her. "But before I could do that, I needed to set things up for us so I could provide a life we could live together."

He pulled into the same parking place he had vacated earlier, got out and hurried around the car to open her door. He paused to rummage through the papers strewn in the back seat until he turned up one he sought, then folded and pocketed it before taking her arm to cross the street.

Sara glanced at her car. "I need to call the service station, get them to come fix my..."

"Battery cable's loose. I'll tighten it. Your car's fine."

Sara stared at him, then stopped to confront him as they stepped onto the opposite curb.

"I staged it," he confessed quietly, grimacing as he looked at her. "I had to...Sara." He hesitated. "Sara," he laughed, repeating her name. "I love your name. Sara." He seemed to drift in and out of memory as he scanned her, tip to toe.

"I had to get back in your life, but I needed to test the water, so I watched you."

He flashed a taunting smile. "I saw you with Rezabec. You were circumspect, curious, cautious. You didn't look all that interested, which was fine with me. Just fine."

She studied him, noting the familiar mannerisms, the way he cocked his head, the way his hands moved, graceful for their size...all confirming that he was who he said he was.

"Anyway," he continued, "right now all you need to decide is, your place or mine?"

"Mine's furnished."

He grinned. "I've got a bed but not much more than that."

Her eyes shot to his face. "I am *not* going to bed with you either place." His laugh stung, and anger snapped inside her like electric sparks. "You think I'm easy, right?"

His rolling chuckle swelled to a loud guffaw as Sara turned and walked briskly through the door into the apartment building, biting her lips, fighting the smile, relieved to know that he was behind her, teasing her, vexing her as he had even as a mute.

Trailing her, his residual laughter dwindled. They both were silent as they by-passed the elevator and trotted up the stairs to the third floor.

Alex took the key from her hand when she was too unsteady to hit the keyhole in two attempts, then it took him another two shots to hit the mark.

He opened the door and mumbled, "...a little nervous."

Inside, Sara felt self-conscious again, as if he were a stranger. "Would you like something to drink?"

"No thanks." He stood quietly, watching her move around the room without taking off her wraps and deliberately avoiding the small hallway to the bedrooms.

"Sara?" He spoke quietly and she whirled to face him. "Would you mind if I took off my coat?" He grinned innocently.

Annoyed with herself, she took his overcoat and hung it in the entry closet, then took hers off and hung it beside his. With exaggerated attention, she brushed a piece of lint from her corduroy skirt.

He slipped a piece of paper from his pocket, unfolded it, produced a pen and eyed the couch. "Come on, sit down a minute, help me fill out this application."

Sara eased onto the couch, settling near but not right beside him. "What's it for?"

He smoothed the creases in the folded page, placing it so she could read the heading. Startled, she turned to stare at his face. "An application for a marriage license? Who's it for?"

He smiled into her eyes without speaking and she dropped her gaze. "Bo...Alex...oh, drat." She shot him another look. "See, it's obvious, we aren't ready for this. I don't even know who you are."

His eyes held hers. "Oh, yes, Sara, you know me. And yes, we are ready for this. Both of us." She stared at him incredulously. "It's the right thing to do, sweetheart. I've loved you all my life, years before I found you tied to the side of my cabin. We have more in common than you can even imagine, and now that I can talk, I can tell you."

She looked at him sharply. "And what about that? What was wrong? Why didn't you talk to me then?"

"I was researching, trying different handicaps. You came along while I was a mute. I'd taken a vow of silence, promised myself not to speak a word for six months. It was very enlightening, especially after you showed up. That was when the deprivation really kicked in.

"I came close to breaking my word because I wanted so badly to say your name. Sara. It's a beautiful name. I'll bet I've said it a thousand times since I left the mountains."

"When did your six months of self-imposed silence end?"

"The day before we went to the Johnsons that last time."

"Why didn't you talk to me then?"

"I didn't want to upset you. Earlier, we communicated just fine without my talking. When things got complicated at the last, I figured my talking might make a tense situation worse."

She grimaced comically. "Are you trying to say I talked enough for both of us?"

He laughed and gave one quick, familiar nod. "You seemed to read my mind, even with most of my face hidden."

"And what about all that hair?"

"If you want to be an outcast, you have to alienate yourself, make yourself so repugnant, nosy neighbors are repulsed or scared of you Hell, I tried to frighten you too. Why do you think I staked you outside

240

that first night? It wasn't stupidity. I wanted to scare you off. But you just kept coming."

"Why didn't you take me to the road that first day like I asked you to?"

"First, because I didn't want Cappy or Franklin getting hold of you again. They would have, if I'd set you down by a road anywhere close. My motorcycle needed work. I was afraid I couldn't take you far enough to keep you out of their hands.

"After I got my machine running right," he looked apologetic, "well, I had been out there a long time and you were so damned pretty..." He let the thought die and swallowed, apparently remembering something else.

"I had all kinds of ulterior motives for keeping you. I liked looking at you. I hadn't realized how lonely I was. You are a beautiful woman, Sara, and I'd been up there two years."

So Krisp had been right—partially. Sara started to interrupt but Bo held up a hand to prevent it.

"Part of your beauty is that you aren't just the usual sexy dolly, posing, letting guys admire her. Your face exposes your every thought. If you're confused, your forehead wrinkles and you squint, like now. When you're mad, your mouth pinches on the ends and you scowl. When you're sad, your bottom lip protrudes ever so slightly. You are completely transparent, if a guy's paying attention." He snorted a laugh. "And I was definitely paying attention."

"The face I like best, of course, is you turned on. When you get hot, honey, you light up the sky. Man..." He took her hand in both of his and smiled, gazing deep into her eyes.

Embarrassed, Sara looked away then tried to change the subject. "I could have gotten away on my own, but I was less afraid of you than of those simpletons in Settlement, and all the other wildlife haunting the woods. Things scared me so much, I was willing to wait for someone to come, and..."

"What?"

She grinned self-consciously. "At first, I thought Bo was old and...well...basically harmless, maybe a little eccentric, but I liked looking at his legs in those leather breeches. Besides, it didn't take me long to figure out he needed a friend—me, or someone. But,

Alex...ah...Bo..." She winced. "Which name am I suppose to call you?"

"Whichever's easiest. I liked 'Bo' better, coming from you. It's more familiar." Casually, he put his hand on her thigh. She shifted, moving away from him.

"Maybe a little too familiar," she said.

He fisted his hand. "Why are you blushing? Don't be skittish with me. I'm the same guy I was at the cabin."

"That was Bo. He...you...didn't look like this at the cabin."

"What? I never expected you to say 'Hair makes the man.'"

"But I thought he was..." She hesitated, her face twisting and looked at the floor. "I felt close to him, you know. To you, I mean. Well, I thought he...you...Bo was like the Phantom of the Opera, scarred and kind of crazy, but wonderful with me, always taking care of me, watching out for me..."

His face softened. "I guess we'll just have to start over again, work our way back to where we were."

She risked a look at him. "I had no idea he would be so...I mean his face, that is, your face..." She groaned. "I don't know how to explain it."

He shook his head, obviously unclear about what she was trying to tell him.

She bit her lips and tried again. "At first I thought Bo was old."

"Don't say 'Bo,' say 'you.'"

"I can't, don't you see? You aren't Bo to me. Let me tell you this my way and then see if you can help me figure out how to make Bo and Alex be one person."

She stood and turned studying him. "I didn't realize it before, but a voice makes a huge difference in figuring someone's age. At first, Bo looked stooped like an old man. And he snarled and grunted like a curmudgeon.

"Also I assumed Bo was hiding something hideously disfiguring under all that hair. I've always prided myself on being a fair person, democratic, able to overlook physical imperfections, concern myself more with the nature and the soul of a person. Naturally, after we were together a while, I felt generous toward Bo. He was so good to me, how could I feel anything but grateful?"

Alex coughed and his expression reflected sympathetic approval.

242

"Those first few days, it took every bit of will power Bo had to keep his hands off you, did you know that?"

She gave him a bewildered look. "You're kidding. He made me sleep in his bed and didn't touch me...inappropriately."

His eyes narrowed. "Every bit of willpower he had."

"Is that why he disappeared that Saturday night when he made me take a bath?"

He nodded, grinning. "Had to ride all night long. Oh, he knew a woman or two who could've helped take the edge off his need, but you were the only woman he wanted."

"And the first time I tried to make biscuits and he put his arms around me."

"And he left for several hours again. Remember?"

She gave him a pained smile. "I thought I didn't appeal to him."

Alex rolled his head back and laughed at the ceiling. "He'd picked up on your vibes and your verbal suggestions that your prior sexual experiences had not been satisfactory. He wanted you to take the initiative. Waiting was hell. He kept maneuvering you into situations where you could make a move on him, but you didn't."

"Like making me sleep in his bed?"

"For all the good it did."

She drew a deep, uneven breath. "Meanwhile, my plan was to brace myself so I wouldn't show any alarm when I saw whatever Bo was hiding under all that hair.

"Of course, when he took off his bearskin coat that first day, I realized he was not stooped, but I still wasn't ready for the shock when he waded out of the river that night leading the mule with little Lutie Johnson on top of it. His clothes were plastered against him and his muscles were flexing and..." She sighed with the memory. "He was magnificent. That's when I realized he wasn't old at all. I wanted to touch him to see if he was real but, of course, I couldn't do that."

He gave her another sympathetic smile. "Of course not."

She regarded him oddly. He was allowing her—even encouraging her—to make observations as if he were someone else. This was weird, still she felt more comfortable than she had.

"Anyway, lying in the shed at night, I thought of him, even when I tried to put him out of my mind. Instead of thinking of ways to escape,

I wondered about the man's self-imposed solitude. I was even more curious about what or who had made him run from life."

She hesitated, gazed toward the window, staring for a moment at the midmorning brightness. "I still don't know the answer to that."

His eyes remained fixed on her face. "You were the cure. We can talk some other time about all the other stuff that ailed him, like a family business, parental expectations, successes that came too easy and too early, pressure, fear about keeping ahead of the game, that kind of stuff."

She gave him a gentle smile. "Anyway, I decided I wasn't the only hostage. I wanted to help Bo escape from whatever was holding him captive, too. He was wonderfully kind, despite the occasional grumpiness. And generous. He shared everything he had."

"Including his bed," Alex interrupted.

She squinted at him from the corners of her eyes. "Including his bed." The squint relaxed. "When Franklin came to get me, I didn't take time to think." She wanted him to understand. "If I had, I wouldn't have gone. That could have been a disaster. It almost was."

Allowing a forgiving smile, he nodded, encouraging her to continue.

"Bo saved me from Franklin and my own stupidity.

"Oh yes," she said, interrupting herself, "that was an amazing knife throw, clipping his fingers like that."

He grinned. "Yes, wasn't it? I was actually aiming for his head. I led him a little too much. I couldn't hit his hand like that again in a million throws. Now, please continue."

She took a deep breath. "Even after I was safe, later that night, I was frightened; too frightened to sleep without awful, awful nightmares. Bo put me in his bed and comforted me. He held me but he didn't touch me in any sexually suggestive way.

"Lying in his arms that night was when I first started thinking I might love him."

Smiling, Alex shifted his position and Sara glanced at his face. He appeared to be uncomfortable, made to feel awkward by her account of her close relationship with another man—another man who was him. She bowed her head. This whole situation was terribly confusing.

"Keep talking." Alex was being kind, encouraging her, like Bo would do.

244

She slid the fingers of both hands together, back and forth, repeatedly. "I *did* love him then, although I kept trying to rationalize, to analyze my feelings. I thought it might just be sympathy, like a bleeding heart might feel for an injured animal."

He touched her shoulder and slid his index finger down her arm. "But you knew it was more than that, didn't you, Sara? And you knew he felt that way too, didn't you?"

She looked intently into his face. "Eventually, yes, I knew. I could tell by the way he looked at me. I mean I thought he might be feeling it too. But he was too kind, too gentle to take advantage of me, as confused as I was, while I was his guest or his prisoner or whatever it was I was."

Alex watched her closely. "But you knew exactly what you were doing when you asked him to take off his shirts that day, didn't you? You weren't so naive as to think that was an innocent request, were you?"

She shook her head, looking at her hands and whispered, "No. I knew. And what happened was what I wanted to happen, only I hadn't really planned to go that far. Things got out of control—at least out of my control—in a hurry.

"After that I loved him desperately." She covered her mouth with one hand, her eyes darting to his face, silently pleading for his understanding. She tapped her fingers on her chin as she continued talking. "I loved him so much he became part of me, inside me, even when he wasn't."

The gorgeous man on her sofa countered quietly. "He loved you before that morning, more than he had ever loved another living thing, Sara. After you made love, he was desperate to hold onto you. Before that, he hadn't dared plan a future with you in it. Afterward, it was obvious, the connection worked both ways. He began formulating long-term plans thinking you could have a life together."

Alex did not attempt to touch her again and she was glad. In her confusion, she was prepared to bolt if he made any move at all. She turned a harsh glare back on him.

"But, after our intimacy—something we repeated again and again—he refused to cut his hair so I could see him. I begged him to. If he loved me, why did he refuse such an insignificant request?"

Alex returned her pensive gaze. "Maybe in his plan, it was important for you not be able to recognize him or to describe his features."

She stared glumly at the easy chair. "I thought he was trying to get rid of me, that he didn't want me to be able to find him again. And that's pretty much what the FBI agent in charge said when he debriefed me."

"Why would Bo have shown you in so many ways how much he loved you, and then abandoned you?"

Her mouth pursed, and she leveled her gaze at him. "The usual reason a man tries to convince a woman he loves her, to get in her pants."

"But you and he had been intimate over the course of several days and, admit it, you could feel him loving you more every single day, couldn't you?"

Her uncertainty became a frown of confusion. "Yes. It was hard to figure out. Except," she said brightening, "I thought maybe he was feeling bad about his girlfriend, a little Mexican girl. Mrs. Johnson called her his 'hot tamale.' The day we were leaving, he took off on his motorcycle to tell his tamale good-bye before he left."

A chuckle burbled in his throat but did not break loose. "That's not where he went. He went to the Johnsons to give them his guns and some other things, including a bill of sale for his livestock, so they could have the benefit of the eggs and milk and the animals. In return, they would feed and care for the stock. They'd have legal ownership, in case anyone came nosing around, asking about their new acquisitions."

"Oh." Sara's scowl dissolved. "That was a good idea. I may not have mentioned; in addition to being compassionate, I think Bo may also be pretty smart."

Alex grinned. "I've thought that about him myself."

"But what about his hot tamale?"

"Not a consideration. He was teaching the young woman to read and write English. Anything else existed only in the minds of the uninformed."

"You mean you...he...spoke to her?"

"No, but he listened to her read English and stopped her when she made a mistake. No one else in her family could do that and none of the other neighbors was willing to do it without strings attached."

Sara's face twisted with her next question. "He asked me to marry him, then it seemed like he took it back. What was that about?"

"You didn't mind fooling around with him in secret, but you were horrified at the idea of wagging him back to meet your family and your friends, of being saddled with a misfit. That was like a knife in his back, your being ashamed of him. He thought you had more character, more depth, than that."

She winced. "Then what made him forgive me?"

"What made it right was your saying you were not only willing to take him with you, but you would try to support him. That was nice. Not necessary, but nice. He's a rich guy, Sara. Money's not a problem."

"Do college professors make that much?"

"No, but a guy whose dad is looking to turn over a small business does, or will."

"Here in Overt?"

"No, in Tulsa."

"But you're here."

"Temporarily. I'm here to teach for a semester and to woo you. When you feel comfortable about us, we are out of here." He hesitated. "If that's all right with you."

Sara regarded him skeptically. He smiled and held his hands out flat, palms up. Frowning at the offered hands, she made no move to touch them. Instead, she peered at him, still puzzling.

"Bo dumped me at a store out in the boonies."

"At a bus stop, and he gave you money for a ticket. It was a place where he knew you were safe from Cappy and Franklin and their family. And you didn't know where he'd gone. With your sense of direction, I'll bet you couldn't have found your way back to the cabin from there. You were able to tell your family and the police the truth when they asked."

"Yes. Well, I didn't tell people exactly the *whole* truth."

"What do you mean?"

She shrugged. "I didn't tell them about sleeping with Bo."

"Why not?"

"Because it was nobody's business."

"And no one knows that?"

"Yes." She suddenly felt defiant. "The agent heading up the investigation, Mr. Krisp. When he was just about through interviewing me, he excused my parents and he asked me some questions privately."

"That was nice of him, to spare you and your parents that embarrassment."

"Yes."

"And in order to reward his consideration, you told him you had slept with Bo?"

"No. I just didn't deny it."

"Was he shocked or disappointed or angry? What?"

"No. He seemed to know already. He was very kind, treated me like I was some goopy teenager. When I assured him I knew what I was doing, he got haughty and insisted Bo was just horny and that I was an opportunity that fell into his lap."

Alex winced. "He may have figured Bo for a letch who snatched women regularly for sex."

"That's not what he thought and it isn't true anyway. Bo would never..." Sara's voice, tense with her sudden anger, faded. She stared into Alex's eyes, perplexed. "This is ridiculous. What am I doing defending you to you?"

"I didn't know for sure you knew I *was* me."

She allowed a pained little laugh. Reluctantly she placed her hands in his open ones, palms down, one on top of the other. He stroked her long fingers with his, flipping each long nail before mischievously capturing her two thumbs with one hand. She looked at his face, startled. He smiled reassurance and lifted the captive thumbs to his mouth.

"Does my face offend you then?" he asked as she watched him kiss one finger at a time.

She shook her head.

"I know you like my body."

She hummed her agreement.

"Is my manner offensive to you? The way I smell? My demeanor? My deportment?"

"No, no, no, and no." She gazed at her hands, which he was nuzzling with his open mouth. "Everything about you is marvelous.

248

Nothing about you offends me."

He lowered his voice. "And do you know I love you?"

Mutely she nodded.

"What else do you need to know, Sara?"

She raised her eyes from her hands, which he held against his mouth, just as he lifted his gaze to hers. "I can't think of...of anything...anything at all when you're doing that."

He stood up, pulling her to her feet. Placing his hands on each side of her face, he lowered his lips to hers.

Familiar? Oh, yes, his kiss was definitely familiar.

He held back, restraining himself. She groaned, the sound lost inside him as she opened her mouth. She sucked at his taunting tongue until he yielded and allowed it to invade. Her breath caught as she welcomed him, her hands tracing the breadth of his arms to his shoulders where they encountered unfamiliar pads beneath the fine worsted wool. Startled, she pulled back.

Holding her gaze with his own, Alex slipped out of his sport coat, removed his tie, unbuttoned his shirt and pulled the shirttail free of his trousers. She stared at his chest, a sight which was also gloriously familiar. Tentatively she pressed her fingers to one pectoral muscle, which he flexed at her contact.

A series of knocks disturbed their ritual before the apartment door burst open.

Libby Cook stood still as the expressions on her face ran a spectrum; from the silly smile she flashed at Sara, to the sultry look as she recognized Alex, to suspicion, realization, and fury as she appraised the freeze frame scene before her.

"What the hell do you think you're doing?" Libby's eyes darted from Sara to Alex and back to settle accusingly on Sara.

Sara took two steps around the sofa, moving to Libby who sidled forward into the room. Sara reached around her friend to shut the door. Alex made no attempt to close his open shirt and Libby gazed unabashedly at his bare chest.

"Libby," Sara began, then hesitated as she suddenly realized it might still be important to keep Bo's identity a secret, indirectly, from the FBI. "Libby," she tried again, "Alex took me to work this morning. I had car trouble."

"I got that much at the office." Puffed up with indignation, Libby reluctantly turned her stare from Sara to Alex and back. "So?"

"I had to come home and he brought me."

"They said you were sick. You don't look sick to me."

"Well, I'm better."

"And?"

Sara turned to Alex and pondered how to explain Libby's anger without mentioning her friend's hands-off warning regarding him. She didn't want to humiliate Libby more than Libby was humiliating herself at the moment.

"Alex, Libby met you first and we have a kind of gentlemen's agreement, you might say, about friends bird dogging friends' friends, if you see what I mean." The statement was more of a plea for help than clarification.

Alex took the hint. "Libby, Sara and I have known each other a long time."

"Odd. She didn't mention it." Libby's voice was acid. "You're so close she didn't recognize you or your name when I mentioned it?"

"I was working undercover when we met, disguised, using an alias. Sara didn't know what I looked like, or my real name until this morning."

Sara's eyes widened in amazement, gawking at Bo/Alex before they darted to Libby. "That's the truth, Libby."

Libby leveled a hard look at Alex. "And what's with your shirt? Is she sewing on a button for you or did I catch you two playing doctor?" Neither spoke. "Or maybe you old friends were merely baring your souls?"

Sara glanced around the room. "Why don't you sit down, Libby? Let me fix us some tea."

Alex shook his head, returning Libby's accusatory glare. "Libby's not staying, Sara." He sounded curt.

Libby's angry stare intensified.

"She's got no business here and I damn sure don't intend to explain us to her. A noodle casserole only buys so much."

Libby gasped and her mouth dropped open.

"Although," he added, pretending to rethink the statement, "the casserole was good." He again focused on Libby. "You'll find your dish outside your apartment door."

Closing her mouth, Libby glowered at Sara once more, then turned on her heel and stormed out the door, slamming it in her wake.

Sara stood frozen in the kitchen doorway.

Slowly, carefully, Alex walked over to her, brushed his shirt away from both sides of his chest and took her hands. Sara didn't object as he covered her mouth with his. He lifted and flatted her hands against his bare chest. At her touch, he closed his eyes and drew a deep breath from inside her mouth.

The gentle kiss opened to one of need, of urgency, hers as well as his.

"You weren't supposed to look like this," she whispered, her lips against his mouth as she pushed his shirt off of his shoulders. The shirt floated to the floor. "I had myself psyched, mentally prepared to accept any kind of deformity. I wasn't prepared for you to be gorgeous. You could have a lot of women, Alex Cadence. Libby, for one."

"Without you," he said, his mouth brushing her ear, his voice soft, lulling her, "I'm like a flashlight with no batteries. A shell. When you touch me," he glanced down at her hands on his chest, "I light up, inside and out. You're my energy pack, Sara, my power supply."

He laced his fingers into her hair, kissing her face, her eyes, her throat. His fingers found the gold chain and followed it down, unbuttoning the top two buttons of her blouse to continue his pursuit.

The hand-carved hickory ring lay between the swells of her breasts. He half laughed, half coughed as he regarded it in disbelief.

"I went back to get this. I thought it'd burned up. I'd have felt a lot better knowing it was here." He sobered as he fingered the smooth white cleavage encasing the ring.

Nudging his chin aside with her forehead, Sara kissed his chest.

Deliberately, moving cautiously, he unbuttoned the rest of her blouse. When it opened to reveal her bra, he allowed a droll little laugh.

She looked up. "What's funny?"

"I forgot we were back in civilization. I'm used to you running around unfettered, without the requisite harness."

Sara reached back to unclasp the bra. Alex removed her blouse and the bra, then stepped behind her. His hands slid deftly along her waist to caress her midriff. He splayed his hands and pulled her tightly to his chest. As he fondled and captured her full breasts, he hummed an audible sigh.

"I've ached to hold you like this again." His voice sounded hoarse. "Sara, my life had no purpose until you tumbled into it. From that first night, you're part of everything I think about. I'll take care of you, my angel. Good, good care of you. I'll feed you, provide you warm, comfortable places to sleep, and protect you from everything—people, animals, weather. You are the center of my universe." His voice dropped. "Marry me?"

"Hmmm," Sara said, affirmatively. Reaching up and back, she clasped her hands around his neck and luxuriated as he continued caressing her. She pivoted in his arms and began unfastening his trousers. Gently, persuasively, he took one of her hands and turned her back toward the couch.

"Let's fill out this form and get blood tests and do whatever else it takes to get the license."

She squirmed out of his grasp. "Let's sleep on it."

He looked skeptically into her eyes and shook his head. "Not until we're married."

"But how do we know we want to get married? Let's live together, fool around for a couple of months first."

His eyes narrowed and the smile faded. "No, ma'am. There's only one way we get back in bed together."

"That's not fair."

"I want you for keeps, Sara." He studied her face, his jaw set. "I don't want a *relationship*. I want a commitment. No more separations, ever."

"But we need to get things straightened out with the FBI."

"Okay."

She twisted, writhing, rubbing her breasts against his bare chest, enticing him. He clenched his teeth and broke away, bending to retrieve her bra and blouse. "First things first." He took a deep breath and shivered as he released it.

She scowled. "*That's* what I thought we were doing, first things first."

"No, we get things straightened out, get married, and then fool around. I don't want any distractions popping through that door when

252

we get to the important stuff."

She sidled closer. He jammed her shirt and bra into her hands. As she took them, she again rubbed her bare breasts against his flesh.

He grabbed her upper arms firmly. "Sara, I'm serious. No sex until.,." He stopped. "You *are* going to marry me, right?"

"Yes."

"Today?"

"I need to talk to my parents. They'll want to come. Won't your family want to be here?"

Grudgingly, he released her and grabbed his shirt. "Sweetheart, family and friends are fine, but all that really matters is that you can make it."

She gave him her prettiest smile. "Oh, I can make it."

"We'll do whatever you want. When?"

"This is Monday." She reached up and patted the side of his face. "How about..."

"Tuesday's good."

"Can you hold out until Friday?"

He slipped his shirt on and she frowned as he began buttoning it. He grinned at her obvious disappointment. "Question is: can you?"

She sighed and murmured, "I guess."

Chapter Twenty-three

"Hear you've got yourself a new boyfriend," FBI Agent William Krisp said, smiling and coming to his feet when Sara walked into his office just before noon.

She was surprised. "How'd you know?"

He reached across the desk to shake hands and motioned her toward a chair. "Sources. Aren't you afraid you and Larchmont will make the hillbilly boyfriend jealous, flush him out into the open?"

She grinned crookedly. She hadn't realized he was talking about her date with Kevin. "Krisp, I need to talk to you about Bo." She chose to remain on her feet as he eased into his chair, regarding her closely.

"I thought that was who we were talking about. Your hillbilly boyfriend. Heard anything from him?"

She ignored his question and leaped instead to one of her own. "Did Bo do anything illegal?"

The agent frowned and slid well back into his chair, waving his hand, indicating she should sit. She eased tentatively onto the edge of one of the chairs facing him across his desk.

Pressing his palms together, Krisp tapped the tips of his fingers and tilted his head back to observe them out of the lower part of his bifocals. He seemed to be thinking. He tapped for several seconds before he stopped and focused on his visitor.

"Conspiracy to kidnap you..."

"You'll have to do better than that. He was as surprised to find me tied up outside his cabin that night as I was to be there."

"Okay, how about aiding in the commission of a felony, harboring fugitives, conspiracy after the fact, little things like that."

"Krisp, get serious. I'm not going to scramble to come up with answers to a bunch of unsubstantiated garbage."

The agent regarded her solemnly.

She stood and started for the door then turned back. "Am I going to have to go out and hire a lawyer to get a straight answer out of you?"

He studied her another moment, then exhaled and leaned forward, elbows on his desk. "Okay, what do you want me to say?"

"I want you to admit that Franklin and Cappy Kindling and their kin folks committed an armed robbery in broad daylight and kidnapped me."

She sidled several steps back toward her chair.

He pursed his lips and drew another deep breath. "I can agree with that. State and federal charges are already filed."

"I want you to admit that no one even resembling Bo was in the store or near that stupid truck or even in the area when the crimes were committed."

He stared another long moment, then nodded grudgingly. "Okay, I admit it. So what?"

"Bo's the hero in this piece, Krisp. He deserves a medal for everything he did. You can't be serious about charging him with a crime...any crime. I know you understand that, don't you?"

The agent narrowed his eyes. "Like I said, so what?"

She plunged ahead. "Krisp, who do you think is going to testify against Bo?"

He sneered. "The Kindlings can't wait."

"Have either Franklin or Cappy ever been in trouble before?"

"Not with us."

She wondered how naive he thought she was not to notice such an obvious dodge. "How about with the local law?"

He smiled a grim little smile and began nodding. "Franklin's got a sheet but not for anything nearly as bad as he gives himself credit for. He's a hoodlum wanna-be, but he's neither well enough endowed nor well enough connected for the part.

"Cappy's a stooge, trailing around trying to hold Franklin's coat, which would be an over achievement, if it happened. Why?"

"I'm your only credible witness, right?"

"Okay."

She gave him a determined look and lowered her voice. "Krisp, a wife can't testify against her husband."

He squirmed and stared back at her. "Sure she can." He hesitated, lowered his eyes and his jowls quivered as he yielded the point. "She just can't be *compelled* to testify, if she doesn't want to." He took a breath and hurried on, not giving her an opportunity to speak.

"Sara, honey, don't go there. A young woman like you can't live in a cabin with no conveniences, have a pack of kids with a hillbilly. He's an ignorant, backwoodsman with little or no education, probably never had any success in his whole life..."

"Except with me."

"No. You only did what you had to do at the time. You can't seriously be thinking about marryin' the man. Sit down with your mom and dad. Talk it out. Don't go leapin' into something you'll regret the rest of your life."

"I don't want Bo Whatever-his-name-is to go to prison for taking care of me. I'll do what I have to do to protect him."

Krisp's face twisted in disbelief. "I don't believe that."

She gave him a determined nod, one reminiscent of Bo. Realizing that, she allowed a wry smile.

Krisp stood up and walked around the desk. He strode by her to stare at the opaque pane in the top half of his office door, shoved his hands deep into his trouser pockets, and stood with his back to her. Finally he turned, locking his hands together behind him, and walked toward her, nodding almost imperceptibly.

"They tell me some new guy's turned up in your world, Sara, girl. He lives in your building." Krisp ran his tongue along his front teeth. "He's been watching you. We've been watching him. I believe you met him this morning. My people tell me he's a clean-cut, smooth talking, well educated, fine looking fellow. Is that about right?"

She nodded.

Krisp nodded back. "You can't tell me you're willing to sacrifice your future with someone like this new fella', or like Kevin Larchmont, just an outstanding young guy, for some hairy old coot of a mountain man."

She felt herself confusing identities again. "I love Bo," she said softly. "And I'm obligated to him, Krisp. I owe him."

"Sara, I think you got a little confused isolated up there with that old hermit. You got to feeling sorry for him, tolerated him, maybe even got to liking his craziness a little. But that's behind you now. You don't owe him a thing."

"You don't know anything about it. Not about Bo, or me, or Bo and me together."

"What is it you think you owe him?"

She shrugged and said the words simply, in a matter-of-fact tone. "Nothing but my life."

Krisp snorted and paced back behind his desk. "Is that what he told you?"

"No. I was there. He saved me over and over again, in some ways I can hardly explain to myself, much less to anyone else. I don't want to forget his humanity, his kindness—him. He's a standard bearer for how people ought to be, for how we all should treat each other. I don't intend ever to forget him."

The agent took a deep breath then let it out. His body language signaled defeat. "What do you want me to do?"

"I want you to drop any federal charges against Bo. I want you to clear up any state charges against him. I want you to make people quit looking for him."

Krisp ruffled. "Hell, girl, we filed those charges against John Doe. 'Bo Doe' sounded too ridiculous. We already quit looking for him because we've got no idea *who* we're looking for, much less where to find him. Unless that hairy bastard turns up back at that cabin, he's beyond us."

"He's free?" she reiterated. "You're through looking for him?"

Krisp nodded.

She pivoted quickly and started toward the door, then looked back at him. There was something else, something he hadn't told her.

"What are you holding back?" Poised, her hand on the doorknob, she regarded him somberly out of the corners of her eyes. "What are you not telling me? And why do I have the feeling you want to tell? Come on, what is it?"

Krisp glanced at her, turned his head, rubbed his mouth with a hand and shrugged. "You are some piece of work, Loomis. Do you know that?" He allowed a grudging smile.

"I've been told." She gave him a questioning look. "Come on, now, spill it."

His grin broadened as he regarded her. "You play a mean game of thrust and parry." He patted his pants pocket. "There is one other little bit of information on your friend Bo. Got it here in my wallet. I figured you'd been through enough. For your sake, Sara, I'm going to trash this little slip of paper and forget all about it. It doesn't seem to have any bearing on this investigation any more anyhow."

Sara looked at Crisp with new interest. "And what information is that?"

He pulled out his billfold, produced a torn half sheet off a legal pad, and smoothed it out on his desk. "I was willing to let you win by default, Sara, let you go away thinkin' you'd outfoxed the fox—that being me—but, you see, it isn't exactly like that."

Her eyes narrowed but she had a good feeling. Something about his demeanor, the warmth in his voice, the twinkle in his eyes, gave him away.

"Okay. What is it exactly like?"

"The agents at the scene assumed the cabin was built by a squatter on land belonging to the U.S. Department of the Interior, part of the Ozark Mountain National Forest."

"But?"

"Out of curiosity—and because I'm a damned good agent—I took a look at the county property records. It turns out, that particular patch of ground is adjacent to the national forest land, not on it. And it's owned by an individual." Krisp paused, but Sara waited.

He thumped a thick index finger on part of a penciled drawing on the sheet. "It seems that several years ago a fellow name of Alex B. Cadence purchased a piece of that quarter section, that forty acres, right there."

Sara struggled to control her facial expression, her breathing. She didn't want to reveal anything. "Is that right?" She concentrated on maintaining an expression of polite indifference. There was another lull. "So Bo squatted on Mr.Cadence's property instead of in the national forest. Is that important?"

"Only in that it reduces the federal government's interest in him, being as there's no encroachment on a federal preserve."

Relieved, she turned toward the door.

"One other little item of interest," he added as she rotated the knob.

Clenching her teeth, she waited, her back to him. "Okay, what?" She refused to turn around to face him. She felt vulnerable and knew Krisp was too sharp not to read her expression, which was probably transparent at the moment.

"That young fellow you met this morning, the clean-cut, clean shaven, young stalwart."

"Yes?"

"What's his name, Sara?"

"Alex."

"Alex B. Cadence?"

"I believe so. Yes."

"Do you know what that 'B' stands for, Sara?"

Agonizingly, she turned, blinking her eyes and biting her lips. "I guess you're going to tell me, right?"

Krisp smirked a little and shook his head, never taking his eyes off her face. "No, Sara. I don't know it for sure myself, at this point. But I fully intend to find out, unless you want to tell me."

Her mouth set in a hard line.

"I'm going to look up that information, Sara Loomis." Krisp scooped up the piece of yellow paper, refolded it and tore it in half, then tore it again and again until it was a pile of shreds. "I'll look into it just as soon as I get a little spare time to spend satisfying my idle curiosity about questions that don't appear to be pertinent to anything I might need to know in an official capacity."

She looked at him, surprised, pleased, suspicious. She had thought he was playing cat and mouse, that he enjoyed watching her squirm, but studying his face, she realized she had been mistaken.

She didn't know how long he had known, but it was obvious that Krisp not only knew Bo's identity, but knew exactly where to find him. And, just as obviously, he was making sure she knew that he knew. Now that he was satisfied that she did, he apparently was ready to let it go.

"I like you, Loomis." Krisp paced toward her. "I've liked you from the git-go. You are a fine, fine young woman with character. In my line of work, we don't ever see too much of that.

"You're the kind of people, Sara, that helps me remember why I keep at this tedious, tiresome, thankless job. I appreciate you for that.

"Have a productive life, young woman. You've got my card. Drop me a line sometime. Let me know how you're doing. I'll remember you. Yes, ma'am, I'll be remembering you for a long, long time, Sara Loomis."

* * * *

His eyes focused on a handful of paperwork, FBI Agent Kevin Larchmont strolled into his own office, which was temporary headquarters for regional supervisor William Krisp.

"How's your social life, Larchmont?" Krisp queried as he gazed out at the street below.

Kevin glanced up from the folder full of papers and grinned. "Great. 'Guess you heard I took Sara Loomis to the show Saturday night. Even kissed her good night. I think she likes me. I'm going to ask her out to dinner this week. I've got a whole campaign mapped out. Going to take it slow and easy."

Krisp watched as the clean-cut Alex Cadence stepped out of his vehicle parked on the street, grinned, and gathered a giggling Sara Loomis into his arms.

Krisp nodded his approval, then sobered and glanced back at his young agent.

"I see. Well, Kevin, my boy, I don't know that I'd get to counting too strong on winning the lovely Ms. Loomis. I'm afraid she's taken."

Larchmont flashed a silly grin. "You mean that hero worship deal with the old mountain guy? Nah, I can get her over him. No problem."

Glancing back out at the scene in the street below, Krisp grimaced. "I'm afraid we locked the barn door on Ms. Loomis, son, after her heart had already been stolen. But there are a lot of other fish in the sea."

"Not like her," Larchmont said firmly.

Having escorted Sara safely into his vehicle, Cadence, beaming, jogged to the driver's side, and climbed in.

Still watching, Krisp took a deep breath.

"No, Kevin, there aren't many like her out there these days," the chief investigator admitted. "But I've found out recently that all it takes is one every now and again to stimulate the old juices.

"Yes, sir, that Sara Loomis is one in a million, son. She is a one-of-a-kind, extremely fine, absolutely *bodacious* woman."

THE END